SPECIAL MESSAGE

NEXT TO DIE

Penny Price is convinced that the person barraging her with threatening phone calls is her father's murderer. Armed with evidence for the FBI, she's branded a target. Penny's only salvation is the playboy next door — Navy SEAL Lieutenant Commander Joe Montgomery. The sole survivor of the worst disaster in SEAL history, Joe has taken to alcohol and living in isolation. Penny refuses to indulge his behavior and a tentative friendship begins, charged with desire. But her father's killer has set his sights on Penny — he will do anything to protect his identity and Joe fears Penny is . . . next to die.

MARLISS MELTON

◆

NEXT TO DIE

Complete and Unabridged

ULVERSCROFT
Leicester

First published in the United States of America
in 2007 by
Warner Forever
Hachette Book Group USA
New York

First Large Print Edition
published 2008
by arrangement with
Little, Brown Book Group Ltd.
London

British Library CIP Data

Melton, Marliss
    Next to die.—Large print ed.—
    Ulverscroft large print series: romantic suspense
    1. Romantic suspense novels
    2. Large type books
    I. Title
    813.6 [F]

    ISBN 978–1–84782–214–7

Published by
F. A. Thorpe (Publishing)
Anstey, Leicestershire

Set by Words & Graphics Ltd.
Anstey, Leicestershire
Printed and bound in Great Britain by
T. J. International Ltd., Padstow, Cornwall

This book is printed on acid-free paper

In loving memory of the three Navy
SEALs who died on June 28, 2005, while
on a reconnaissance mission in support
of Operation Redwing, in Afghanistan.
Michael Murphy
Danny Dietz
Matthew G. Axelson
and the sixteen Special Operators who
sought to rescue them and also perished.

Lastly, to the sole survivor —
This is not your story, but your heroism
inspired it.
God love you, Marcus.
Carry on, down the Good Road.

'A light shines above them, and an angel comes down to them — beckoning them to come. The angel is dressed in a WWI-style infantryman's uniform. He tells them, without words, not to worry. Warriors take care of their own in Heaven, he says. They have been expected, and there is a big reception planned.'

A Tribute to the Fallen,
CMDR Mark Divine

Acknowledgments

There are so many souls who deserve credit for helping me write this story. The most outstanding contributor would be a reader-turned-collaborator, Janie Hawkins. Janie, you have painted my world in Technicolor! Thank you from the bottom of my heart for your contributions to my characters, their stories, and every last line of this book. Here's to the next project; I can't wait!

Thank you, Kevin McPartland, Special Agent FBI, retired. You were with me at the conception of this story and answered all of my silly questions along the way, with patient faithfulness. I'm thinking you deserve a story of your own . . .

Commander Mark Divine, thank you, sir, for checking the accuracy of my facts and for your unintentional influence when you wrote in your *Tribute*, 'What if it were me?' In some ways, this story answers that question.

Thank you, Sam the SEAL, for taking the time to hash out details that changed the whole gist of my story and made it more real.

For Sharon, who helped tremendously in determining the personality types of my characters and for the articles you've sent my way.

For Cathy, Kerri, and Lisa P., who helped me get started, and everyone else who has contributed a portion of this shared project.

Thanks to physical therapist, Carrie Hewitt, for contributing your expertise and making Joe's therapy more credible.

Above all, thank you, loyal readers, for urging me to carry on with the SEAL series. Without you, I'd be writing to myself. Bless you all!

Prologue

Northern Afghanistan

'Break contact,' Joe whispered through the interteam radio, and he and the three SEALs in his command stepped off the trail to descend as quietly as possible into the wooded ravine. Wending through the cypress forest that glowed green in his night vision goggles, Joe counted the seconds that elapsed before the staybehind — the claymore that he'd placed on the trail — exploded.

' . . . nineteen, twenty.'

Bang! The loud crack was accompanied by the screams of Taliban insurgents, the same men who'd surprised them four miles up the trail when they swarmed from an underground cave. The SEALs had retreated, taking and returning heavy fire. It was a long way back to the landing zone, made longer still with forty men or more, equipped with night vision capabilities, raining bullets at them in a firestorm that echoed off the surrounding mountains.

The SEALs had dropped their backpacks on the trail to speed their retreat. And with just six rounds of ammo per man, they were running low on both ammunition and energy by the time the landing zone, or LZ, came into view.

There it was, on a plateau on the adjacent mountain, the side of which had been riddled by aerial cannon fire that incinerated the scrub brush and cratered the earth. The only way to access the LZ was to pass through a precipitous wooded ravine and climb the other side.

Once deep within the ravine, the SEALs remained hidden and, for the time being, safe. In the wake of the claymore's destruction, gunfire gave way to moans and shouts. Wind whistled eerily through the limbs of stunted evergreens.

If the SEALs were lucky, the explosion and their subsequent disappearance would send the insurgents back into their caves, away from the LZ.

This reconnaissance mission, thought Joe, darkly, had been cursed from the moment Chief Harlan spiked a high fever, prompting Joe to take his place. The Spectre gunship that had swept this mountain an hour prior to their drop-off had completely overlooked the presence of unfriendlies on the trail. Worse still, the gunship was nowhere within range of the four SEALs now. If it were, one simple radio call would bring the AC-130 screaming to their rescue like a mother eagle protecting her fledglings. Its minigun was capable of knocking out the forty or so insurgents with the precision of a surgeon's blade.

Driven into retreat, Joe's squad had only one option remaining: to call for extraction. If the insurgents didn't leave before the helicopter's arrival, and if — God forbid — they were carrying rocket-propelled grenades in their arsenal, then this cursed mission would officially be classified a goatfuck.

At the bottom of the ravine, Joe checked his watch. The window was open, the satellite in position, for Curry to get on the SATCOM radio and request a hot extract.

'Bravo, report,' Joe said into his mouthpiece.

'Curry here,' whispered the corpsman.

'Smiley,' acknowledged their sniper.

'Nikko,' said their gunner. 'Shit!'

Joe hesitated at the swear word. 'What is it?'

'I wondered what the fuck was running down my leg. Oh, shit!'

That didn't sound good. 'Rally up,' Joe instructed, bringing the squad into a tight perimeter.

Four shadows drifted together. Nikko was

breathing hard. He collapsed next to Curry the corpsman, who kneeled to assess his wound. Joe did the same, taking in the severity of the hit that was illuminated by Curry's penlight. 'Shit' was not the expletive that leaped into Joe's mind. Nikko'd taken a bullet in the thigh, close to the femoral artery. Given the gunner's pallor, he'd lost a lot of blood already. Didn't it figure, since they would have to climb with the agility of mountain goats to make it up to the LZ?

They needed to call for extraction immediately, or Nikko was a goner.

With Curry frantically stanching the gunner's wound, Joe took the radio from him, set it up a short distance to one side, and made the call to their task force commander, Captain Lucas.

'Helo's on the way,' Lucas assured him.

'Blackhawk?' Joe requested, praying for a sleek and stealthy craft.

'Can't get one in the air,' Lucas admitted grimly. 'We're sending in a Chinook.'

With a sinking sensation in his gut, Joe dismantled the SATCOM. The thunderous arrival of the Chinook helicopter would not be overlooked by the insurgents they'd left on the trail, who — given the way this mission was going — most certainly carried missiles.

'Let's go,' said Joe, infusing his tone with

optimism. As the officer in charge, his most important job was to keep the squad motivated and functioning smoothly.

The men scurried to obey him. Curry pulled Nikko to his feet and propped him under one arm. Smiley stepped forward and relieved the gunner of his M60, which would lighten Curry's load, but the corpsman still faced the daunting task of getting both him and Nikko up to the LZ.

Armed with Nikko's gun, Smiley took point. Lean and agile, the twenty-year-old darted out of the cover of trees to tackle the near-vertical incline. Ascending fifty meters, he ducked behind a boulder and shouldered his rifle, covering Nikko and Curry, who hobbled painstakingly after him, leapfrogging his position and pausing farther up the ridge.

Then it was Joe's turn. Physically, he was as fit and robust as the younger men, but the soil slipped beneath his boots. His raw-boned body strained for speed as he dug his toes in, scrambling hand over hand to reach his destination, an outcropping of stone that resembled a Tyrannosaurus rex. Over the pounding of his heart, he heard the *whop-whop* of the approaching helo.

No doubt the insurgents could hear it, too. *Come on*, he urged both the helo and his men. It wouldn't take the enemy long to spy the four SEALs clambering up the opposite mountain, not with a four-ton helicopter landing at its height. To make matters worse, the first hint of dawn was silvering the sky.

It was Smiley's turn to take off. He pushed to his feet and bounded up the incline, seemingly unhindered by the weight of Nikko's M60. At the same time, the Chinook surged closer, its blades chopping the air like the wings of a thousand angels. Any minute now its shape would materialize out of the charcoal canopy above.

Yet Nikko and Curry struggled now to make their ascent. Joe was about to abandon his position to give Curry a hand, when both men slipped and took a tumble that had Joe scrambling after them in consternation.

The Chinook thundered into view, yet they were nowhere near the LZ yet.

'Curry, Nikko!' Joe called, reaching them at last.

'I couldn't hold him, sir,' Curry explained. Nikko had passed out.

'Get his feet,' Joe urged. Together they heaved and struggled to carry Nikko uphill.

But then a half-dozen missiles streaked overhead. 'Son of a bitch!' He and Curry threw themselves on top of Nikko. Grenades punctured the very earth around them, sending up spumes of rock that peppered their backsides as they succumbed to gravity.

Finding himself intact, Joe peeked up at the helo. It still awaited them, rotors whirring impatiently. 'Let's go!' he yelled, preparing to haul Nikko, without stop, to the ridge.

Neither Nikko nor Curry made reply. Joe nudged aside his NVGs. 'Curry!' he cried in disbelief. Curry's skull had been crushed, presumably by falling rock.

He thumbed his mike. 'Smiley, get down here. Both men are down.'

He glanced up again, praying the Chinook would linger. Smiley's shadow made a quick and steady descent as four more missiles sizzled across the ravine at them.

Joe gritted his teeth and ducked, bracing himself. *Boom, boom, boom, boom!* The mountainside trembled. It vomited rock and dirt, all of which fell in a merciless rain on Joe's back. When he looked up, Smiley was gone. Joe groped for his NVGs, but they were gone, too.

His last hope was the Chinook. Its ramp was down, with reinforcements pouring out, bearing grenade launchers. Joe pushed to his knees and waved them down. He needed hands to pull his men up, get them into the belly of the Chinook, and bear them home again — dead or alive.

But it wasn't to be.

Another missile shot across the ravine like a falling star. And there wasn't even time to make a wish.

In the next instant, the helicopter exploded into a giant fireball that mushroomed outward, blasting Joe with heat and flaming shrapnel. The force of the explosion thrust him backward, tearing him away from Nikko and Curry.

He felt himself falling.

He hit the ground and rolled. The earth beneath him was vertical. He grappled to slow his descent, but he was moving too quickly, glancing over rock and shrub. He tucked and rolled, protecting his head and extremities. He crashed through the boughs of an evergreen, struck the base of a tree, bounced off it, and rolled again.

He dropped, hit the ground, and spun around, sliding on a carpet of foliage.

At last, he skidded to a stop.

Cracking open an eyelid, he found himself peering through cedar limbs to see flames dancing from the remains of the Chinook. Spumes of smoke darkened the brightening sky. Joe sucked a slow and painful breath into his lungs. The stench of burned flesh made him cringe.

Jubilant cheers floated over the ravine, followed by volleys of gunfire as the guerillas sounded their victory.

Oh, Jesus. Oh, God.

Not a soul aboard or near the Chinook could have survived that explosion. His men were either dead or dying.

So this is defeat, Joe thought, losing consciousness. It was worse than anything he'd imagined.

1

The chiming of Lieutenant Penelope Price's doorbell elicited a groan. She had just sunk onto her overstuffed couch to watch the six o'clock news while indulging in a slice of cheesecake. Penny's hands and feet ached. She deserved a little downtime, having worked extra hours at the naval hospital, seeing to her own patients plus those of the physical therapist on maternity leave.

'It better not be a salesman,' she muttered, leaving the cheesecake on the coffee table. As she crossed her two-story foyer toward the front door, she tightened the sash on her velour bathrobe. Perhaps it was her neighbor, the Navy SEAL, back from his assignment and looking for his cat.

But the face peering through the door's glass oval wasn't that of the too-hot-to-handle Commander Joe Montgomery. It was Penny's twenty-four-year-old drama queen of a little sister, Ophelia.

'Hi,' said Penny, braced for trouble. 'What's up?' Crisp October air surged inside, bearing the scent of dried leaves.

'Um, I need to stay here a while,' Ophelia

answered, casting a nervous glance over her shoulder. 'Can I park my car in your garage?'

Penny tucked a strand of copper hair behind one ear, deliberating. 'You can't keep running to me every time you break up with a boyfriend, Lia,' she chided.

'I'm not,' Ophelia reassured her. 'But I need to put my car in your garage, now. Please,' she added.

It was the lack of theatrics that persuaded Penny to cooperate. 'Okay,' she agreed, flicking a glance at Lia's rustbucket of a ride. 'Hold on a sec. I'll need to move some stuff first.'

Moments later, the '91 Oldsmobile was parked snugly in the single-car garage and Ophelia stepped out of it, dragging a suitcase with her.

Penny eyed the suitcase with dismay, a sure sign that Lia had failed to pay her rent — again. 'How long are you planning to stay?' she asked as the garage door rumbled shut behind them, leaving the sisters in darkness.

'I don't know,' Ophelia admitted. 'Let me tell you what happened, and you can decide for yourself.'

Oh, dear, that didn't sound too promising. With concern pooling in her belly, Penny led the way through the laundry room into her hard-earned three-bedroom single-family home. It was supposed to be the house she would live in with her husband and babies, but, at twenty-nine, she still wasn't married, and if her sister kept landing on her doorstep, she might never lead a normal life again.

Ophelia dropped her suitcase in the foyer and headed toward the kitchen, wringing her hands as she went.

'I have leftovers if you're hungry,' Penny offered, taking note of Lia's longer locks. Her hair was like Penny's, only layered, with a hint of whimsical bangs. While the elder sister dressed comfortably and sensibly, Ophelia liked to test the limits of fashion using sequins, tie-dye, lace, and beads.

'That's okay, I'm not hungry.' But spying the opened box of cheesecake, she pounced on it, serving herself a giant slice.

'So what happened?' Penny prompted.

Ophelia ignored the question. 'Hey, I didn't know you had a cat,' she said, pointing her fork toward the family room.

Commander Montgomery's tomcat was crouched over Penny's dessert. 'Felix!' she scolded, rushing over to scoop him up. 'He's not mine. He belongs to my nextdoor neighbor.'

'The Navy SEAL?' Lia's slender eyebrows shot up as she stuffed her mouth with another huge bite. 'Are you sleeping with him?'

'Of course not,' Penny answered, seeing through her sister's delay tactics. 'He's on assignment somewhere. One of his girlfriends is supposed to be pet-sitting, but she's unpredictable and Felix likes to eat — don't you, big boy?' She scratched the cat's broad head. 'Now can we get to the point of your visit?' she demanded.

Ophelia's shoulders drooped. She put her plate abruptly on the counter, pushing it away. 'Well, first of all, the tourists have gone home, and I'm not making much money waitressing.'

'Right,' said Penny, who had advised Lia to get a real job when this same thing happened last year.

'But that's not the only thing,' her little sister added with a miserable sigh.

Penny thought of the worst possible scenario. 'I hope this has nothing to do with Daddy's journal,' she pleaded.

'I'm afraid it does,' Ophelia admitted in a small voice.

'Oh, no. What did you do?'

'I called Eric,' Lia admitted, begging Penny with her pretty turquoise eyes to understand. 'I was pissed. I wanted answers.'

'What did you say to him?' Penny asked, clasping the cat more firmly, furious that her sister might have blown their chance to seek justice.

14

'I asked him how he slept at night, okay? I didn't accuse him of stealing the ricin or murdering Dad.'

'And what did he say?'

'Nothing. He couldn't say anything. You know how he talks. He started stuttering and stammering, and — believe me — his stutter is even worse when he's nervous, and he wouldn't be that nervous unless he was scared.'

Penny regarded her sister over Felix's twitching ears. 'Did he threaten you?' She didn't know whether to slap her sister or comfort her. 'Is that why you hid your car in my garage?'

'I told you. He can't even talk. He just breathes into the phone.'

'Breathes? You make it sound like you've talked more than once.'

Lia swallowed visibly. 'He's called a few times since then. But like I said, he doesn't say anything.'

Penny shivered as she caught a whiff of Ophelia's apprehension. 'Oh, boy,' she murmured. Lia had taken their discovery to a whole new level, and now she was paying for it.

'I'm sorry,' her little sister added, with uncharacteristic humility. 'I don't know what made me call him. I was just so upset.'

Penny's worry subsided into pity. 'I understand, honey. I was upset, too.' She considered their options. 'Well, I guess it's not going to change anything for Eric to know that we're onto him. Unless he disappears between now and then, the FBI will still be able to arrest him.'

'Have you shown them Daddy's journal yet?'

'No, I have an appointment on Thursday.'

'Oh, good,' said Lia, rubbing her arms as if chilled.

'I'm glad you're moving in with me for a while,' Penny decided suddenly. 'We're better off sticking together on this.' She didn't like the thought of Ophelia being scared.

Lia sent her a grateful smile.

Over Felix's purrs, Penny overheard the newscaster mention something in the news about Navy SEALs. She turned her attention to the television, hushing whatever Lia was about to say.

' . . . northeastern Afghanistan, the worst disaster in Special Forces history,' the female anchor was saying. 'Known casualties include the sixteen men aboard the Chinook helicopter and three SEALs found dead nearby. Taliban leaders claim to have beheaded the fourth SEAL. An unprecedented search continues, despite those claims. The identity of the missing SEAL has not been released.'

As the anchor moved to a bombing in neighboring Iraq, Penny directed her gaze out her window to her neighbor's dark, empty home, and her heart constricted with empathy. She wondered if Commander Montgomery knew any of the casualties personally. The Special Forces community was especially tight-knit.

'Do you think your neighbor was involved?' Ophelia asked, following her gaze.

'No,' Penny answered definitively. 'He's a high-ranking officer. He'd never be out in the field. But he probably knew a lot of those men,' she added, aware that the tragedy would have touched him deeply. When a neighbor had returned from Iraq half-paralyzed last year, the SEAL built a handicap ramp and organized hospital transportation for the man. He was considerate like that.

He was also six feet three inches of sculpted muscles, with sun-streaked hair and khaki green eyes. Penny'd had a crush on him for years, but with gorgeous women jumping in and out of his hot tub with him, she knew she never stood a chance. Besides, he'd scarcely even spoken to her, except in polite greeting.

17

He had no idea that she cared for his cat and kept his front yard tidy while he was out playing commando.

With a hidden sigh, she retrieved her half-eaten cheesecake and carried it to the kitchen. 'I'd better go to bed,' she announced, rinsing the plate and sticking it in the dishwasher. 'I have to get up early for work,' she added. 'I think you'll find everything you need upstairs.'

'Thanks,' said Lia, who'd flopped into the recliner and was flipping through channels.

As Penny slipped into bed minutes later, she remembered the nineteen men who'd lost their lives. As a lieutenant in the United States Navy and a proud patriot herself, her heart ached for them and their loved ones. She considered the commando still missing. *Let him be alive*, she prayed.

Then, as her mind had a habit of doing, she conjured an image of her awe-inspiring neighbor. His first name was Joseph; she'd overheard his friends call him Monty. But to her, he was more of a Mighty Joe. Given the concern he'd shown the injured vet last year, she just knew that Mighty Joe was taking this tragedy very personally, and she wished with all her heart that she could comfort him.

★ ★ ★

I'm going to die here, Joe thought, collapsing in the meager shade afforded by a rock overhang.

He panted, hungry for oxygen to feed his fast-beating heart. Near the height of this mountain chain, fourteen thousand feet above sea level, the air was terribly thin. It was warm by day, but at night the temperatures plummeted, leaving him shivering in his dust-covered uniform.

The relentless wind chapped his lips and stung the burn on his cheek. His mouth was so parched that his tongue had swelled. If he didn't find water soon, he'd have to steal it from the soldiers hounding him. And wouldn't that be fun?

The escape-and-evasion plan was weak, another oversight of this botched mission. Joe would have been better off slipping through enemy lines to reach coalition forces than he was penetrating the Hindu Kush to seek the E & E extraction point. For four endless days, he'd been chased by guerillas familiar with the terrain. And all he'd had to eat in that time was a lizard, caught basking on a rock.

He'd come so close, so many times, to being caught. But the fear of death — especially death by beheading, which the Taliban were notorious for — kept him moving, to no avail. The extraction point remained elusive.

He was stuck in a death trap where nothing made sense. How could everything have gone so wrong so quickly? Why couldn't he find his way out of this labyrinth of terror?

The sound of distant bombing was his only connection to reality. The Americans were retaliating.

Then a remote-controlled drone darted past him, diving down into a valley. It was searching for him, he realized, shedding tears of frustration.

There was no way to signal his location. Along with his floppy hat, he'd lost the glint tape he kept Velcroed to the underside of the brim. He'd ditched his infrared strobe when he'd ordered his squad to shuck their rucksacks. His E & E kit, with signal mirror, was lost when he fell four days ago. There was no other way on this barren mountainside to signal an SOS.

His only choice was to stay on the move or risk capture, but he'd driven himself to exhaustion. He lay in the scant shade afforded by the rock beside him, panting what might be his final breaths.

Was he turning delirious? He thought he heard voices, where before there was only the howl of the wind.

He tried to rouse himself, but he could scarcely crack an eye. As he pulled his knife free, it clattered from his clumsy fingers and rolled away.

Shit, he'd just given himself away.

The voices stopped talking. Cautious footsteps came closer.

Be merciful, God.

He struggled to his elbows.

Through bleary eyes, he blinked at the vision of two men, swathed in cream-colored robes and wearing turbans. Angels? he wondered, blinking to bring them into focus. But then he heard the bleating of sheep; no, they were herdsmen.

They approached him cautiously, conferring between themselves, casting glances all around. The only word Joe recognized was 'Amerki,' American.

One of them produced a knife and he flinched, expecting the worst. But it was his own knife, which they'd retrieved. The older of the two laid it on Joe's abdomen. The man reached under his robe for a goatskin canteen and offered it, his eyes watchful and concerned.

'Thank you,' Joe managed to rasp. He lifted a hand to bear the canteen to his lips, but he was shaking too badly.

The stranger helped him. As Joe sipped the rejuvenating liquid, fighting the impulse to guzzle it, the older man said something to the younger. 'Come,' he added to Joe, urging him to sit up.

Joe hesitated. Who was to say these men wouldn't turn him over to the Taliban? As if sensing his distrust, the man said again, 'Amerki.'

Hope made Joe's extremities tingle. Maybe, just maybe, they were going to help.

★　★　★

Eric Tomlinson's persistence paid off. On his third visit to Ophelia Price's apartment, a German woman, with her hair in rollers, stuck her head out of the opposite apartment and demanded, 'Vy do you knock every day on Lia's door ven you can see she isn't home?'

With a bead of cold sweat sliding from his temple to his jaw, Eric summoned a ghastly smile for her. 'Do you know . . . w-w-w-where she is?' he asked.

'Vy shoult I tell you?' the woman asked, running a wary eye over his gaunt frame.

'I have to . . . t-t-talk to her.' His body twitched with the effort needed to get the sentence out.

'No, I don't know vere she is,' insisted the frau. She stepped back, intending to shut her door.

'Wait!' Eric threw himself across the breeze-way, putting a shoulder against the door before

22

she could fully close it. 'You do know,' he accused. He could see it in her fleshy face as she battled to push the door shut.

'Go away. She vent to stay vith her sister, okay? She vill haf friends stayink here. Dat's all I know!'

He stepped back suddenly, and the door slammed shut. Her sister? Ah, yes, Danny's Price's older daughter. Eric had preferred her over the impious Ophelia. But Sonja, his wife, had liked the younger daughter. *Isn't she beautiful*, she would say about her red-gold hair and turquoise eyes.

Yes, he would agree, *but the older one is smart, like Danny.*

Danny's insight had brought Eric to the brink of ruin five years ago. Danny'd died because of it, taking Eric's secret to the grave.

Or so Eric had hoped.

Ophelia Price seemed to know the truth. *How do you sleep at night?* she'd demanded of him.

He hadn't slept a wink since her call.

How could she have guessed, he agonized, unless Danny left a note, a clue, a message from the grave? It wouldn't take long for the elder sister to get the feds involved.

He would have to silence both of them, or they'd all be sorry.

2

Afghanistan

The hospital facility at Bagram Air Base was
made of prefabricated materials and powered
by generators. There was no hot water.

Having requested a real shower in lieu of a
wipe-down, Joe found himself in a communal
bathing area, shivering under the trickle that
came out of the showerhead. Soap in hand,
he set about scrubbing a week's worth of filth
from his body, mindful of the treated burn on
his right cheek, which he'd been told to keep
dry.

Soap stung the cuts and blisters on his
hands. His sunken abdomen, jutting hip
bones, and torn skin gave testament to just
how desperate his plight had been.

The men who'd rescued him were a tribal
elder and his son. They sent word of their
discovery to coalition forces, and six men
from the Joint Special Operations Task Force
had flown up to the remote mountain village
to escort their ops officer back to Bagram. He
was fussed over and cared for and denied
even a moment's isolation in which to mull

over his role in the disaster.

Joe's commander, Captain Lucas, had blamed the Taliban. *God, it's good to get one of you back, son, he'd said with tears in his eyes. Who would have thought they'd score a hit like that with a thirty-year-old SAR, an SA-16 Gimlet? It sure as hell did the job for them, though, damn them to hell!*

He was sending Joe home to recuperate. *You'll need time to deal with this, Monty, he* said, his hands heavy on Joe's shoulders.

How could it have happened? Joe wondered, watching the water swirl down the drain. He'd done everything he'd been trained to do. Those men should not have died.

He put a hand against the shower wall, fighting to inhale. The crushing weight on his chest made him want to double over.

He'd never known defeat could hurt so much. Until this impasse, all he'd ever tasted was glory.

Sure, he'd known a sliver of doubt at BUD/S, when for the first time ever he'd found himself in the company of men as fit and focused as he was. But even then it hadn't taken long to prove himself, to rise above.

The sound of a door closing snatched Joe from his misery. He turned off the water and reached for the towel. Girding his hips, he pulled aside the shower curtain, only to freeze at the sight of Chief Harlan — 'Harley' — planted in the center of the locker room.

He'd come to talk to him.

Sean Harlan wasn't a tall man. Not only did Joe tower over him, he significantly outranked him. But rank didn't mean much in Special Ops. Wearing crisp desert cammies over his athletic frame, his head shaved as smooth as a baby's bottom, with blue eyes and a mobile mouth that worked in tandem, Harley cut an intimidating figure. Those eyes and that mouth could go from warmly amused to coldly unimpressed in under a tenth of a second.

Right now, both were flat, concealing his thoughts.

From the moment Harley'd joined the JSOTF, he had garnered Joe's respect. With sixteen years of experience in the field, he knew more about SEAL tactics, techniques and procedures, weapons, demo, and mission planning than any SEAL Joe knew, including himself.

Joe acknowledged him with a nod. 'Chief.' Harley was supposed to have been the OIC on the mission gone wrong, but when he'd spiked a fever, Joe had opted to take his place at the last minute, rather than postpone the time-critical reconnaissance.

Harley's stare centered on Joe's bandage. 'Sir.' His blue gaze then raked Joe's frame, as if seeking evidence of his travail.

Joe had lost fifteen pounds. His cheeks were shrunken and sunburned, his lips blistered, his feet and hands swollen.

When Harley finally looked him in the eye, the grim set of his mouth was not without compassion. 'I'm glad you made it, sir,' he said gruffly.

An invisible noose looped around Joe's throat. 'Thank you,' he managed.

'I want to know what happened,' Harley demanded, in a voice that grew gravelly with emotion and, to Joe's horror, accusation. Moisture glittered in his bright blue eyes. The hands at his side curled into fists. 'Those were *my* boys,' he added. 'I was responsible for them.'

At the possibility that Harlan was blaming him, a cold sweat bathed Joe's pores. 'Everything went wrong at once,' he sought to defend himself. 'We were compromised and had a running gunfight with about a hundred of them; the gunship was nowhere within range. Nikko got hit and went under; we had to get him out fast. The tangos had mortars and our ammo ran dry.' He couldn't begin to summarize the odds they'd faced.

But Harley was shaking his head. Obviously, he'd heard the underlying causes and they weren't enough. 'I should've been with them,' he insisted.

'You were sick,' Joe reminded him. At the same time he wondered if he'd made a mistake in taking Harlan's place. If he'd waited a day or two, or if he'd sent Harlan in with a fever, would things have turned out any different?

'I told you not to take my place,' Harley reminded him, tripling Joe's sudden uncertainties. 'I could have gone in, sir, fever or no fever.'

Feeling light-headed, Joe widened his stance. He would have sworn it was the right thing to do. There were forces in the field awaiting the results of their mission. But what if he'd unconsciously longed for one last stint in the field? 'The same thing would've happened if you were there,' he insisted.

'Maybe so,' Harley conceded, 'but those were *my* men.'

Joe's knees trembled. Maybe Harley wasn't blaming him. Maybe he was just coping, like Joe was, with the overwhelming knowledge that the soldiers they'd trained with, eaten with, swapped stories and tender moments with were gone.

'They were my men, too,' Joe countered,

holding the man's burning gaze with difficulty. 'And I'm sorry, Sean,' he added, bringing a tremble to the chief's chin. 'I'm so fucking sorry that it ended this way.'

Harley's hard expression softened with resignation. Silence fell between them, as deep and hopeless as a mortal wound. 'I hope that burn heals for you, sir,' he said, nodding at Joe's wound.

'Thank you.'

Drawing himself upright, he snapped off a tight salute.

With a leaden arm, Joe managed to return it.

Swiveling on his boots, the chief performed an about-face and marched quietly out of the bathing area.

Joe waited three seconds before wilting on one of the benches that lined a wall of lockers.

Jesus, what if it was his fault?

He dropped his face into his hands and shuddered.

$\star$ $\star$ $\star$

It took three days of debriefing, paperwork, packing, and travel to finally arrive home. Joe nosed his soft-top black Jeep into the driveway of his suburban four-bedroom family home in Virginia Beach, cut the engine, and stared.

In the past, he viewed leave time as a necessary but annoying lull between missions. This time, there was no future mission to anticipate. He would not be returning to his team.

You're too senior to remain the operations officer, Captain Lucas had explained. *It's time to assume your own command. Go home and wait for a detailer to give you a call.*

Yet home seemed strangely unfamiliar. When he'd left Virginia back in May, the dogwoods were still blooming. It was late October now, and the ten-year-old maple in his front yard had turned orange. Its brilliance set his white house apart from the others, as did the landscaped flowerbeds. He'd paid some kid to cut his grass over the summer. Someone must have raked his leaves, because the yard looked pristine.

Too apathetic to be grateful, Joe pushed out of his vehicle, grimacing at the pain it caused him. It'd become apparent that he'd injured his back in the fall he'd taken on the heels of the explosion. Yet he'd refused the medication prescribed to him. Pain kept his thoughts off the tragedy.

He had just shut his door when a flurry of

grass-muffled footsteps had him turning his head. His next-door neighbor — what was her name again? — was hurrying across her lawn to see him, cradling his black and white tomcat in her arms.

'Sir!' she called out in a friendly voice. Her shy smile wavered as she beheld the nasty burn on his face, but she pinned it right back in place. 'You're home,' she observed, drawing to a halt by his front tire.

'Yes,' he agreed, his tone abrupt. He was happy to see his cat again but not in the mood for cheery small talk.

Her aqua blue eyes broke over him like a warm Caribbean wave. 'I was worried,' she admitted, causing him to drown in her next words. 'I heard about the tragedy on the news, and I'm so sorry. You must have lost some very good friends.'

Her sincerity was just too much. 'Thank you.' Joe had to look down at his cat. 'Felix, you big mooch. What are you doing taking up this lady's time?' He stepped forward to pet the cat's head.

'Oh, it's not a problem,' the neighbor assured him. 'Felix just realized he could get a steadier diet by coming to my door. Your — ah — cat-sitter isn't terribly punctual.'

Her cool reference to Barbara, his girl-friend, had Joe glancing up. He caught the neighbor taking in the scabs and scratches on his hand, and he snatched it back, turning away to reach into the Jeep's back seat for his duffel bag. As he dragged it out, the weight of the bag made him groan. He turned back, freeing one hand to take the cat. 'Thanks for watching him,' he muttered.

With concern creasing her brow, his neighbor relinquished the feline. 'If there's anything I can do to help . . . ' she offered.

'Thanks,' he said again, more remotely. His true feelings were anything but remote. He felt raw and vulnerable and utterly off balance.

'I'm glad you're home,' she said, backing away. With another shy smile and a flutter of fingers, she retreated, walking crisply across her lawn. She didn't sway her hips — not intentionally, at least.

Bemused by her friendliness, Joe dismissed her from his thoughts and hefted his cat to eye him with admonishment. 'You've been playing the field, haven't you?'

Felix offered him a self-satisfied smirk. 'Nnnro,' he replied, butting Joe's chin with the top of his head.

'Liar,' Joe muttered, heading toward his front door. Every step sent pain shooting up the right side of his back.

★ ★ ★

32

Penny slowly closed her door and put her back against it. Gracious! Her neighbor hadn't looked like that when he left. He was gaunt and sunburned, with more cuts and scrapes on him than on an active three-year-old. And that wound beneath his eye! What, besides an intentional branding or an awful accident, could have caused such a severe burn?

Poor man! Recalling his groan when he'd pulled his bag from the Jeep, she realized he was in pain. What was hurting him, his back?

As a physical therapist at the Portsmouth Naval Medical Center, Penny tended all kinds of injured patients. One look at the lines of pain on Joe Montgomery's face and it was apparent: He'd been through hell.

But why? Commanders sat in their offices, delegating. They sent junior officers and enlisted to do the dangerous work. He must have been in a car accident. That would explain his condition, the wound on his cheek, as well as his back injury.

That had to be it. She pushed from the door, dismayed but satisfied by her conclusions.

★ ★ ★

At ten o'clock that night, she wasn't so sure. 'Hey, it looks like your SEAL's home,'

Ophelia announced, blowing in from the waterfront. 'Every light in the house is on.'

'I know,' said Penny, who sat on her couch, biting off a hangnail. It was out of character for her neighbor to run up his electricity bill. Something was wrong with him. 'So how was work?'

'Slow,' Ophelia admitted, dropping onto the couch and reaching for the remote control.

'Why don't you get a real job?' Penny suggested, glancing at Lia's Hooters T-shirt.

'Real jobs are boring,' her sister retorted, flipping through channels.

Penny was tempted to throw her hands up in despair. Would Lia ever learn to take life seriously? 'I need to ask you a favor,' she said firmly.

'What?' Lia asked with an anxious look.

'I found out today that I have to work tomorrow. The other PT is on maternity leave, and we're short-handed until her replacement comes in. I can't make that two o'clock appointment with the FBI.'

'Can't you reschedule it?'

'Sure I can, if we wait two more weeks, but I don't think that's smart, considering Eric knows of our suspicions, do you?'

Ophelia just looked at her. 'So what are you asking me?'

'I need you to go in my place. Take the evidence and explain our suspicions to an FBI agent.'

Ophelia flopped back against the couch and groaned. 'I was afraid you'd say that.'

'Oh, come on, honey, you can do it,' Penny assured her. 'FBI Headquarters is in Norfolk, right off of 264 and Military Highway. You won't get lost. I'll even give twenty dollars to cover your gas,' she bribed.

Ophelia grimaced. 'Fine, I'll go,' she relented.

'Great,' said Penny, rolling to her feet. 'The journal and gas money are already on the kitchen counter. Don't forget to show them the printout of that e-mail.'

The phone beside the couch rang, startling them both.

'That can't be for me,' Penny pointed out. Her friends were all married, cuddling up with their husbands or putting their babies to sleep.

Ophelia reached for the phone and cautiously lifted the receiver. 'Hello?' she said.

Penny strained her ears to hear who was on the other end.

'Hello,' Lia said again, and the tension in her face let Penny know, instantly, that this was another prank call, like those that had chased Ophelia from her apartment.

'Go to hell,' said Lia hotly before slamming the receiver down. She wrung her hands. 'It's Eric again,' she confessed.

Consternation made Penny's stomach cramp. 'Just take the phone off the hook,' she advised. 'He can't bother us if we don't answer.'

'True.' Ophelia jammed the receiver between the couch cushions.

If only it were equally easy to bury their concern that Eric would interfere before they handed their evidence over to the FBI. 'Be careful tomorrow,' Penny added. She didn't want to alarm Ophelia further, but it paid to be cautious. 'And call me at the hospital as soon as you get back,' she added. 'I want to know what the FBI's going to do for us.'

Surely the authorities would have something to say about Eric stealing and selling a deadly toxin.

'I will,' Ophelia promised. 'Good night, Pen.'

''Night.' Penny checked the doors before going to bed. She settled into her wide and cozy bed, but a nagging sense of danger kept her from falling asleep. She remained awake, even after her sister had retired to the guest room across the hall.

The lights shining from the neighbor's house, a mere twenty feet from hers, brightened Penny's bathroom, yet she couldn't bring herself to get up and shut the door.

Mighty Joe was home. He was safe. The world was still rich for his presence. But something awful had happened to him. She could *feel* it.

What if she came right out and asked him? He'd probably guess that she was smitten with him. What woman with a view of his hot tub wouldn't be? He was ruggedly beautiful, from the top of his golden-brown head to his tan calves. The scar on his face couldn't touch that. He carried himself with so much self-assurance that it was hard to believe there was anything he couldn't do. A man like that wouldn't appreciate her gushing concern.

Yet something deeper than a polite hello had passed between them today. Or was that just wishful thinking? He'd looked at her with those deep-set, army-green eyes, and she'd sensed that for the first time ever, he'd taken note of who she was.

It wasn't exactly the start of a beautiful friendship, but it was something. With a sigh, Penny closed her eyes, dreaming of getting to know her neighbor better.

3

Lia found the dark brick façade at the FBI Headquarters in Norfolk as intimidating as she'd imagined. Perhaps it was the fact that it was enclosed by cement barriers and monitored by myriad security devices. The guards weren't content to X-ray her enormous purse, either. They pawed through it, seizing both her sister's cell phone and her own can of pepper spray. Her embroidered jeans and coral-colored mesh sweater met with frowning disapproval.

In an environment that epitomized the rules and regulations she regularly flouted, Lia felt like a fish out of water. She nearly fled the building in defiant terror, except that the special agent who came to fetch her from the waiting room was scarcely older than she, with flame-red hair and a ready smile. She wore a honey-colored pantsuit that appealed to Lia's sense of style.

'Hi, I'm Special Agent Lindstrom,' said the woman, offering a handshake. 'You can call me Hannah.'

'Ophelia Price,' said Lia, standing up. The other woman had to be six feet tall; she made

Lia feel diminutive. 'I'm here for my sister, Penelope.' At the woman's raised eyebrows, she added, 'We were named after our grandmothers.'

'Aha,' said the agent. 'Well, why don't you follow me?'

She escorted Lia from the reception area, down a hall, to a private room barely larger than a closet. 'This is where we do our interviews,' she explained, slipping behind a desk and motioning for Lia sit in one of the two chairs. 'Can I interest you in coffee?' she asked, indicating the percolator perched atop a tray table.

'Oh, no thanks. I'm nervous enough.'

'There's no need to be nervous,' Hannah reassured her, lacing her long fingers together. A sizable diamond winked on her left hand. 'What can I do for you?'

Lia rummaged in her purse and produced the journal Penny'd instructed her to bring. She withdrew a square of paper from the back of the notebook and unfolded it. 'Our father died five years ago, when his car went off the road. The accident was deemed suspicious, but nothing came of that. Penny just found this in Daddy's journal.' She handed the printed e-mail message across the desk.

The special agent skimmed the paper with

apple-green eyes. 'Who is Eric Tomlinson?' she asked.

'He used to be my father's partner. They worked together at BioTech, a biochemical lab outside of Langley Air Force Base.'

The agent nodded, indicating that she'd heard of it.

'Just before my father died, a toxic by-product called ricin went missing from the lab. There was a big stink about it in the news.'

'Ricin,' repeated the agent, with a spark of interest. As she studied the text, her auburn eyebrows drew together. ''Sixty-four thousand dollars was wired this morning to the account specified,'' she read out loud. 'Why would your father have kept this?'

'He suspected Eric of selling the ricin. It says so right here in his journal in the last couple of entries.' Lia opened the journal to the appropriate page and gave it to the agent to peruse. 'My sister thinks that when our father saw the e-mail, he confronted Eric and gave him time to do the right thing.' She pushed their suspicion through a tightening throat. 'But Eric was more concerned with covering up his crime.'

The gaze that rose from the handwritten journal was thoughtful, relieving Lia's fear that their suspicions would be mocked. 'And all this happened five years ago.'

'Is that a problem?' Lia asked.

'If we're talking murder with malice aforethought, then there's no statute of limitations that would prevent us from pressing charges,' Hannah reassured her. 'The problem here is whether the trail has gone cold.'

'Five years is a long time,' Lia conceded.

'Can you tell me where your father died?'

'Somewhere close to Morgantown, West Virginia. He was on a business trip.'

'Do you have a copy of his death certificate?'

'Penny would,' Lia said, realizing that despite her grief, Penny had managed to contact their father's insurance company, meet with lawyers, plead for Social Security benefits. Meanwhile, Lia had simply taken up a drug habit. She owed Penny bigtime.

'I'll need you to fax me that certificate as soon as you find it. I'm assuming the car was totaled and hauled to a junkyard. If it hasn't been scrapped, we can examine it, as well as take a look the first investigation.'

Lia tugged on a dangly earring. 'Do you think you'll find anything, after all this time?'

'You never know,' said the agent with a shrug. 'There ought to have been plenty of information documented right after the ricin went missing. We might be able to build a case on that.'

'You don't, um, offer bodyguard services, do you?' Lia inquired.

The agent's quick glance gave nothing away. 'Why do you ask?'

'Well, I think I might have blown it by confronting Eric over the phone.' Lia bit her bottom lip.

'You made contact with the suspect,' the agent confirmed.

'Yeah, when Penny told me about the journal, I kind of flipped out,' Lia confessed. And that was probably an understatement. She'd been furious to think that the father she'd adored with all her heart had been murdered by his friend and partner, of all people. His death had cast a pall over what ought to have been the best years of her life.

Hannah reached for a pen. 'What exactly did you say to Eric Tomlinson?' she asked, pen poised over a legal pad.

'I identified myself.'

'Yes?'

'He . . . made a sound of surprise. Then I asked him how he slept at night, considering what he'd done.'

'You didn't mention the ricin?'

'No, but I think he knew what I was talking about.'

Hannah jotted herself a note. 'What did he say to you?'

'It was hard to understand him because he stutters. But he did say something that sounded like 'You're gonna regret this.'' She hadn't told Penny that part.

'Is that the last time you spoke with him?' the agent asked.

'Not really. He's been calling me. I sublet my apartment and moved in with my sister to avoid his calls, but last night he found me again.' She shivered at the recollection.

'What does he say when he calls you?'

'Not much,' Lia admitted. 'He can barely get a word out.'

Hannah Lindstrom tapped her pen on the legal pad. 'We don't issue personal body-guards,' she said, answering Lia's earlier question. 'If a witness in a major case is being intimidated, we'll ask the U.S. Marshal's service to protect them. That's not exactly the situation here.'

Lia blushed, feeling chastised.

'If you feel threatened, you can call your local phone company and give them permission to identify your caller,' the woman suggested. 'The police handle misdemeanors like harassment.' She pulled a business card from the holder on the desk. 'Here's my card. If you come across anything else related to the ricin, be sure to let me know.'

'I will,' said Lia, dropping the card into her purse. She realized, with a cinching in her chest, that the FBI wasn't going to rush out and arrest Eric tonight. 'So, what now?' she asked.

'I'll take a look at the earlier investigation and give you a call. I have your contact information,' she added, referring to the sheet that Lia'd filled out in the waiting room. 'I assume you're going to stay with your sister for a while?'

'Yes,' Lia acknowledged with a grimace. As much as she'd like to be back in her own apartment, she couldn't afford to return, anyway.

A vulnerable feeling accompanied Lia out of the building and into her car. She eased away from the FBI compound with her returned pepper spray, only to find herself stuck in the heavy traffic pouring out of the Norfolk Naval Operations Base.

'What is it with sailors getting off at three in the afternoon?' she groused, wanting desperately to get back to Penny's in Virginia Beach.

She hadn't felt safe being in possession of the journal. Now that the FBI was holding it, she strangely felt less safe.

It was a bleak and overcast October day. It

wasn't particularly cold, yet Lia shivered and cranked up the heat in her Oldsmobile. Keeping an eye on the rearview mirror, she scanned the drivers behind her.

Would she even recognize Eric after all these years? She'd met him only a couple of times when he and his wife came to their house for her father's Christmas dinner. She'd freak out if she saw him behind her now. But what could he do to her, run her off the road and drag her out of the car? She'd blast him with her pepper spray if he did that.

She'd owned the can of pepper spray for three years now and never used it. Oh, crap, that stuff didn't go bad, did it?

As she grubbed in her purse, the traffic inched forward. Leery of being cut off by a lane switcher, Lia accelerated abruptly, only to brake again. With one hand in her purse, she sifted through the sea of makeup.

Mascara, lipstick, lip gloss, eyeliner. Aha, pepper spray.

She withdrew the can and turned it over. Where was the expiration date on this thing?

Bam!

With an exclamation of horror, Lia looked up to realize that she'd plowed into the back of the Honda Civic she'd been tailing. She dropped the pepper spray and clutched the steering wheel in consternation. Oh, my God, not another accident!

The driver's door on the smaller car opened slowly. Out stepped a scowling young man in battle dress uniform. Lia had to blink because for a second there she thought she was seeing Al Pacino, the way he looked in *Scarface*. And oh, my God, he was coming toward her car to talk to her. What if he got violent? She groped for the pepper spray she'd just dropped.

'What did you think was gonna happen with you tailgating me like that?' he demanded.

She cracked the window just enough to say, 'I barely tapped you.'

'Tapped me?' His eyebrows shot up. He gestured at the back of his car. 'Obviously, you haven't seen the damage, any more than you were looking where you were going.'

'I was looking!' she retorted with heat.

'Bullshit. You were too busy looking at yourself in the mirror and reaching for your cell phone.'

'I don't even own a cell phone, asshole.' If he wasn't going to be civil, then neither was she. 'I was reaching for this!' She held the pepper spray up to the crack in the window.

'Whoa.' He stepped back, throwing his hands up. 'Put that away. Are you crazy?'

'Yes, I'm crazy. Now get back in your car

46

and drive. The traffic's starting to move.'

He eyed the damage done to the back of his car, then looked at her larger car in disgust — it was probably totally unharmed. 'Hell, no,' he said. He went back to his car and came out with a cell phone. With a challenging look, he punched three numbers and held it to his ear.

He was calling the cops. 'Stop!' Lia unlocked her door and struggled to get out, breaking a fingernail. 'Ouch! Damn it! Stop,' she pleaded. 'You don't need to do that!'

His brown eyes seemed to take a snapshot of her body as she rose from the car. In the next instant, he was slipping the phone into his camouflage trousers. 'Oh, so you have insurance?' he asked her, on a far more reasonable note.

'Er, not exactly.' She'd tried to pay her car insurance two months ago, but it was just too much money.

His mouth curled with renewed contempt.

'But I'll pay you whatever you need to get your fender fixed.'

He stepped back. 'Stop waving that thing in the air.'

'Oh. Sorry. I think it's expired anyway.' She lowered the pepper spray. 'Listen, I'll write you a check. Just give me a ballpark figure.'

'Do you think I'm stupid?' he asked her on

a note so incredulous that she took closer stock of him.

Maybe he was a boy genius in uniform, but not likely. 'No,' she said carefully. He looked about eighteen years old, but his uniform made him appear important. His black hair was cut so short that the blustery wind had no effect on it, unlike her own locks, which were blowing into her eyes.

'Look, let's start again,' she proposed. 'I'm sorry I tapped your car, okay? I'm a little distracted this morning. Do you want me to pay for the damage or not?'

'Oh, you'll pay,' he said, in a way that had her snatching her hair out of her eyes. 'But I'm not taking a check.'

Perplexed, she tipped her head back to glare at him. He was amazingly good-looking, with chocolate-colored eyes and lush, lush lashes. 'Well, a check's all I've got,' she countered, ignoring the sudden tug of sexual attraction. 'It's not like I carry a bunch of cash with me.'

'Come on,' he chided. 'I can tell with one glance at your car that your check would be useless.'

She gasped, outraged by his assumption.

'And if my instincts are right, you've got some unpaid speeding tickets.'

'Listen, young man,' she snapped, before

he issued any more accurate statements, 'I don't have to take this kind of slander from you. Why don't you get in your car and drive home to mommy?'

He quirked an eyebrow and cocked his head, like, *You did not just say that.* 'Tell you what,' he said, with a hint of humor lacing his Philadelphia accent. 'How 'bout you take me out to dinner and we'll call it even.'

'Are you crazy?' she cried, amazed by his presumption.

'Then you'd prefer I press charges,' he said with a shrug. He made to retrieve his cell phone.

'Wait!' Her heart was thumping and her thoughts were still muddled, but she could think clearly enough to realize that there was yet a way out of this predicament. 'You're going to forget about this accident if I take you out to dinner?' she clarified, giving herself time to plot.

'I'm partial to seafood,' he added with a gleam in his eyes. She suspected he was laughing at her, only he didn't so much as crack a smile.

'How do I know that you're not psycho or something?'

He shrugged again. 'You don't.'

'Oh, great. That's reassuring. What are you, like eighteen years old? Do you have a thing for older women?'

'Age isn't the only mark of maturity,' he said, utterly unperturbed.

'Right.' She glanced back at her car, gauging her ability to jump inside it and take off.

'I've memorized your license plate number,' he added, as if reading her thoughts. 'I will call the police.'

Lia envisioned Penny's reaction to the police showing up at her doorstep.

'Meet me for dinner tonight at Peabody's at seven,' he persisted.

Yeah, right. Like she'd really go out with a kid like him, even if Peabody's was the hottest spot in town. 'Okay,' she lied. 'I'll be there.'

The traffic had begun to flow around them. Someone blew the horn. They were getting dirty looks.

'Give me that necklace you're wearing.'

'What?' From the necklace dangled a cameo pendant that once belonged to her grandmother.

'If you want it back, you'll show up tonight.'

'I am not giving you my necklace,' she snapped indignantly. 'Here, you can have my ring.' She twisted the opal ring off her right ring finger. It'd been a gift from her last boyfriend, the jackass. She'd never miss it.

He accepted the offering with a suspicious frown.

'Now leave me alone. I'll see you soon enough,' she added, raking the faces of the drivers passing them, wondering if Eric was having a good laugh.

'You owe me dinner,' the soldier reminded, following her to her car. 'Don't break your word.' He shut her door for her. 'Seat belt,' he added, tapping on the glass.

With a growl of annoyance, Lia whipped the seat belt across her chest and snapped it into place. She looked up to see Soldier Boy slipping fluidly into his car. He skewered her with a look in his rearview mirror, and then he took off, his motor roaring loudly.

'Annoying brat,' Lia muttered, her own car lurching into drive. She was shaken by the incident, but it served at least to take her mind off greater worries, like whether Eric knew she had gone to the FBI and whether he was plotting his reprisal.

* * *

At seven-thirty in the morning, Penny stepped out of her house in her uniform, relieved that it was Friday. She paused on her front stoop to savor the crisp air drawn in by last night's rain. The sun edging over the house across the street had turned the sky a buttery yellow. She would have preferred to watch it rise over the Atlantic Ocean, but duty called and she had to go. At least she would have the weekend off for working overtime.

The thud of a closing door drew her gaze to Joe Montgomery's house. She watched him limp toward his Jeep. He wore his dress blues, complete with golden tassels and brass buttons that fairly gleamed, topped off by a smart combination cap. She wondered what function he was headed to, dressed like that.

As if sensing her perusal, his head turned and his stride faltered. Despite the shadow cast by the brim of his cap, she could see lines of pain etched on either side of his mouth.

'Good morning,' she called across the lawn. Had he slept at all since his return? He'd left the lights on every night.

'Morning,' he growled back. Averting his gaze, he continued doggedly toward his Jeep.

She watched with concern as he shut himself inside and backed the vehicle slowly out of his driveway.

He used to drive like a bat out of hell.

With a shake of her head, Penny told herself not to fret over him. There were plenty of patients at Portsmouth Naval Medical Center who welcomed her attention.

Joe wanted to die. The pain in his chest took up so much room, there wasn't space for oxygen. His eyes burned. His knees quaked as he stood in formation with the other SEALs in attendance at Smiley's funeral.

Arlington National Cemetery was a palette of autumn hues. Pots of colorful mums flanked the myriad headstones. Vermillion maples and golden oaks fortified the perimeter of the graveyard. Was Nature mocking him? How could she seem so vibrant in the presence of death?

The air was saturated with the scent of lilies. In the midst of dripping blossoms lay Smiley's coffin, draped with the stars and stripes of the American flag.

The bugler lifted the horn to his lips to emit the purest notes Joe had ever heard. They cut straight through his heart.

Day is done. Gone the sun. From the lakes. From the hills. From the sky. All is well. Safely rest. God is nigh.

Boom. The first volley of the seven M14s cracked into the silence. Joe locked his knees to keep them from buckling. In his mind's eye, Nikko passed out, dragging Curry down with him.

Boom. Mortar rounds punched into the earth and made the mountain tremble.

Boom. The fireball within the helo mushroomed outward, thrusting Joe away on a wave of incinerating heat.

He swayed. The men standing at attention on either side of him shifted closer. 'Sir?' one of them inquired beneath his breath.

'I'm fine,' rasped Joe, but he wasn't.

If the men around him knew he'd been Smiley's OIC, they were circumspect enough not to mention it. If they didn't know, they would never guess. Middle-aged officers didn't take the place of savvy, experienced chiefs. It was unheard-of, a put-down to the enlisted man's integrity.

So why had he done it?

Beyond Smiley's mourning family, there stood the press, momentarily subdued, oblivious to the fact that he was the sole survivor of that hideous disaster.

God, keep it that way.

I have to get through this, Joe told himself, digging deep for composure. It was nearly over. The funeral detail stepped forward to fold the flag in a shape reminiscent of the tricorn hats of the Revolutionary War. Admiral Johansen presented it to Smiley's mother, who cradled it in her arms like a baby, the way she'd once cradled her son.

Joe squeezed his eyes shut. He couldn't watch.

The honor guard withdrew. It was the SEALs' cue to merge and form a line. Joe fumbled to remove his trident pin. His fingers were still swollen, tender. He couldn't see through his tear-blurred eyes. He trailed the man in front of him. And then it was his turn to hammer his pin into the lid of the coffin.

Boom. Half-blinded by tears, he somehow managed to align his pin with the others. His teammates went to shake hands with family members. Joe broke rank and limped toward his car.

Once inside his vehicle, he clung to the steering wheel and let his chest heave. The salt of his tears stung the wound on his cheek.

Help me, God. The pain in his heart was getting worse, not better.

Twenty minutes later, Joe drew his first full breath.

With a sharp sniff, he lifted his gaze at the coffin, awaiting burial at the height of the hill. Smiley's family still hovered around it, loath to leave their beloved Richard.

I'm so sorry, thought Joe, looking up at them. *If my arrogance and ambition got him killed, please forgive me. 'Cause I can't forgive myself.*

Twenty-eight trident pins winked in the sunlight.

Commander Montgomery was finally back. Penny rolled over as the headlights of his Jeep strafed her ceiling. He cut his engine and slammed his door shut. *Now I can sleep*, she thought, snuggling deeper into her pillow.

But then strange noises seeped through the window she'd cracked to counteract the higher thermostat setting Ophelia preferred. Thuds and shouts snatched her from her sleep. She slitted an eye and realized that, in contrast to the previous nights, her neighbor was keeping the lights off. What on earth was going on with him?

It was out of character for the SEAL to make any noise. Certainly he'd thrown a couple of parties that got loud, dragging on until three in the morning. But the commander by himself was so stealthy that Penny never noticed his comings and goings.

Until tonight. Something was terribly wrong. Penny had dealt with wounded soldiers too long not to sense it. And she couldn't sleep because of it.

Another thud reached her ears, followed by a sound like a roar.

That's it. Throwing back the covers, she rolled out of bed. What if he was hurt and shouting for help? Her professional role would not let her turn a blind eye.

She snatched up her bathrobe, wriggled her feet into slippers, and left her room.

A peek into the guest room showed that Lia was sleeping soundly. Penny went downstairs, fetched her house keys, and locked her sister inside.

The keys jingled in her pocket as she crossed the lawn toward his dark house. An early frost crunched beneath her slippers. Her breath came out in a snowy vapor. She arrived at Joe's door, chilly in her night attire, and knocked.

What am I doing here? Penny wondered, hearing nothing but silence coming from inside her neighbor's house.

She reassured herself that she had every right to be concerned. If he rebuffed her, she would at least tell him to tone it down.

She raised a hand and knocked again.

Nothing. Perhaps he'd finally gone to sleep.

Lovely. She could go back to her own bed. But as she turned to go, the sound of shattering glass wrested her attention. A lurid curse followed.

Not only was her neighbor still awake, but he sounded like he'd just hurt himself. Penny swiveled toward the door and knocked more loudly, calling, 'Commander? Are you okay?'

She put her ear to the door and overheard

a loud thud followed by a moan. She reached for the doorknob and found it locked.

Okay, she had a choice: help herself to the key that she'd seen Barbara, the cat-sitter, use, or walk away.

She started to leave. Three steps from the door, she sighed and doubled back. Retrieving the key from under the third flowerpot, she let herself in.

'Commander?' she called with a shiver of uncertainty. 'It's your next-door neighbor, sir. I'm coming in.'

4

Penny slipped inside Lieutenant Commander Montgomery's front door and shut it quietly behind her. Not only was the foyer dark as pitch, but his house was bigger than hers, the layout unfamiliar. She pocketed his key alongside her own and waded into shadow.

A light, shining from deep within the recesses of the home, was her only beacon. As she felt her way past a flight of stairs, something silky rubbed against her calf, emitting a yowl. 'Felix!' she breathed, her heart hammering.

The hardwood under her slippers transitioned into steps that descended to a sunken family room, a space scantily illumined by the light, which she now saw was coming from the kitchen. Across the distance, she spied broken bits of glass glinting on the countertops amid a spattering of blood. The potent scent of whiskey reached her nostrils. 'Commander?' she called in consternation.

A shackle seemed to close around her right ankle. It startled a hoarse screech from her throat as it yanked her off her feet. She threw out her arms out to break her fall and landed across the hard body of a man lying concealed in shadow.

He wasn't content to bring her down, either. He grappled and rolled her to the floor. In the next instant, she was lying on her stomach with her right cheek embedded in the carpet and her left arm locked behind her back. A heavy weight pressured her spine. Her legs were immobilized.

'Who're you?' he growled in her ear, his words slurring together.

Something warm and wet plopped upon her cheek.

'Lieutenant Penny Price, sir,' she said breathlessly, 'from next door.' He was bleeding on her, she realized, catching the scent of blood.

'Penny.' Some of the pressure eased from her spine. 'Copper penny,' he mused on a strange note. 'Never knew your eyes were blue.'

There was no way he could see her eyes in the dark, which meant he'd noticed them the other day. 'Sir, I believe you're hurt. I'm in the medical profession. I can help you,' she added in a no-nonsense voice.

'Cut my hand on glass,' he corroborated. He grew abruptly heavier, and she feared he was passing out on top of her, in which case, she might never get out from under him.

'Commander!' she said sharply.

He lurched to attention. 'Hmmm?'

'You're hurting me. Do you mind getting off me, sir?'

'Sorry.' He withdrew his weight, and she rolled to one side until she made him out, struggling to sit back on his heels. A dark stain streaked down one side of his face, coming from a cut above his right eye. He hadn't gotten that by picking up glass.

'Let me help you,' she repeated. Clambering to her feet, she sought to help him rise. 'Up you go, sir, before you bleed all over your carpet.'

He went up easily enough, but then he nearly pitched over again, and she had to muscle him upright, propping herself beneath his armpit. 'Which way to a bathroom, sir?' she asked, wanting to avoid the kitchen and all that broken glass.

' 'hind you.'

Sure enough, there was a door in the opposite wall. 'Okay, let's get you cleaned up.'

She half-dragged, half-carried him toward the opening in the wall. It was impossible not to notice how hot, big, and lean his body felt, draped heavily over hers. 'Watch your eyes,' she warned, fumbling inside the door for a light.

As he flinched and groaned, she took in the

room beyond her with second thoughts.

Oh, dear, this was his bedroom.

And what a bed he had, she marveled, her gaze momentarily glued to the California king. It was covered with a thick black comforter that reflected the rest of the room's decor — black and khaki geometric patterns. His dressers and bed were of Scandinavian design, with clean, uncluttered surfaces.

He started toward the wide, inviting bed.

'Oh, no, in here,' she urged, tugging him toward what had to be the bathroom.

As she wrestled him into the room and flicked on the light, she noticed more blood dripping from his right hand. So he *had* cut himself picking up glass. Was that before or after he cut his brow ridge?

She positioned him in front of the vanity, noting in her peripheral vision the burgundy wallpaper and handsome brass-and-marble fixtures. 'Let's have a look at you.'

Propping him against the sink, she craned her neck to assess the cut just beneath his eyebrow. Blood still pulsed in a sluggish trickle. Meanwhile, two fingers on his right hand were bleeding all over the tile floor.

'We're going to treat your hand first,' she decided, cranking on the water.

'What happened?' he wondered, squinting at his reflection. He touched the cut. 'Ow!'

'Help me out here, Commander,' she said crisply. Pulling his hand under the water, she lathered him with the liquid soap found in the dispenser, noting the number of scabs and calluses. Could he have damaged his hands like this in a car accident? How, trying to pull someone from the wreckage? 'Do you feel any residual glass in your fingers?' she asked, patting him dry.

'No.'

She grabbed up a handful of tissues and applied pressure.

'Feel stupid,' he admitted. Closing his eyes, he swayed on his feet.

She threw an arm around his waist. 'Don't fall again, sir. Here, do you want to sit down?'

'Yes.'

She helped him settle onto the closed toilet seat. 'Keep pressure on your fingers while I take a look at your eye.'

His whiskey-laced breath could have lit a fire if she'd had a match. Oddly, the scent of it was not unpleasant as it rose into her nostrils. If anything, it made her feel a little intoxicated herself.

She wet a clean washcloth and gently dabbed the blood from his face while he sat in a silent stupor. 'You really ought to get a stitch or two,' she commented, stifling her awareness of him. 'This cut is deep.'

'No medic,' he insisted, coherent enough to make his wishes known.

She pursed her lips in disapproval, but she didn't argue. The cut would leave a scar if it went unattended, but compared to the burn on his left cheek, who was going to notice?

'I don't suppose you have a first-aid kit — '

Her request was cut short by the sudden weight of his head against her breasts. He'd nodded off, burrowing his nose into the deep V of her bathrobe.

Her heart leapt. Only in her wildest fantasies had she imagined her neighbor nuzzling her breasts. She cupped his face and forcibly brought his head up. 'Do you have a first-aid kit?' she inquired firmly.

His deep green gaze tried to focus on her mouth. 'Under the sink,' he said.

'Sit still,' she told him. 'Don't move.' She took her hands off him long enough to locate the box, marked with a red cross. 'This is good,' she praised, finding it well stocked. From the corner of her eye, she noticed the SEAL assessing her figure in the frumpy velour robe.

'How'd you get in here?' he asked her, sounding suddenly more sober.

'Let's not worry about that now,' she said in her best bedside voice. 'Hold still while I put this bandage on you.' As she affixed it across his handsome eyebrow, she examined the wound on his cheek. 'How did you burn your face?' she asked him casually.

'Shrapnel,' he said without giving it much thought.

'Not a car accident?' she queried. It wasn't any of her business, she knew. But the only way to really comfort him was to know what he'd been through.

'No,' he said, his eyes growing glassy.

She sensed dark memories rising inside him and wondered if there was anything she could do to dispel them. Perhaps if he talked it through . . . 'Let me see your fingers.' As she taped bandages over his cuts, she dared to ask him, 'I take it you had a pretty tough day, huh?'

Moisture put a glitter in his bloodshot eyes. 'Yeah,' he rasped.

'Where'd you go this morning?' she asked, keeping her tone light.

He was quiet so long, she thought he wouldn't answer. 'Funeral,' he said at last.

Her breath caught at his pained admission. 'Who died?' she asked with gentle concern.

'One of my men,' he said in a hollow voice.

'I'm so sorry. That must have been awful for you.'

His Adam's apple bobbed. To her dismay, tears flooded his eyes, only he was too drunk to care or notice. But the sight of them tore at her heartstrings. She should have realized that Mighty Joe would be the kind of leader to take the loss of a junior SEAL seriously. 'How old was he?' she asked, encouraging him to unburden himself.

'Like ... twenty,' he answered as tears streaked his face.

Penny found herself smoothing a curl on the top of his head. Soft and silky, it was the color of maturing oak leaves. 'He was just a baby,' she commiserated.

'Yeah.' With a start, he noticed that his face was wet. He wiped the tears with an impatient swipe of his hand. 'Shit,' he swore, clearly perturbed that she'd caught him crying.

'Why don't you get some sleep?' Penny recommended. 'Maybe you'll feel better in the morning. Where do you keep your pajamas?' she asked, eyeing his blood-stained button-up shirt.

The question seemed to confuse him. 'My what?'

'Pajamas,' she repeated, checking the hook on the back of the door.

'I don't wear any,' he said, preparing to push to his feet.

'Oh. Well, you can't sleep in that.' She tackled his shirt buttons with efficiency, steeling herself against the thrill of baring his shoulders. He wore a sleeveless T-shirt that highlighted the breadth of his torso, making him look like a superhero, or every girl's wet dream.

She filled his sink with cold water and left his shirt and washcloth soaking. 'Would you like some privacy?'

He was squinting at her. 'What for?'

'Never mind,' she said, hot in the face. 'Let's get you into bed.'

She helped him to his feet and, keeping a firm grip on his elbow, steered him toward his mammoth-sized bed. He'd lapsed into silence — embarrassed, no doubt. She pulled back the covers and moved him closer. 'In you go.'

He put one hand on the mattress, but with his world still reeling, he lost his balance and grabbed her to slow his descent.

Penny ended up sprawled on top of him for the second time that night. Only he didn't wrestle her down. Instead, he groaned with pain, his grip on her arm almost painful.

'Are you okay?' she asked in consternation.

'Don't move,' he begged with his eyes squeezed shut.

She remained still, loath to cause him any more discomfort, but she couldn't help but note that she was sprawled across his dense body like they were lovers.

Bit by bit, the grip on her arm eased, and then he gave a sigh, as if a spasm had passed.

'Go to sleep, sir,' she whispered, thinking he'd just passed out.

He rolled without warning, causing her to slip into his embrace as he turned onto his side, captured her face in one hand, and lowered his mouth.

She let it happen, stealing a purely selfish moment to gauge whether her fascination with this man was warranted. With stealth that made her gasp, he swept his tongue between her lips and kissed her, with one purpose only. Penny's adrenaline skyrocketed. She told herself she would pull back shortly.

But the whiskey-laced kiss intoxicated her. It went on and on until the encroachment of his palm on her breast roused her to reality. 'Good night, Commander,' she muttered, squirming away from him.

To her relief, he let her go. She slipped off the bed and scuttled to the door. Snapping off the light, she shut it behind her.

He didn't say a word back. Perhaps he'd passed out already.

Penny tottered into his family room. Mercy! No wonder women flocked to his door! The man had skills that would make the devil jealous. Too bad *that* would never happen again; she was sure he hadn't known he was kissing the lieutenant next door.

As she crossed his still-dark family room, she made out the silhouette of a table lamp, lying on the floor. Curious to see what other damage he'd done, she flicked the light switch and caught her breath.

The room was a disaster. It looked like a bomb had detonated, especially with all that blood smeared across the cream-colored carpet. 'Oh, no,' she murmured. The carpet would be ruined by tomorrow — unless someone got the blood out tonight.

Envisioning Joe's response tomorrow to the destruction he'd wrought, she groaned. He was already heartsick over the death of one of his men. He didn't need to deal with this and what promised to be a monstrous hangover. That left only one thing to do.

With a sigh and a squaring of her shoulders, Penny headed for the kitchen in search of carpet cleaner.

★   ★   ★

Joe felt like he was being stabbed in the eye with a needle. It turned out to be a ray of sunlight piercing his blinds. He groaned and turned toward the wall. That move prompted pounding in his head and a wave of nausea.

Oh, God. What had he done to himself?

69

At least he was safe in his own bed, though he was still dressed in his clothes, for the most part.

What time was it? He blinked at the clock. It took several seconds to process that it was afternoon already — three o'clock in the afternoon, to be precise. Jesus. How late had he stayed up? He tried to remember and drew a blank.

Careful not to jar his pounding head, he scooted off the bed and plodded into the bathroom to pee. There was blood on the floor, under his feet. His shirt was soaking in blood-stained water.

He blinked at the bandages on his right hand. Glancing in the mirror, he found a third bandage crisscrossing his eyebrow. He leaned closer to the mirror in disbelief. Damn, he'd given himself quite a shiner.

A vision flickered and he seized it, recapturing a memory, followed by another, and then another. He cursed in dismay.

The lieutenant next door. She'd been in his house. She'd washed the cuts on his hand and patched up his brow, her tone both efficient and firm.

She'd asked him questions. Lots of questions.

He put a hand to his forehead, trying desperately to remember. What had she gotten out of him last night?

Shit, the last thing he needed was others to know who he was. The press was on a quest to find him, to publicize his story. Other SEALs knew better than to say anything. They would fiercely guard his identity. But what if his nosy neighbor was eager for money or fame? What would stop her from exposing him?

With his thoughts in a tailspin, Joe washed his hands and splashed water onto his face. He brushed his teeth and helped himself to headache medicine.

Resentment simmered. It was hard enough living with the thought that his choice to take Harlan's place might have cost nineteen men their lives. Christ, he didn't need the media asking him if he blamed himself. He shut the medicine cabinet with more force than necessary.

Obviously, he was going to have to face his ministering angel and find out just how much she knew.

Stalking out of his bedroom, Joe was halfway across his TV room when the realization hit him: The carpet under his feet was damp. Someone had scrubbed it. And the room smelled of rug cleaner.

His gaze flew to the kitchen. He knew he hadn't left it like that, with every surface gleaming.

She had some gall cleaning up his house,

like she was his wife or something. He'd planned on eating breakfast first — cancel, make that lunch. But with his temper at a boil, he couldn't stomach any food.

He wanted an explanation, and he wanted it now.

★ ★ ★

Penny backed down her porch steps to admire the life-sized scarecrow she'd just stuffed. It guarded her front door from a lawn chair, a festive reminder that Halloween was less than a week away. All she needed now was a cornucopia of gourds and several pumpkins to complement the chrysanthemums that graced each step.

'We need to talk.'

With a gasp, Penny whirled to find her neighbor standing less than a yard away. Heavens, where had he come from? She put a hand to her pounding heart, aware that its beat was not subsiding beneath his glare. Sober and in the light of day, he looked ten times more dangerous, more forceful, and — God help her — more appealing than ever.

The memory of his kiss warmed her like a ray of sunlight.

'Of course,' she said, forcing a smile. Questions whirled, like just how much of last night did he remember and what, exactly, did he have an issue with? 'Why don't you come in?'

With neighbors taking advantage of the sunny Saturday, he nodded in favor of that suggestion.

She led the way inside, guiding him through her foyer to the kitchen. 'Would you like a cup of cider?' she asked, hoping to set a friendly tone.

'This isn't a social call.' He crossed his arms and planted his feet.

Penny drew a breath and turned to face him. He stood a foot taller than she, with a frown that formed a crease between his eyebrows. It was all she could do not to appear as intimidated as she felt. 'Okay, then. How can I help you?'

'You broke into my house last night,' he accused quietly, his expression grim and watchful. 'How'd you get in?'

'You keep a key under a flowerpot.' She'd put it right back where she found it. 'I could tell by listening at your door that you were hurt, sir. I'm sorry for entering without permission.' Since he didn't want to be neighborly, she fell back on military speak.

His eyes narrowed at the intentional formality. 'Did it even occur to you that I would rather have been left alone?'

Penny considered whether that was true. 'With all due respect, sir, you weren't in any state to know what you wanted.'

Anger flashed in his khaki green eyes. 'Whatever state I was in, in my own home, is none of your goddamn business, Lieutenant,' he growled back, addressing her by her inferior rank.

'Correct, sir,' she said, swallowing her intimidation, 'but your physical well-being is my business, as is the well-being of any serviceman or woman,' she added, impersonalizing the incident.

His hot glare raked her from head to toe. 'If you tell a soul about last night,' he warned, articulating each word, 'then you can kiss your career goodbye. Is that clear enough?'

Puzzled, Penny sought the reason for his threat. What on earth was he afraid of? That she would accuse him of indecent behavior? Did he even remember kissing her? 'Crystal, sir,' she said, searching his locked features for an answer. 'Perhaps you'll tone it down next time, so that I'm less privy to your business,' she suggested, indignant that he would think her capable of such low behavior.

A dull blush highlighted his cheekbones, and she felt a little better for it.

'I don't know what kind of game you're playing,' he added, revealing his confusion,

74

'but whatever it is, you're wasting your time.'

'I don't play games,' she told him, dropping the 'sir' from her statement.

Her answer made him hesitate. She could see him struggling to understand her.

'You cleaned my rug,' he said, his tone still accusing.

'Yes, I did.'

'Why?'

Did he really want an honest answer? 'Because I thought you'd already dealt with enough.'

His frown became ferocious. He took a step forward, and Penny took a cautionary step back. 'Leave me alone,' he said through his teeth. 'I don't need a nosy neighbor prying into my business.'

Penny was too hurt by the word 'prying' to make a quick reply. Uncertainty chased across his face in the wake of his anger, before he pivoted, stalking toward the door. It closed quietly behind him.

Five seconds elapsed before the silence was broken by the sound of running feet. 'Oh, my God!' Ophelia cried, bursting into the kitchen, her face a reflection of outrage. 'Was that your SEAL?' she asked, seizing Penny's arms. 'Who does he think he was, talking to you like that?'

Penny blinked away her numbness. Consternation rose in its place as she realized that

Ophelia had just overheard every word Commander Montgomery had said. 'Don't worry about it,' she answered firmly. 'He wasn't threatening me; he was protecting his privacy.'

'What do you mean he wasn't threatening you?' Lia cried. 'I heard what he said. He implied that he was going to ruin your career. And for what? All you did was patch up his cuts and clean his carpet.' Penny'd had to explain why she slept until ten this morning.

'I said forget it,' Penny repeated. 'He's been through enough, okay? He didn't mean to threaten me. If he really knew me, he wouldn't have bothered.'

'Oh, come on!' Ophelia propped her hands on her jeans-clad hips. 'There's no excuse for him talking to you that way! He's the one who got drunk last night.'

'You need to forget about that, too,' Penny cautioned.

'What?'

'Stories like that can damage a man's career. He's hurting inside. Try to be sensitive to that and forget the rest, okay?'

Her sister eyed her with the same incredulity as the commander had moments before. 'I can't believe you're just going to let that pass,' she marveled.

'Well, I am,' said Penny calmly. 'He's

grieving,' she added, wondering if perhaps he'd watched his man die and even tried to save him. He'd been hit by shrapnel, he'd said, implying that there'd been an explosion.

Ophelia's eyes flew suddenly wide. 'You're crazy about him,' she exclaimed. 'You have to be. Otherwise you'd never let him talk to you that way.'

Penny tried to deny the truth, but she'd never been good at lying. 'I admire him for his commitment to this country,' she answered unconvincingly. 'Now leave it alone, Ophelia. I don't want to talk about this anymore.'

Thoughts glimmered in Lia's jewel-like eyes. 'Whatever,' she said airily.

That wasn't the reassurance Penny was looking for. 'I mean it, sis. Don't even look at him if you see him again.'

'Okay,' said Ophelia, throwing up her hands.

With a sigh of mistrust, Penny moved past her, en route to fetch her purse. 'I'm going to the store to pick up pumpkins,' she said, expecting her sister to tag along. Ophelia had developed a habit of shadowing her lately. 'Are you coming?'

'No, I don't want to miss *Oprah*,' she said.

With a sound of disgust, Penny headed to the door. 'Why don't you work on your résumé?'

'I'll think about it.'

Which was all she'd ever done with her journalism degree. 'I'll be back in an hour,' Penny added. As she shut the door behind her, she scanned the street, as was her habit, to make sure that Eric wasn't stalking them.

According to the FBI agent, Hannah Lindstrom, the FBI was scrutinizing all previous investigations. Penny had faxed them a copy of her father's death certificate, which made reference to a hit-and-run. If the FBI could show that Danny Price was murdered, Eric might be arrested, and his freaky prank phone calls would come to an end.

The sooner the better, Penny thought, slipping into her powder blue Toyota Matrix. As she backed out of the driveway, she sneaked a peek at her neighbor's house.

He'd closed the blinds in all of his windows. Now he was blocking the world out, hiding in his lair.

What secret was he guarding? she wondered. She couldn't just dismiss the question, any more than she could stop Joe Montgomery from commandeering her thoughts.

5

Lia waited for Penny's car to disappear before she stalked out of the house and across the adjoining lawns to the neighbor's front door. Undeterred by all the closed blinds, she pounded on the oak veneer, tugged her sweater over her glittering belly ring, and waited.

This Montgomery fellow didn't realize it yet, but he was the first man Penny had shown an interest in since Brad, the fiancé who'd dumped her. And since half the reason Brad left was Penny's devotion at the time to Lia's rehabilitation, Lia figured it was her duty to set the SEAL straight.

It took forever for him to answer. When the door yawned open, she wavered at the unfriendly look on his face. 'I'm Penny's sister,' she announced. Her training in journalism kept her voice strong and steady. 'And I'm here to give you a reality check.'

His bandaged eyebrow quirked, but he didn't try to stop her.

'Number one, Penny is the most selfless, hard-working, nurturing person you will ever have the privilege of knowing in your entire life.'

His eyes narrowed, but she was just warming up.

'That you could speak to her in the way you did, after what she did for you, staying up half the night to scrub your carpet, makes you the most selfish, self-righteous jerk I have ever laid eyes on. If you knew what Penny gave up for me when our father died, you'd be licking the soles of her feet.'

She could feel the incredulity building in him, but she refused to back down. 'Don't even think about saying another word to her that is less than humbly apologetic. Who do you think has been raking your leaves and feeding your cat, for God's sake? You need to wake up and get a life!'

With that, she whirled away, chin angled into the air as she cut through his mulch bed to hike it back to Penny's.

Her pricked ears caught the words he finally growled. 'Well, I'll be damned.'

She was dying to look back but worried that the smirk on her face might push him over the edge. He'd looked a little unpredictable there toward the end, and it wasn't her intent to incite him to violence, just to open his eyes to Penny's virtues.

* * *

Dazed, Joe shut the door against the cold.

He stood in his chilled foyer, processing the awful fact that a third person had witnessed the exchange between him and Florence Nightingale. He cringed to consider that she'd probably heard every nasty word he'd said.

Her scolding words returned to him. *If you knew what Penny gave up for me when our father died, you'd be licking the soles of her feet. Who do you think has been raking your leaves and feeding your cat, for God's sake?*

Okay, so Lieutenant Price had tended his yard and fed his cat while he was gone. Go figure. Apparently, in addition to being nosy, she was quite the do-gooder. He applauded her selflessness, but he'd never asked for her help.

He limped back to his leather sofa and eased painfully onto one end while checking the score to see what he'd missed. On the widescreen TV, his alma mater, USC, was getting the snot beat out of them.

His gaze flickered to the carpet. If Penny Price hadn't scrubbed it last night, he'd have cleaning professionals crawling all over the room.

With a mutter of annoyance, Joe snatched up his beer bottle. 'So that makes me a selfish, self-righteous jerk?' he asked his cat, taking a swig.

Felix sat at his feet, glowering, and Joe realized that he'd forgotten to feed him. With a groan, he pushed to his feet.

Okay, so maybe he was a little self-absorbed, enough to keep him from seeing what his neighbor was up to. Honestly, he'd never given her much thought, except to notice that she was in the Navy, just like him.

She wasn't the type of woman he tended to notice. She had a trim but unremarkable figure, did nothing with her hair, wore very little makeup.

He dumped the contents of the can into Felix's bowl and slowly straightened. Her face was pleasant but not striking. In fact, only her Caribbean blue eyes could truly be called beautiful.

They seemed to see right through him, which he found totally disconcerting.

She'd looked at him like that last night, when he'd been sitting ignominiously on the toilet seat. His breath caught as snatches of their conversation returned to him.

Where'd you go this morning?

Funeral.

Who died?

One of my men.

I'm sorry. That must have been awful for you.

Shit. He'd prided himself on being circumspect about SEAL business. The Inquisition could not have gotten him to confess the tiniest detail of any given mission. But with two short questions, Penny Price had him telling all and blubbering like a baby.

He'd actually cried in front of her!

With a gagging sound, Joe tossed the can in the trash. How humiliating!

His memory fast-forwarded, and he froze at the vision of her lying in his arms, her eyes glimmering like aquamarines in the semidarkness. He could still feel the texture of her lips under his. She'd tasted so sweet, almost familiar.

'Oh, no!' Joe breathed, as the possibility that he'd slept with her had every hair on his body prickling in alarm.

He couldn't have.

He wouldn't have. Or would he?

He dragged his fingers through his hair. God forbid that she accuse him of sexual misconduct. Wouldn't that be the nail in his coffin?

He swiveled and hobbled to his bedroom. Thrusting his door open, he approached the rumpled bed, seeking evidence that might suggest what he'd done.

His beige sheets appeared pristine, hardly used at all.

He stripped them, all the same, and carried them to his laundry room to run a load of wash. As the washer hummed and swished, Joe took a long, sobering shower, then shaved the bristles off his face.

What does she want from me? he wondered, so distracted that he nearly cut himself with his razor.

For the most part, he liked women. They were entertaining, mysterious, with physical attributes that drove him crazy. But in his experience, they were also ambitious, conniving, and calculating. Women wanted Joe for what he could give them. Some were after his money. Others got off on the fact that he was an officer, with plenty of prestige. Some just wanted to be with him so they could screw around when he was overseas. The way he figured, Penelope Price wasn't any different.

She would bear watching, he decided. If she turned out to be as selfless as her little sister insisted, he'd apologize. On the other hand, if she became a thorn in his side, she'd soon regret it. He valued his privacy above all things.

★   ★   ★

Vinny DeInnocentis pounded on the apartment door in a tidy but aging complex two blocks from the ocean-front. A peek through the window revealed a lavishly furnished, whimsically decorated apartment. It looked exactly like the kind of place where the flame-haired beauty who'd crashed into his car would live. He nearly had her now.

'Can I help you?' demanded a voice from across a breezeway.

Vinny found a middle-aged woman glaring at him. She wore curlers and a housecoat, her feet stuffed into pink slippers. 'Yes, ma'am. I'm looking for the young lady who lives here, Ophelia Price?' He'd passed her license plate number to a friend in law enforcement, who, in turn, gave him her name and mailing address. 'Do you know when she'll be back?' he asked respectfully.

The woman took quick inventory of his battle-dress uniform. '*Nein*, she von't be back. She mooft out last veek,' she said, revealing German origins.

'But her furniture's still inside,' he pointed out.

'She rents the place to friends of hers,' the frau replied, tightening her robe against the cold.

'Well, do you know where she went to?' Vinny asked, doubting the woman's story. Perhaps she was Ophelia's self-appointed watchdog.

'How many more men vill come around askink me that question?' the woman groused, rolling her eyes.

Vinny didn't like the way that sounded.

'She don't vant no strange men comink after her,' she insisted, hunching her rounded shoulders.

'I'm not a stranger, ma'am; I'm a friend. I just want to give her this ring back.' He pulled it from his pocket and crossed the breezeway to show it to her.

The frau seemed to recognize the ring. 'Vell, you don't seem like a bat man,' she allowed. 'Vat do you do?' She gestured at his uniform.

'I'm a Navy SEAL.' He was also a student, taking classes at the local community college, and this was his first night off in a week.

'Oh, *ja*? My son is in the Navy.' Her frown grew more relaxed. 'Ophelia vent to stay vith her sister,' she suddenly divulged.

Her sister! Vinny's heart faltered. 'Where does she live?' he asked. Not far away, he hoped.

'Just a minute,' she said, disappearing into her apartment.

Vinny waited, his blood thrumming impatiently. Thoughts of the copper-haired beauty who'd crushed in his taillight had obsessed him all week. Her feisty tongue and slippery

86

tactics had amused him. She was about to find out that Navy SEALs were tenacious sons-of-bitches and they didn't like being stood up.

'I forward her mail to her,' admitted the frau, coming out again. She had an index card, which she handed to him.

Vinny glanced at the Virginia Beach address and nearly let loose a war cry. He bestowed the woman his best Boy Scout smile. Of course, he'd never been a Boy Scout. 'Thank you so much, ma'am,' he said, slipping the card into his pocket as he turned away. 'She'll be grateful to you.'

'I hope so,' said the woman. 'You're not like the other man.'

Vinny turned slowly back around. 'What was he like?' he inquired blandly.

'Older,' she said. 'Quiet and . . . creepy.'

Vinny nodded. He'd already guessed, given Lia's apparent driving history, that she had some serious skeletons in her closet. 'You have a good day, ma'am,' he called, turning away.

He wondered how she handled surprises.

★   ★   ★

'The therapist will be in shortly,' smiled the petty officer who'd taken Joe's pulse and blood pressure and left him to change into a patient's gown.

Once changed, Joe eased onto the hip-high table, grimacing at the pain that simple act caused him. The room was chilly, and the gown barely reached the tops of his thighs. A draft blew down the back where the ties failed to meet.

He hadn't wanted to seek medical help, but the spasms in his back had prompted an appointment with a doctor, who'd subjected him to an MRI, informed him that his serratus posterior inferior was strained, and written him a prescription for physical therapy. Joe didn't know what the future held for him beyond his R&R, but if he wanted to continue as a SEAL — and there wasn't any question about that — he needed to recover fully.

Light footfalls approached the closed door. He pictured the therapist, Lieutenant Sparks by name, pulling his chart from the holder. She gave a knock and stepped in briskly. Only total mastery of his facial muscles prevented Joe from revealing his dismay as his neighbor stepped into the room.

'Lieutenant Commander,' she greeted him with poise, having had the advantage of seeing his name on the chart. 'Lieutenant Sparks had her baby early,' she explained, 'and I'll be standing in for her.'

Her tone was so impersonal, so professional, that it threw Joe even more off balance. 'I'd like to be seen by another therapist,' he croaked.

With the slightest firming of her lips, she answered coolly, 'I'm the only therapist available until Lieutenant Sparks comes back. If you'd like to wait three months . . . ?' She shrugged to convey that was his choice.

Joe hunched his shoulders, thinking hard. He could go to a civilian therapist and pay out of pocket, or he could suck it up and keep their exchange impersonal.

He cut a critical glance at her khaki uniform. She wore standard work attire for officers: a tan-colored blouse and skirt. Her hair was in a tidy bun. Navy-issue pumps made her look a little taller. Aside from those eyes, and that soft mouth, she was unremarkable. So why did she rattle him so much? 'I'll stay,' he muttered.

'Let's talk about your back,' she invited, frowning down at the referral sheet his physician had given him. 'It says here that you've strained an intermediary muscle, the serratus posterior inferior. How'd you do that?'

'I hurt it in a fall,' he admitted.

She laid the chart down and walked around

the table. Stepping onto a stool, she unlaced the ties at the back of his gown and slipped a cool hand to through the opening. 'How far was this fall?' she asked.

Her touch made him jumpy. 'I don't know. A long way.'

'You don't remember?'

He ground his molars together. 'No,' he said shortly.

She pressed her thumb into muscle, making him flinch. 'I'd say you've gotten an accurate diagnosis. Here's what we're going to do,' she said, stepping off her stool. 'We'll start with moist heat packs on the affected area for twenty minutes, followed by a brief ultrasound treatment, then a fifteen-minute massage to increase blood flow and relaxation.'

She was going to massage him? Joe's mouth went dry. His heart palpitated.

'Have you been taking the meds you were prescribed in Afghanistan?' she asked, picking up his chart again.

'No.'

'Good,' she said with a quick, pitying look, 'because you're not supposed to mix that stuff with alcohol.'

A humiliated flush heated Joe's face. He looked down at his healing hands, clenched and unfurled them.

'I'll send in a corpsman to set you up with

those heat packs. See you in twenty minutes,' said Lieutenant Price, snapping the file shut and heading for the door. It closed quietly behind her.

Joe glowered, cursing his luck. Of all the therapists in the Navy, his had to be his next-door-neighbor. The corpsman burst into the room with his arms full of steaming packs but drew up warily. 'Sir,' he hedged. 'Can I get you to lie on your stomach?'

Joe was left alone, weighted down by lovely warm, moist packs that put him instantly to sleep. He was jarred awake by Penny's entrance. She wordlessly removed the heat packs and wheeled the ultrasound machine closer. To Joe's consternation, she rolled the elastic of his boxer-briefs down past his butt crack, then squirted warm gel all over his back.

She had to be humiliating him on purpose.

The machine buzzed and crackled as she sent healing sound waves deep into his tender muscles. She didn't speak but worked the handheld device in a circular motion over his back. Remembering the threats he'd practically hurled at her, Joe wrestled with his conscience. Maybe she'd done all the right things because it was her nature to be helpful. In that case, he'd stepped over the line by threatening her. But he had to be sure first.

'Lieutenant,' he interjected, making her pause.

'Yes, sir?'

'How much did I tell you the other night?' He had to know.

She moved the device again, in a slow, circular motion. 'You said that you were hit with shrapnel,' she replied, her tone sympathetic. 'One of your men died, presumably in the same incident. At first I thought it was a car accident, but given the fall you don't remember, I would also have to consider a helicopter crash.' She waited for him to deny or confirm her guess.

He did neither. Her assumptions were amazingly astute. He needed to tread with caution, or she'd come up with the truth on her own, if she hadn't already.

'What I do is classified,' he said, guarding his secret.

He thought that would be the end of it, but then she added, 'The only recent downing that I've heard of didn't have any survivors, though,' she added. 'A helo was blown up while rescuing four SEALs on the ground. Three of them died and only one came back alive.'

He tried not to tense, but every muscle in his body flinched.

'You knew those men,' she guessed, her

tone filled with compassion.

He stayed quiet. To his relief, she didn't press him for an answer.

Instead, she turned off the machine, mounted a stool for some much needed height, and commenced with the soft-tissue massage, her hands cool and remarkably efficient.

He didn't want to enjoy her touch, but he did. The pressure she placed on his tender muscles was exquisite.

Aw, man. He'd gladly put up with her nosy questions if he got a massage like this every time. *Oh, yeah, right there. Ahhh.*

And yet, for some reason, her touch stirred memories he wanted to forget.

He remembered plummeting backward, falling slow-motion through space while the fireball of helicopter chased him. The torso of one of his comrades issued from the explosion — no legs, just the trunk and head.

Joe silently cursed, wishing the vision had stayed where it was, repressed in his subconscious mind.

But Penny had brought up the crash. She'd brought it right into this room.

He didn't know whether to be relieved or disappointed when she removed her hand and wiped his back with warmed wet wipes. 'How do you feel?' she asked, dusting his back with powder, massaging it in, quickly and lightly.

He shivered at the pleasant, almost sensual caress. 'Good,' he admitted. 'Relaxed.'

'I'm glad to hear it. I want you to use a cool pack every night, when you're watching television or as you go to sleep.'

He was wriggling in an attempt to unfurl the elastic of his boxer-briefs.

'Do you need help turning over?' she asked.

'No, I got it.' The last thing he wanted was to humiliate himself by revealing a semi-aroused state. It wasn't his fault that a woman's hands on his body did that to him.

Using the gown as a shield, he rolled over and swung his feet over the side. *Not a twinge*, he marveled. She'd really loosened him up. 'Wow,' he murmured, thinking she was quite talented.

'I'd like to see you again on Thursday,' she said. 'We'll run through the same treatment.'

He looked forward to it. Maybe then he'd even be able to look her in the eye and not feel like a loser.

'Check with the receptionist on your way out,' she added with a small, professional smile. Her skirt swished and her heels tapped, and she was gone.

Joe heaved a sigh of self-recrimination.

Maybe little sister was right. Penelope Price didn't seem like the type to expose him. She had integrity. And given the magic in her fingers, he was probably lucky to have her as his neighbor, not to mention his physical therapist.

★ ★ ★

Penny shut herself up in her office and dropped into her desk chair. Bringing her aching fingers to her nose, she savored the scent of clean male and fresh laundry. The feel of his hot, smooth skin replayed itself in her kinetic memory. His densely powerful muscles were a playground to her tutored hands. She could have spent hours massaging his body, starting with those perfectly toned butt muscles peeking out of his boxer briefs.

With a sigh, she released such unprofessional thoughts. Her infatuation with Joe was pointless. He'd made it clear that he resented her meddling. And yet, his visit today had only stoked her fascination. There was something going on with him that she couldn't put her finger on . . .

She tapped her chin, thinking.

He refused to talk about the accident that had left him scarred and another SEAL dead. When she'd mentioned the downing of the helicopter filled with men, he'd gone rigid, almost like he'd witnessed it. But he couldn't have. He was a commander.

And yet, there *was* one lone SEAL who'd survived that fiasco. He'd been chased for days by Taliban insurgents, only to be later found and rescued. That could not have been Joe.

Or could it?

Penny glanced questioningly at her computer. She swiveled in her chair and jiggled the mouse, performing an online search for articles regarding the recent disaster. While skimming one article, she read, 'Military officials said the survivor was knocked off his feet by the blast of a rocket detonation during fighting with insurgents and slid down a mountainside in the steep terrain.'

Penny's ears started ringing. She skimmed the rest of the article, her certainty growing with each printed word. *Joe was the survivor.* Everything in print dovetailed with his circumstances: his sudden arrival at home, his physical condition, his refusal to talk about what had happened.

'Oh, my God,' she breathed, understanding why he was so vehement about protecting his privacy. The last thing he would want was publicity. 'Oh, Joe.'

She leaned back in her chair, envisioning

the hell he'd been through and reeling at the heartache she knew he was left with.

The urge to comfort him was overwhelming. It was also futile. She had no desire to join the ranks of women he'd loved and left, nor could he have made his desire for privacy any clearer. Her only option was to give him physical relief. She could help to heal his body. But who would heal his broken heart?

6

'You must be Monty.'

Joe lifted a startled gaze from the magazine he was reading in the clinic's waiting area. He'd been well aware of the older man standing immediately in front of him, clutching a cane and watching everything Joe did. But he'd assumed the man was either senile or lost in his own thoughts, not that he was pondering Joe's identity. 'Yes, sir,' He set the magazine aside, thinking, *Do I know this guy?*

'I'm Admiral Jacobs,' divulged the stranger. He wore civilian clothing and sported sparse silver hair atop his egg-shaped head.

An admiral. Joe rocketed to his feet. 'Sir, nice to meet you, sir.' He snapped off a salute, which the admiral half-heartedly returned.

'At ease, there, Commander,' the old man growled. 'We're all in civilian clothes, here.'

'Would you like to sit, sir?' Joe asked, offering his chair, though there were several empty seats in the waiting area.

'Oh, no. Sitting makes me feel confined. Brings back memories of 'Nam.'

'You were a POW, sir?'

'Yes, I was. Spent a hundred and three days in a South Vietnamese jungle camp with two shattered kneecaps. Enemy shot down my parachute,' he added.

'I'm sorry to hear that, sir,' said Joe, who remained standing. 'If you don't mind my asking, how is it that you know me?'

For several seconds, Admiral Jacobs just looked at him with pale blue eyes. 'I've done my research, son,' he finally answered. 'When any of my boys get lost, I take it personal.'

Joe swallowed against a dry throat. It unsettled him a bit that this man knew him, but he'd never heard of Admiral Jacobs.

The man narrowed his eyes, 'You ever ask yourself if someone's to blame for the hell you've been through?'

Joe wavered on his feet. 'Yes, sir,' he admitted, realizing with sudden clarity that he blamed himself. If he'd let Harley go in or waited another few days, there might have been no casualties.

'Where was that AC-130 when you needed it?' continued the admiral in a hushed voice. 'And who in his right mind would send a Chinook into compromised airspace?' A vein appeared on the man's wrinkled forehead. 'That's like standing in an open field flailing your arms and yelling, 'Here I am! Shoot me down!'' A fleck of spittle appeared on one corner of the admiral's mouth.

The possibility that someone else was to blame left Joe light-headed with mixed shock and relief.

'My only son was a marine with the Third MEF,' the admiral volunteered unexpectedly.

It took Joe a second to remember that the Third Marine Expeditionary Force had been wiped out by friendly fire at the start of the war. 'The incident outside of Nasiriyah,' he remembered. 'I'm sorry to hear that, sir.'

With a nod and wetness in his eyes, the old man looked away.

An aide leaned out of the door to call the next patient 'Admiral Jacobs? Your turn, sir.' Without a glance back at Joe, the admiral hobbled toward her.

Joe waited for him to disappear before sinking back into his seat. Could someone other than himself be blamed for the clusterfuck that had killed so many?

Closing his eyes, he dared to think back. He was belted into the belly of the UH-60, awaiting that fateful jump that would place him and his men on the LZ. The thrumming of the rotors, the thinness of the air, grains of sand stuck in his teeth. He remembered as if it were yesterday.

As operations officer, he'd pored over maps

with the original four SEALs and talked with intel operators. They'd assured him that there were no rebels on the mountaintop, and even if there were, the AC-130 would be right there on call to take them out. Nothing should have gone wrong.

Joe's eyes sprang open. For a second there, he'd teetered toward the trap of cynicism that Admiral Jacobs tried to set in his mind. God, it was tempting to blame someone else for a night gone wrong.

Only Joe couldn't do that. His colleagues at JSOTF were thorough. His superiors had served in the Gulf War and knew the cost of self-inflicted casualties.

It was bad luck, pure and simple, that those insurgents had been hiding in caves. Bad luck that the AC-130 had been summoned elsewhere, that they couldn't get a Black-hawk in the air instead of a Chinook.

The only person who could have altered the events of that night was himself. A different day, a different OIC, and the tragedy might have been avoided.

★ ★ ★

Admiral Jacobs's cell phone gave a shrill ring. Penny, who was about to remind him that cell phones weren't permitted in the hospital, kept her mouth shut. Who was she to tell an admiral what to do?

'Jacobs,' he growled, wincing as Penny bent his knee and put her weight into the joint, forcing it to stretch beyond the comfort zone.

As the caller identified himself, Penny felt the admiral stiffen. 'What the hell do you want?' he growled.

Mercy, thought Penny, releasing pressure to extend his leg fully. She'd never seen this gruff side to the admiral, who was always sweetly affable during his biweekly appointments. She moved to his left leg.

'I thought this matter was settled,' the old man blustered.

'Bend your leg, sir,' Penny reminded him.

He did so, distracted by whatever it was that the caller was telling him. The news was bad enough to make him put a death grip on the phone. 'Are you certain?' he demanded.

The reply made the admiral's jowls quiver. 'Fine, then. Do whatever it takes,' he acceded. With a sad shake of his head, he severed the call and fell back, clutching a hand to his heart.

Penny sent him a look of concern. 'Is everything all right, sir?' she inquired, applying more pressure to his bent leg.

'Oh, as all right as it can be, I suppose,' he

replied, his eyes still closed. He sounded so weary.

She felt sorry for him. Poor man, he'd lost his son early in the war and never quite got over it.

Penny couldn't fathom losing a child to war, let alone to blue-on-blue engagement. 'That's it for today, sir,' she told him gently. 'I'll see you next week at the same time. Keep up the exercises,' she added, placing her hand briefly over his.

His skin felt so cold!

She left the room, dropping off the admiral's chart, then hurried down the hall to snatch up the chart belonging to her next patient. Recognizing Joe's name, a flush of anticipation heated her cheeks. All day she'd looked forward to this session.

With a warning knock, she peeked inside. 'Good morning.'

She drew up short at the sight of Joe propped against the table, wearing nothing but black boxer briefs. Her gaze skittered over his washboard abs to the bulge below, and her skin seemed to shrink.

'Morning,' he said, clearly unabashed at being caught half-naked.

'Where's your, um, gown?' she asked, dragging her gaze upward. Heat rose to her face, no doubt turning her complexion bright red.

'There wasn't one in here.' His green gaze mocked her discomfit.

'I'll get some more,' she said, fleeing the room.

When she returned, he was lying facedown on the table, weighted with moist heat packs. The corpsman had gotten his session under way. Penny stowed the gown for later use and left the room.

Twenty minutes later, she returned. 'Do you, uh, want to put the gown on now?' she asked, removing the cooled heat packs.

'What's the point?' he asked sleepily.

'Right.' But with the gown on, she could pretend he was dressed and not practically naked — a circumstance that disturbed her sensibilities. 'How's your back been?' she asked, wheeling the ultrasound closer. She rolled his briefs down, squirted warm gel on his back, and spread it, delighting in the texture of his skin.

'It was good for a day, and then the spasms came back.'

'That's why we need to see you more than once,' she answered, turning the machine on. She applied the wand over the affected muscle group. She gave in to the childish urge to write a cursive L. L for love, lust, and let-me-touch-you-everywhere, lover boy. He couldn't possibly guess the game she was playing, so why not?

Precisely seven minutes later, she cut the machine off, eager to get to the part she enjoyed most. She climbed her stool and put her hands on him. *Oh, yes.*

The term *soft tissue* was a misnomer on Joe. There wasn't anything soft about him. He was all fibrous, toned muscle, the density of which left the joints in her fingers aching, yet she would happily have continued for hours.

'You think you could work on my shoulders some?' Joe's sleepy voice seemed to echo her own reluctance to bring their session to an end. 'They've been kind of tight lately.'

Her impulse was to say, 'I'd love to,' but she focused instead on the fact that Joe hadn't yet apologized for his behavior the other day. From her perspective, he owed her something first. 'I don't know,' she said, holding out. 'You might have to do something for me.'

'Like what?' he countered.

She rolled her eyes at his obvious consternation. What did he think she was going to ask for, sexual favors? 'Like carve those two pumpkins I put on your porch.'

'Oh,' he said, silent for a moment. 'I figured you put them there.'

'Halloween is a week from today. You carved four jack-o'-lanterns last year. The neighborhood kids will miss it if you don't

105

make at least two,' she pointed out.

'I'll think about it,' he said noncommittally.

'Not good enough,' she countered, pressing her thumb into a knot to release the tension.

'Uh!' he groaned, half in pleasure, half in pain.

'You could also keep an eye on my sister, Ophelia, while I'm at work.' It wasn't so hard to make demands in this position.

'Her?' he countered in accents of horror.

'She's been getting prank phone calls,' Penny explained, thinking why not give Joe something to do other than brood over what couldn't be changed. 'From a guy who killed our father,' she added.

'When was this?' came the confused question.

'About five years ago. My father worked in a biological warfare lab, where they tested ricin, among other things. That's a toxic biowaste — '

'I know what it is.'

'Well, several grams of ricin went missing five years back, and not long after that, my father was killed in a hit-and-run. We think his partner sold the ricin to terrorists, who then killed my father for knowing too much.'

Joe craned his neck to look over his shoulder at her. 'Have you gone to the cops with this?' he asked incredulously.

'The FBI is looking into it.'

'Well, that's something.' He lay back down again.

'So . . . ' She swept a hand up his spine to play along the ridges of his shoulders. 'How much do you want that shoulder massage?'

'I'll keep an eye out,' he promised grudgingly.

'Thank you.' With a satisfied smile, Penny tackled his shoulders. Never in her life had she gotten to mold shoulders so broad, so powerful, or so tight. She pressed and rolled his muscles, pleased to hear the groans of ecstasy he couldn't keep to himself.

'God, you're good at that,' he admitted.

'Too bad I'm not a masseuse,' she countered, reaching for wet wipes to clean the gel off his back. She sprinkled him with powder and briskly spread it out to absorb the gel. 'Other patients are waiting for me,' she added, concealing her disappointment.

The face he lifted looked sleepy and satisfied. 'Thanks,' he said gruffly. 'When do you want to see me next?'

'Let's say Monday,' she decided, dismissing the thought that he looked like a man who'd just had sex.

'I won't be back till Monday night.'

'You're going out of town?'

'Quick trip to Florida,' he said shortly.

'Are you driving or flying?' she wanted to know.

'Why so many questions?' he fired back.

'Because you shouldn't sit still for more than two hours at a stretch,' she retorted, coolly.

'I'm flying to Orlando and driving to Daytona.'

One of the SEALs who'd died was from Orlando. Penny had read that in one of the articles yesterday. Joe was going to pay his respects to the family, she guessed. 'That'll be good for you,' she said with sympathy.

He narrowed his eyes at her. 'What will?'

'Paying your respects.'

A long silence, fraught with tension, passed between them. 'Did Admiral Jacobs tell you something?' Joe demanded.

'Admiral Jacobs? No, do you know him?'

'No, I don't. But he knows me and, apparently, you do, too,' he accused.

She sighed and clutched his chart closer. 'Why is that such a threat to you?' she asked, watching in fascination as his expression darkened. 'I have no reason to tell anyone that you're the one survivor of the Special Ops disaster.'

There, she'd said it and he didn't deny it. But the look that crossed his face nearly broke her heart. 'I'm so sorry for what happened,' she added quietly. 'I know this has got to be a nightmare for you.'

His eyes glazed over with that horror-filled look she'd seen before. He couldn't even answer her.

'Be careful in your travels,' she said, wanting to spare him the indignity of losing his composure — again. 'I'll see you Tuesday.'

She left the room quietly, leaving him to grapple with his demons.

⋆ ⋆ ⋆

Joe put his weight back into his couch cushions and sought oblivion. If he could turn off his thoughts and let Barbara have her wicked way, it might yet come. But that wasn't as easy as it sounded, not even when her itty-bitty red dress rode high enough to reveal that she wasn't wearing panties.

The tall blonde straddled him, breasts brushing his chest as she nibbled the column of his throat, interspersing words of desire.

Had she had another breast enhancement? Or was he comparing her curves to someone else's?

'Oh, Monty,' she whispered, sliding down his legs to kneel at his feet. 'I've missed you so much.' Unzipping his jeans, she murmured her appreciation, finding what she was looking for.

Barbara was practiced and lusty, the way Joe liked his women. Her mouth felt nice — hot, wet, and hungry. Yet he could scarcely maintain his enthusiasm, especially when she fumbled to sheathe him with a condom.

She climbed on board and kissed him. Her lips strayed to his jaw, his ear, his cheek as she lowered herself atop him. 'Mmmm, I love the scar,' she murmured, tracing it with her tongue. 'It makes you look like such a bad, bad boy.'

Her words brought everything back in an instant: the explosion, the fireball, body parts flying at him as he reeled backward. His arousal fled. He felt suddenly sick to his stomach. 'Get off,' he said quietly.

Barbara pulled back, her eyes enormous. Immediately she seemed to realize her mistake. 'I'm sorry,' she whispered.

'It's not your fault,' he forced himself to say. 'I've got some issues right now.'

'Is there . . . anything I can do?'

'No. Thank you. I think you should go home,' he suggested.

With a gasp of hurt and disbelief, she leapt off him, yanked her dress down, and sought her shoes. Joe got up and went into his bathroom.

Splashing water on his face, he stared at the scar marring his reflection. How could any woman find that attractive? Every day for the rest of his life he would look at it and think of the men he'd watched die — men who'd been like brothers and sons to him. He detested the scar. At the same time he vowed never to surgically fix it. It was part of him, as much as those men had been part of his life.

The front door thudded shut. Joe let Barbara leave, knowing he'd never see her again. He didn't particularly care. Their attachment had been physical and little more. She wasn't the kind of woman he could trust with confidences.

She wasn't like . . . Penny.

Thoughts of his neighbor had him glancing out his bathroom window. The lights in her house were on. She was home, as was her sister, who'd pulled up in her Oldsmobile when Barbara rang his doorbell.

Joe found himself heading for the door. He'd made a promise to keep an eye on Ophelia while Penny was at work. As far as Joe was concerned, both sisters were susceptible while working with the FBI to catch a criminal. If their father's partner was that ruthless, what was to stop him from seeking retribution?

Jamming his feet into sneakers, Joe donned

a denim jacket and left the house. Barbara's car was already gone.

It was a brisk October night. The full moon illumined the lawn as he crossed it to Penny's house. Since he was leaving in the morning, this was a good time to tour the perimeter and gauge any vulnerabilities.

Penny didn't have a fenced yard like his. As he rounded her house, he noted the thick garden beds. An early frost had left her rosebushes bare. If their thorns weren't enough to deter intruders, the prickly holly bushes planted under each window would.

He came to a neat brick patio, complete with an outdoor fireplace, wrought-iron table, and chairs. The cozy setup tempted him to take a seat and listen to the crickets chirping in the dark corners of the yard.

But then a light came on overhead, and he glanced up to find the shutters of a bay window standing open. To his astonishment, a naked Penny appeared at the glass and closed the shutters, oblivious to his presence below.

Joe's head spun. Her uniform had definitely down-played the curves she possessed. His body tingled unexpectedly before he ripped his gaze away, annoyed.

He didn't want to find his neighbor appealing. On his first day home, she'd rocked his world, like some kid at the swimming pool doing cannonballs and making the water choppy. She'd been a thorn in his side ever since. Sure, she was his physical therapist, and she meant well. She had magic in her fingers and the ability to dispel his physical complaints, at least for days at a stretch. But he didn't need or want to know her any better.

And yet she was making demands on his time, worming her way into his cloistered existence.

With a scowl, Joe went back to assessing her home's security. He checked the French doors that led to the patio. They were tightly locked, but with the kind of deadbolt that could be twisted from the inside. Any intruder could break out a pane of glass and reach inside to unlock it.

He continued around the house, finding the remainder of the windows and the front door secured. At least she wasn't careless.

Obligated to point out the vulnerability, he approached Penny's front door and knocked, eyeing her scarecrow as he waited.

Awful Ophelia opened the door.

'Hi,' he said, nonplussed to see her. 'Tell your sister to get a different deadbolt for the French doors in the back. She needs to buy one that locks with a key.'

113

'Okay,' said Ophelia, looking puzzled. She wore a silk bathrobe. 'You want to come in?' she asked.

He didn't trust her as far as he could throw a stick. 'No, thanks.'

'Suit yourself,' she said with a shrug, 'but Penny's baking a pie.'

She was trying to set him up with Penny, Joe realized. 'Sounds good,' he said backing away. Oh, no. Penny Price was not his type. He dated women who weren't into long-term relationships, women as adventurous and thrill-seeking as he was. 'Next time.'

'You don't know what you're missing,' she called as he all but ran for his door.

There wouldn't be a next time, not for Penny. The women he got involved with understood that a love affair was just a temporary thrill. He liked it that way, and as long as he remained a SEAL, it was going to stay that way.

Perhaps when he settled down, stopped traveling, he'd consider emulating what his parents had — a close-knit symbiosis of passion, affection, and trust. But for now, he couldn't trust his heart to any one woman. Women came to him because of what he was, not who he was. That wasn't the foundation he wanted to build on, and so he refused to build any foundation at all.

Heading straight to his kitchen, Joe found Felix waiting for his evening meal. He fed the cat, then opened his liquor cabinet. 'Guess it's just us guys tonight,' he said to his cat. 'You, me, and J. D.'

He poured himself a shot of whiskey and tipped it back, feeling the burn all the way to his stomach. The vision of Penny, naked from the waist up, seared his memory.

He poured himself a second shot to drown it.

But he already knew that memories floated to the top. The most he could hope for was to pass out cold tonight. That way he wouldn't dream.

7

Having flown into Orlando, where he rented a car, Joe did not arrive at the oceanfront city of Daytona until dusk. At the thought of facing Nikko's widow, his stomach churned. The sweat dampening his shirt was more a result of his dread than of the muggy weather.

Two miles from the oceanfront, he turned into a neighborhood of modest ramblers. The two young boys playing Wiffle ball in the street were Nikko's. They had the same dark hair and olive complexion as their Greek-American father. With dread pooling in his limbs, Joe parked along the curb several yards away and watched.

He tried to step out of the car, but he couldn't.

The sinking sun washed the sky in hues of violet. The brothers were close in size, maybe six and eight years old. Ignoring their lengthening shadows, they took turns swinging at the plastic ball while a fruit bat darted overhead.

Nikko would never play with them again.

Just get out of the car, Joe. Get it over with.

He turned the ignition off and cracked the door. He was about to push to his feet when the porch light blinked on and a dark-haired woman emerged. 'Alex and Marcus, it's time to come in,' she called.

Both boys ignored her.

Their mother tried again. 'It's too dark to play out here. Put the ball away and come into the house, now!'

'Five more minutes,' insisted the older boy. Joe sensed defiance in both his voice and body language.

Nikko's widow put her hand to her forehead. The weary gesture tugged at his heartstrings. Now she was the sole enforcer of the family.

With a vice around his chest, he watched her square her shoulders. She marched into the street and wrested the bat from the elder boy, who, for a moment, looked ready to retaliate. But then he glimpsed his mother's expression and relinquished the bat. The threesome trailed quietly into their house. Nikko's wife shut the door.

Now was the time to go talk to her.

Only Joe couldn't. Guilt burned in him like toxic waste. He shut the car door and started up the engine. With a tire-squealing U-turn, he fled the neighborhood.

Stabbing at the window button, he brought

a gusty ocean breeze into the car. The glow of neon lights lured him to the boardwalk. He paid three dollars to park at the beach.

Kicking off his shoes and socks, he plodded toward the incoming tide, barefoot. The warm sand squished between his toes. He walked straight into the surf, where the shock of cold water hit his calves, his knees, his thighs. He did not stop walking until it smashed into his hips, nearly knocking him off his feet.

He stood there, letting the water numb him. Memories of SEAL training flashed back to him. The Coronado Bay was colder at this time of year than the Atlantic Ocean. He and his fellow candidates were made to lie in the surf at dawn, clinging to each other while the waves crashed into them. It was a team-building exercise that taught them that together, they could endure anything.

Only they hadn't. They'd been overcome by overwhelming odds and circumstances beyond their control.

Would Nikko's widow understand that, or would she blame him the way he blamed himself? He would rather let the water close over his head than face her tonight, but the memory of Nikko's smile had him turning around.

With his pants soaking wet, he got back

into his car. He returned to Nikko's quiet neighborhood, got out, and walked barefoot to the front door. Hearing the banter of a television show host, he knocked.

A shadow blocked the light in the peephole. 'What do you want?' He had to look suspicious, standing there in sodden pants.

'I'm a friend of Nikko's,' he rasped. 'I was with him when he died.'

The door cracked open. A dusky face peered out.

'My name's Joe,' he said, putting out a hand.

Her hand was slim and small. Holding it put a choke-hold on Joe's vocal cords.

'Victoria,' she said. 'Do you want to come in?'

'I'm all wet.'

'Please,' she insisted, opening the door wider.

She found a pair of Nikko's sweatpants, long enough to fit him, and threw Joe's slacks into the dryer. Then she and Joe sat across from each other in the dining room, where he spooned down the soup she insisted on feeding him. The boys poked their head out of the bedroom, but she shooed them away.

She waited for Joe to finish eating before demanding, 'Tell me what happened.'

He told her everything, not withholding the fact that he'd taken Chief Harlan's place. He braced himself for accusations, but they never came. She remained stoic right up to the point where he related how Nikko had passed out from lost blood, dragging Curry down with him. As the rest of his story unfolded, her brown eyes filled with tears.

'Then he never knew what happened,' she concluded, reaching for a napkin to cover her trembling lips.

'No, he never knew.'

Her face contorted with grief as she nodded her understanding. Joe's composure slipped. The lump in his throat ached unbearably.

'Thank you for telling me.'

Her gratitude shook him. His eyes burned. His vision blurred with tears. 'I'm sorry,' he added, appalled to hear his voice crack. 'I'm so sorry I couldn't save him.'

'It wasn't your fault,' she reassured him, her eyes benign with forgiveness. Then she reached across the table and seized his hand, holding it fast. 'Don't blame yourself,' she added. 'He died doing what he loved.'

Her acceptance humbled him. He couldn't stop the tears that poured from his eyes.

Victoria offered him the guest room for the night, but Joe declined. Leaving an hour later in his dried slacks, he felt as if he'd been cut free from an enormous weight.

As he eased into his car with the intent of finding a motel, he spared a thought for Penny.

You were right, Lieutenant. That was good for me.

* * *

Joe was back.

Penny parked her car in front of her house and smiled at the lascivious-looking jack-o'-lanterns glowing across the darkness at her. He'd faced them deliberately in the direction of her home so she wouldn't miss seeing them.

Apology accepted, Commander. Happiness warmed her like a flame as she peered into his windows, wondering how his trip had gone. A bluish flicker told her that the TV was on. But then she caught sight of a second vehicle parked behind his Jeep, and her happiness disintegrated. The green Volkswagon belonged to yet another one of his girlfriends.

He was back in action. Well, she sighed, it beats drinking himself into a stupor.

Yet loneliness enveloped her as she gathered her groceries from her trunk and carried them into her dark and empty home. Lia hadn't left a single light on when she left for work.

Dumping grocery bags on the kitchen counter, Penny went to hang her jacket in the closet. Was it too much to ask to find a helpful husband, someone with whom to share life's everyday burdens, to snuggle with on the couch? She pictured Steven Parks, the surgeon who'd eaten lunch with her every day last week. He'd promised to call her this weekend, but he hadn't yet. Perhaps he'd called while she was out.

She hastened to the kitchen to check her answering machine. The flashing light had her pulse accelerating. 'You have one new message,' announced the digitalized voice. The machine gave a beep, but no one spoke. The sound of heavy breathing chased away Penny's expectations.

Eric was at it again. To her amazement, he began to talk. 'W-w-why're doin' this? Why? You're gonna ... end up d-d-d-dead, like your father!' The phone clicked, and the digitalized voice on Penny's machine said, 'End of call.'

Penny could only stand there, rocked by the heavy beating of her heart. But then she realized the recording was just the evidence they needed.

She snatched up the phone to alert the authorities. Special Agent Lindstrom's business card was pinned to the corkboard. Beside it, on a scrap of paper, were Joe's name and number, scrawled in Lia's handwriting.

Penny eyed the information as she dialed Hannah's number. How had Lia gotten their neighbor's number, and why?

The agent's phone bumped her over to voice mail, and Penny left a concise but shaken message, requesting Hannah to call her back.

She hung up and waited, suddenly conscious of how dark and quiet her house was. What if she wasn't alone? She strained her ears and listened. A muted sound seemed to come from upstairs.

Fear had her snatching the phone up a second time. She tapped out Joe's number, refusing to ask herself why she was calling him, of all people.

'Montgomery.'

Just the sound of his voice sent warmth rushing through her. 'Hi, this is Penny. I know you're busy, but can you come over for a sec?'

His leather sofa creaked. 'What's wrong?' he asked, obviously picking up on her fright.

'I want you to hear something on my

message machine.'

'Be right there.'

She dashed to the porch to wait for him, too rattled to put away her groceries.

★ ★ ★

Joe found Penny standing on her front porch, trying not to wring her hands. Her enormous eyes hit him like a punch in the gut. 'What happened?' he asked again.

'Come inside. I want you to hear this.' Casting a wary glance up her staircase, she led the way to the kitchen, where groceries had yet to be put away. She ignored them, pushing a button on her wall phone.

Joe listened to heavy breathing and then a panic-stricken message, while Penny wrapped her arms around herself.

'He admitted to killing my father,' she marveled, when the message came to an end. 'That's all the proof we need.' She was trying to sound cool, like the call hadn't rattled her, but she didn't fool him.

'This is the guy who's been harassing you,' Joe guessed, forbearing to mention that the caller hadn't admitted to killing anyone.

'My father's former colleague,' she confirmed, 'the one who sold the ricin to terrorists, we think.'

'And then murdered your father,' he added, for clarification.

'Yes.'

'I thought you said the FBI was working on this.'

'They are. I just called the agent in charge of the case and left a message. Hopefully she'll call me right back.'

'I'm sure she will.' Her wide-eyed vulnerability made her look especially feminine, as did her civilian clothing — soft, faded jeans and a stretchy pink sweater that highlighted her perfect little breasts.

'I'm glad Ophelia wasn't home to take this call,' Penny said breathlessly. 'She would have totally freaked out. But hey, now we have we have his recorded confession. That should help speed up his arrest.'

Her quick chatter betrayed agitation. On instinct, Joe stepped forward and offered her a reassuring squeeze. 'He'll be out of the picture in no time,' he comforted.

He didn't mean the hug to be personal, but it unsettled her enough to blurt, 'So how was your trip?'

'Good,' he said, letting his arms fall. 'I'm glad I went.' He could actually breathe again. Yes, some awful things happened that night, but he didn't need to blame himself entirely.

'Thanks for carving the pumpkins,' she told him, with a wry little smile that drew his gaze to her full mouth.

'No problem.' A current of awareness passed between them. 'You, uh, you want me to have a look around?' Joe offered. 'Make sure nobody's lurking upstairs?'

'Would you?' She sounded relieved.

'Sure.'

He poked his head around the first floor, then took the stairs two at a time as Penny trailed behind. He peered into closets and under beds, taking silent but approving note of the understated traditional decor. Her bedroom was tidy and neat, filled with a light, rosy fragrance. The room Ophelia used was a wreck.

'All clear,' he said, having assured himself that she was home alone.

They paused at the top of the staircase, next to their merging shadows. 'Thank you,' Penny said, gripping the banister.

'You want to come to my place till the feds get here?' he offered. She was obviously still shaken.

'Oh. No, thank you. You already have a guest,' she added with a fluttering gesture.

'Cindy was leaving when you called.'

'Oh, well . . . I should wait for the agent to call me back,' she explained.

'Right,' he agreed. 'So you're going to be all right, then?'

'Sure,' she said, pinning on a bright smile.

'Okay.' He started down the stairs. The last impression he wanted to give was that he was coming on to her.

'Thank you,' she called, seeing him off.

''Night,' he called back.

On his way to his house, he heard Penny's phone ring.

★   ★   ★

Under the glow of her desk lamp, Special Agent Hannah Lindstrom flipped through Eric Tomlinson's folder one more time. She had to be overlooking something. If Tomlinson had sold the ricin to terrorists, then why was there no trail?

She flicked a glance at her silent phone, willing it to ring. Last night, the police had left Miss Price's home armed with evidence of harassment, if not an implicit statement of guilt, and promising to arrest Tomlinson the next day. Hannah had waited since then to hear that they'd made more headway questioning him than the FBI had.

The man would not confess to selling the ricin.

Nor was there any proof to suggest that

he'd murdered his partner: no accounts, foreign or domestic, in his name, holding mysterious sums of money; no history of an e-mail account from which the printed e-mail had been sent, not even on microfiche.

To make matters worse, the original investigation of the ricin theft had been headed up by an old-school detective who'd scoffed at forensics. Hannah could only guess that the man had had his palm greased for slapping a lid on the case. She'd never reviewed a sloppier investigation.

The jangling of her phone cut through her bleak thoughts. She flashed out a hand to answer it. 'Special Agent Lindstrom.'

'Sweetheart.'

Her stomach tightened with mixed guilt and pleasure. 'Oh, hi, honey.'

'I thought you'd be home by seven.'

'Oh, yeah, you know this case is hot.' What a lie that was. As cases went, this one wasn't even lukewarm. The police had grounds for arresting Tomlinson — on a harassment charge — but the FBI still did not.

'I know what you're doing, baby,' Luther chided.

She loved it when he called her baby. It made her melt.

'You don't have to hide from me,' he added. 'If you're not ready, you're not ready.'

She wanted to be ready. No man in the world would make a better father than Luther. She could picture him down on the floor wrestling with a brown-haired toddler. It was herself as a mother that she couldn't quite see. But the fact that Luther so completely understood that made her want to please him all the more.

She slapped Eric's file shut. 'I'll be home in ten minutes,' she promised, feeling breathless and scared and excited all at the same time.

'I love you, sweetheart.'

Sweetheart did the same thing that *baby* did. She hung up the phone knowing she was doing the right thing.

Snapping off her desk light, she grabbed her purse and hurried for the exit. ''Bye, Emilio,' she called, waving to the janitor as she disappeared.

Back in her office cubicle, the telephone rang again. On the fourth ring her voice mail picked up.

The caller left a muted message. 'This is Sergeant McCaully with the State Police. Uh, getting back to you regarding Eric Tomlinson, we still do not have the suspect in custody at this time. We do have a warrant, but he's flying low. He's in the NCIC, so if we get a hit, we'll pick him up and hold him. Just thought I'd let you know.'

Eric huddled in his car on a dirt road that dead-ended behind him, surrounded by trees and falling leaves. With what felt like a block of ice in his chest, he reached for the gun in his glove compartment, checked his arsenal, and left it on the seat beside him.

The Price sisters lived just a block away. He'd been watching them, waiting for the right moment to confront them. At the same time, he could sense the enemy closing in. The vultures were circling.

Danny's daughters hadn't heeded his warning. They'd gone and gotten the cops involved. Stupid, stupid girls. Because of them, he was forced to take more drastic measures.

8

Ophelia applied her eyeliner with dramatic strokes. She scowled as she considered the likelihood of an unprofitable evening ahead of her.

Penny was right. Waitressing was not a career — at least not in this tourist town. She couldn't live like this forever, with cash to burn one month, empty pockets the next.

The worst thing was subletting her apartment to a couple of friends because she couldn't afford to pay the rent herself. She trusted them to care for her cherished stuff, but it felt just awful to leave everything behind, like a traveling gypsy.

Assessing the results of her heavy hand with a frown, she realized she looked just like a gypsy. With a grimace, she reached for a tissue to wipe it off. But then the door-bell rang.

She was home alone.

Penny wasn't due in until six o'clock, two hours from now.

Peering out of the powder room, Lia eyed the front door. The visitor was a man. She could tell as much by his silhouette, visible through the oval window with a pink-washed sky behind him.

What if it was Eric? The police were on the prowl for him, but they hadn't found him yet.

It didn't look like Eric. The caller was of average height, while Eric was tall and spindly.

Wetting her glossed lips, Lia tiptoed to the door for a better view. The man had turned away. All that she could see was a broad back and short black hair. There was something vaguely familiar about him. It definitely wasn't Eric.

She pulled the door open.

The stranger turned, and she gasped her dismay. It was Al Pacino's young look-alike, the driver of the Honda Civic, only he was wearing a T-shirt and jeans, which made him look even younger. She went to slam the door in his face, but he was faster than she was, jamming a foot between the door and the threshold.

'Go away,' she said, pushing with all her might. The door didn't budge.

His gaze fastened with amazement on her orange Hooters T-shirt, paired with tiny black shorts. 'You're a Hooters girl?' he demanded with his Philadelphia accent.

It was none of his business. 'Get lost or I'll call the cops,' she told him coldly.

'Oh, I don't think so. You didn't want cops to come last time, remember?' he said. He cracked a cocky smile, displaying strong white teeth.

'Look,' she said, alarmed that he'd gone to such lengths to find her, 'I don't want you here. What part of get lost don't you get?'

'You owe me a debt,' he stated simply.

'And I offered to repay that debt. With a check,' she reminded him. 'I don't date younger guys, got it?'

'A bad check ain't gonna fix my car,' he pointed out, gesturing broadly.

She glanced at the Honda Civic parked at the curb. 'Your car's already fixed,' she snapped. He obviously didn't need her money. The chain dangling from his neck looked like eighteen-karat gold.

'You still owe me,' he said with a glimmer in his chocolate eyes, like he was laughing at her.

'Look, I don't have time for this. I'm going to be late for work.'

'So I'll go with you.'

'The hell you will!'

'Is there a problem?' cut in a third voice.

It seemed to come from the bushes, but then the next-door neighbor cruised around the corner of the house. He must have been in his backyard, about to slip into his hot tub,

because all he was wearing was a towel, and
— holy crap — no wonder Penny was half in
love with the guy!

Little Al turned to face the newcomer. The
size and stature of the man didn't have the
effect Lia expected, other than to eradicate
his smile. He cut a bland look at her. 'Who is
this?' he asked with a jerk of his chin.

'I said, is there some problem here?' Joe
repeated. His tone was so cold that even Lia
shivered.

'Um, sort of,' she admitted. 'This boy
won't leave me alone. Now I'm going to be
late for work.'

'Sounds like you'd better take a hike,' Joe
said to Little Al.

But the young man stood his ground. 'Isn't
he a little old for you?' he asked Lia with just
a hint of disgust.

'Not really.' She tossed her head.

Joe ascended the porch steps. His body
language indicated that this was all going to
stop right now. 'Is this the person who's been
harassing you?' he asked.

Instead of turning tail, Little Al widened
his stance. Hands fisted loosely at his sides,
he gave every indication that he was prepared
to duke it out.

Lia couldn't watch this. 'Hold on a sec,' she
cried, leaping between the pair. 'This isn't

Eric, obviously; he's too young,' she said to the SEAL, 'so you don't have to kill him. He's just some kid who's mad because I back-ended his car and crushed a taillight. This guy' — she turned to Young Al while pointing at her neighbor — 'is a Navy SEAL. You do not want to mess with him. Now leave me alone.'

Young Al seemed to blanch and snapped to rigid attention. 'PO2 Vinny DeInnocentis, Team Twelve, at your service, sir!' he barked. 'I'm sorry, sir, I didn't realize.'

What?

The menace went right out of the neighbor's face. He took in Lia's open-mouthed astonishment and smiled. 'Joe Montgomery, lieutenant commander,' he countered, extending a hand. 'Nice to meet you, Vinny. I live next door.'

The two men sidestepped Ophelia and pumped hands.

Just like that, they were buddies. They both looked at her, as if considering a mutual problem. 'She owes me a dinner,' Vinny explained.

The name fit him even better than Little Al. 'I am *not* taking you out to dinner,' she snapped, still reeling at how the tables had turned. They were both Navy SEALs? What were the odds of that?

'Deal's a deal,' Vinny insisted. He pulled a ring out of his pocket. 'She even gave me this ring as a token of her honor.'

Commander Montgomery frowned his disapproval. 'Does your sister know about this?'

Ophelia snatched the ring out of Vinny's fingers and jammed it onto her right hand. 'I'm twenty-four friggin' years old. I don't have to tell my sister everything,' she ground out.

'Then act your age,' he suggested mildly. 'You said you'd take him out to dinner.'

'Fine,' Lia said, throwing up her hands. 'We're going to Hooters. I'll pay for your dinner there.'

The commander looked inquiringly at Vinny. The boy SEAL shrugged. 'That'll work,' he said easily, but his eyes brimmed with mischief.

'See you around, PO2,' called Joe. With a nod at Lia, he pattered barefoot down the steps and across the lawn.

'You'll have to follow me,' Lia said to Vinny. 'And try not to get me into any more trouble than I'm already in for being late.'

He didn't say a word to that.

★　★　★

Between the boxing match on the wide-screen TV and the action in the restaurant

136

behind him, Vinny didn't suffer a dull moment. He jump-started his five-course meal with an appetizer: raw oysters on the half shell.

As Ophelia sashayed past him with her tray, he worked the mollusk from the shell, balanced it for a delicate moment on the tip of his tongue, relished the silky meat, and then swallowed it with ecstasy.

She pretended to be unimpressed.

An hour crept by, and his appetite stirred enough to request an entrée. Torn between a Philly cheesesteak and snow crab legs, he ordered both, chuckling at the look of dismay on her face as she realized how much their 'date' was going to cost her.

'Are you really going to eat all of that?' she snapped, breaking to a halt beside his stool.

He picked up an empty crab claw, working it open and closed. 'Don't worry, *cara mia*. I can still eat you for dessert.'

'Grow up,' she scoffed, leaving him in a cloud of spicy-sweet perfume.

Her words didn't faze him. Vinny was used to being teased about his age. In SEAL/BUDS training, he'd been dubbed Mowgli, after the wild child from *Jungle Book*. It had taken him only two years to prove that he was any SEAL's match, and his code name became 'the Godfather,' thanks to his resemblance to Al Pacino.

As man of the house growing up, he'd assumed responsibility early on. Only the toughest survived on the east side of Philly, with gangs and drugs on every corner. From the day his father'd up and left them, to the day of SEAL graduation, there wasn't an obstacle that Vinny hadn't tackled head-on. Winning over Ophelia couldn't be that hard.

The Philly cheesesteak made its appearance. He ate half before setting it aside and ordering key lime pie. The next time Ophelia passed him, he swirled whipped cream on his finger. 'You want a lick?' he asked with a straight face.

'No,' she said flatly, but her lips twitched.

She was glancing his way when her foot caught the leg of a chair and her tray went flying, upsetting several half-empty glasses. Soda splattered the wall. Ice chips sprinkled the carpet.

'Shit!' Her gaze flew with dismay toward the office at the entrance to the kitchen, and sure enough, the manager poked her head out.

'Is that you, Lia?' the woman demanded, her lips pursed into a red knot.

'Sorry,' Ophelia said. 'I'll clean it up.'

'You have customers waiting for refills,' the manager snapped. 'I'll get this.' She snatched away the towel that Ophelia had grabbed. 'I swear to God, if you don't learn how to carry a tray, I'm going to have to let you go.'

Observing the interchange, Vinny waited for Lia, as everyone called her, to tell the woman to pack sand. Instead, she nodded to the barkeeper's helper to pour more drinks and said, 'It won't happen again.'

With grudging admiration, Vinny made a point to catch her eye. 'Hey,' he called out, 'she's just jealous 'cause she can't fit her fat ass into those shorts you're wearing.' He made sure his words were loud enough to be overheard.

The manager shot him a look that could kill.

Ophelia made a choking sound. He couldn't tell if she was grateful or contemplating murder as she bore her refills to the waiting table.

The sky outside turned from pewter to black. The restaurant began to empty. Vinny watched the ninth round of the boxing match. Out the corner of one eye, he saw Lia take a biker couple's order. He thought he saw the old man put his hand on her ass.

'Did that old lech just feel you up?' he asked as she approached the bar.

She looked at him blankly. 'I don't think so.'

'What do you mean, you don't *think* so?'

She shrugged. 'It happens all the time. It's no big deal.'

'You don't think?' If she was his little sister — Isabella — he'd make a big fucking deal out of it.

'Relax, Little Al,' she told him. 'I know how to handle it.'

He was too startled by the nickname, which was surely a reference to Al Pacino, to summon an argument.

He kept a watchful eye on her as she carried two Long Island iced teas back to the table. Sure enough, the hairy geezer with tattoos on his forearm put his hand right below her heart-shaped bottom.

With a forced smile, Lia removed it, put it back on the table, and gave it a pat.

Good boy. Down, boy.

She called that handling it?

Vinny stood up. This was wrong.

As she turned toward the kitchen, she intercepted his path. 'Go back to your chair,' she warned him. 'Don't you dare get me into trouble!'

'I'm just going to talk to him.'

'Oh, no you're not.' She darted an uneasy glance at the manager's open door.

'Is there a problem, Lia?' The woman's voice was like nails on a chalkboard.

'Not at all,' she retorted.

'Actually, there is,' Vinny countered, turning to the matron. 'Do you allow your waitresses to be groped by customers?' he demanded.

'Of course not,' the woman huffed.

'Well, that old guy just put his hands on her backside. What are you going to do about it?'

'Well, I hope you told him to stop,' she said to Ophelia.

'Yes, of course I did. There isn't a problem.' She tried to move past Vinny, but he wrested the order booklet out of her hands.

'How 'bout you take their order?' he said, thrusting it at the manager.

'Excuse me?' the woman huffed. 'I am not a waitress. Tending tables is Lia's job, not mine.'

'Looks like you'd better take over,' said Vinny, grabbing Lia's hand, ''cause she just quit.'

'Oh, no I didn't,' Lia countered, trying to break free.

'You know what?' the manager shot back, 'I'm glad for an excuse to let you go. Take a hike, and take this hot-head with you — *after* he pays for his food.'

Vinny whipped his wallet out and tossed forty dollars on the counter. Retrieving Lia's purse from behind the bar, he dragged her toward the door. 'Come on, *cara mia*, let's go,' he urged.

With her jaw dangerously set, she let him tug her toward the door.

'Do you have a jacket?' he asked as the door whooshed shut behind them.

'In my car.'

As they marched toward her car, he sought the keys in her hippie-style purse. She snatched it from his hands, pulled out her keys, and tried to get in, but Vinny held her fast.

'Let me go. I can't believe you did that!' Her voice shook with fury.

'You're not driving anywhere right now,' he said. Spying what looked to be her sweater, he edged her aside and lunged for it, then locked the car up tight. 'Let's go for a walk,' he suggested, pocketing her keys.

'I'm going to kill you.'

'How 'bout you count to thirty and then I'll let you hit me,' he suggested.

She wrenched the sweater out of his hands and stormed ahead of him, throwing it on as she stomped across an enormous parking lot toward an indoor shopping mall.

Vinny followed close behind. 'Are you counting?' he inquired.

'Thirty!' She whirled without warning. He

caught a fist in the gut and a cuff on the side of the head.

'Ouch, that hurt.' He was impressed.

'I can't believe you just got me fired,' she ranted, shoving him with both hands. 'Who the hell do you think you are? I needed that job. I'm completely broke, you jerk. Thanks a lot!'

'No problem,' Vinny murmured, smiling to himself.

He knew from experience that you had to hit rock bottom if you wanted to push your way to the top.

★   ★   ★

Hearing the break in her voice, Lia fled across the parking lot, scattering the seagulls who were hunkered down for the night.

A car that was backing up blared its horn as she stepped into its path. The driver shouted obscenities. Lia shouted one back.

How was she going to pay her rent now? There weren't any jobs near the beach this time of year. She'd be crashing at her sister's place till springtime, providing Penny didn't kick her out first. She had to be tired of having Lia around.

Hell, Lia was tired of herself these days.

Tears of frustration stabbed her eyes. She

was so intent on putting distance between her and the boy SEAL that she didn't see the manhole cover jutting out of the sidewalk. She tripped over it in classic Ophelia style and pitched to her knees on the unforgiving concrete.

Crushed, she rolled onto her bottom, bowed her head over her scraped knees, and willed herself not to cry.

The air shifted. 'You okay?' Vinny asked matter-of-factly.

'Fuck. You,' she gritted. She kept her head down so he wouldn't see the self-pity pooling in her eyes.

'Yeah, you can do that later,' came the cocky response. 'So, did you hurt yourself? Lemme look.' He lifted the hem of her sweater and peered at her knees. 'Scraped 'em up good.'

No shit, Sherlock.

'Come on, I'll help you up.' He put his arms around her and lifted her to her feet. 'Let's go inside,' he said, gesturing to the mall doors. 'Maybe something's still open.'

They hobbled through the entrance to find that the only establishment in operation was a dimly lit Irish pub.

Jerking free of Vinny's touch, Lia limped into what was clearly a locals' hangout. The handful of patrons glanced their way as they headed to a booth.

'I'll be right back,' said Vinny.

He was gone for ten seconds, enough time for her to verify that her pantyhose were shredded and one knee was worse off than the other. When Vinny returned, he pushed into the space beside her and reached for her legs.

'Don't touch me.' But then she saw the damp paper towels in his hands and grudgingly submitted to his aid.

'Sit sideways,' he said, swinging her legs over his thighs.

It wasn't like she had much choice. 'How's that feel?' he asked, pressing the makeshift compresses to her knees.

'Better,' she admitted, unsettled by his touch. He had strong, tanned fingers and thighs made of granite.

A waitress stepped up to their table. 'What can I get you?'

'Think you could come up with a bag of ice?' he asked.

'I'll check,' she said, moving away.

Vinny stroked the bare skin behind Lia's right knee. 'You have beautiful legs,' he said with reverence.

'Look,' she said, steeling herself against his flattery, not to mention his caress, 'I don't know how to get this through your thick skull. I'm not interested in getting to know you. I don't go out with guys my own age, let alone guys that are younger than me.'

His chocolaty eyes skewered her, and her words seemed to roll like water off a duck's back. 'You still owe me a debt,' he reminded her. 'Who paid for my dinner? I did.'

'That's because you got me fired, you idiot!'

'Come on,' he chided softly. 'You deserve a better job than that, and you know it.'

The compliment confused her. She closed her mouth with a snap and considered her options. 'Fine. I'll buy you a beer, how's that? Or are you even old enough to drink?'

'I'm old enough to die for my country,' he pointed out.

Alrighty, then.

The waitress reappeared with a glass full of ice. 'I couldn't find a baggie,' she explained, putting it in front of him.

He drew the glass closer. 'The lady's going to buy me a Heineken,' he said, lifting out an ice cube.

'And what'll you have?' the waitress asked Lia.

'I'll take a rum and Diet Coke. Captain Morgan, please,' she specified.

The waitress left, and Lia gasped as Vinny put an ice cube on her knee. He circled the abrasion, careful not to touch it directly. A shiver of pleasure moved up her thigh. The ice melted fast, dampening the frayed edges of her pantyhose.

'I'm training to be a medic,' he volunteered, sending her a quick glance.

His eyelashes were ridiculously thick and curly. 'Are you really?'

'Yeah. I like it. I think I'll go to med school eventually.'

She reassessed him. Obviously a brain went with all that brawn. It was a shame that he was so young. Maybe if he were ten years older . . .

'How long have you been a SEAL?' she asked. Not that she wanted to know him any better.

'Three years.'

No way. 'What? Were you like twelve when you joined?'

'Hah, hah. No, I was seventeen. And you don't join the SEALs. You're selected through one of the world's most rigorous training programs. Only fourteen out of sixty-six candidates graduated.'

Wow. Okay, that said something for him. Questions crowded her brain, but she stifled them, not wanting to give him false encouragement.

'I'm half Irish, half Italian. Know what that means?' he added, clearly needing none.

'No.'

'It means I'm stubborn and passionate. When I see something I want, I go after it.'

'Really,' she drawled, stifling an involuntary shiver.

'When I was seven, I saw a documentary on the Discovery Channel about the Navy SEALs. It looked like something I wanted to do.'

'And now you want to go to med school,' she added.

'Well, sure. I also like challenges. Which is probably why I like you.'

She tingled at the confession. 'You're wasting your time.'

'We'll see. Of course, if I want to go to med school, I'll have to finish college first,' he continued, despite the interruption. 'Every semester I take two classes.'

'You sound busy,' she said.

'I bet you went to college,' he wagered.

'Yes, I did.' And she'd partied like a frenzied animal.

He fixed his penetrating gaze on her. 'What'd you study?'

'Journalism.' *When I went to class.*

'And you graduated?'

'Yeah.' Thanks to Penny, who'd typed up many a paper for her and drove her to rehab till she got her act together.

'So what're you doin' waitressing? You

should be on TV or radio or somethin'.'

'I could if I wanted to,' she said with false confidence. 'I like the idea of snooping around, finding stories.'

'You should do it,' he said. 'What's stopping you?'

'I don't know,' she admitted, chugging down her drink. The Captain Morgan went straight through her empty stomach into her bloodstream.

'I think you'd look hot on TV,' he persisted, his deep voice like a caress.

It had to be the liquor making her face warm. 'No one's going to hire me,' she admitted. 'My grades were bad. I wouldn't have graduated if my sister hadn't helped me. 'Course, she lost a fiancé in the process, and that was my fault . . . ' She shut her mouth abruptly, unwilling to say too much.

'You know what I think?' he said after a reflective sip of his beer. 'You lack self-confidence, that's what it is.'

She bristled at the accusation. 'Excuse me? I do not.'

'Prove it,' he challenged.

'I don't have to prove a damn thing to you.'

'Not to me.' He gestured with his chin. 'Prove it to yourself.'

Lia felt a scowl coming. Wasn't this totally annoying? A barely twenty-year-old boy was telling her what to do with her life. 'Do you want another beer?' she asked him, her temper flaring anew. 'How many is it going to take for you to leave me alone?'

His eyes narrowed briefly, but then he gave his patented crooked smile. 'The repairs on my car came to two hundred and twenty dollars,' he let her know.

Lia swallowed hard.

'At three dollars a beer, that's . . . just over seventy-three beers,' he added, proving himself adept at mental math.

Her gaze flickered over him. There was more to this boy than met the eye. 'You're pretty smart, huh?' she commented, testing him.

He gave a shrug that said, Yeah, so what?

'So why didn't you go to college instead of SEAL training?'

His expression turned suddenly remote.

'Forget it,' she added. 'I don't even want to know.'

'My mother got sick. She couldn't work anymore.'

'Oh.' In two short sentences, he managed to cast himself in a totally different light.

'I had a scholarship to wrestle at Penn State, but . . . ' His sentence trailed off. 'It worked out better this way.'

She couldn't keep from asking. 'Did your

mother get better?'

'Yes, she did.'

'Well that's good.' Lia thought of her father and her heart gave a familiar, painful squeeze.

The conversation lagged.

'Did I say something?' Vinny asked a moment later.

'What do you mean?'

'You just dropped off a cliff there,' he pointed out.

She was feeling the effects of the drink she'd sucked down. She suddenly felt weepy and tired and defeated, especially when she thought of her beautiful apartment, the one she couldn't afford to return to. 'I'm just tired,' she said. 'I want to go home.'

'No problem,' he said. 'Stay right here. I'll go get my car.'

She didn't understand. 'Why?'

'So you don't have to walk.' He was already on his feet, jingling the keys in his pocket. 'Be right back.'

In a blink of an eye he was gone. Lia sat for a stunned moment feeling lonely. The loneliness grew when she reflected that he'd gone off with her car keys. What if he decided just to dump her here? She hadn't been very nice to him.

A couple of minutes crept by. She paid the waitress and reapplied her lipstick, covering up the fact that she was nervous. But then

Vinny was back, reaching for her hand.

'I'm parked illegally,' he volunteered, helping her to her feet.

'I'm not a cripple,' she said, but his hand was so warm and steady that she didn't tug free. Besides, she felt wobbly on her feet; she'd managed to get tipsy off just one drink. She didn't want to walk into a wall.

His car was parked with two tires on the curb. He held the door for her as she eased into the passenger seat. Cozy and warm, the interior smelled like Windex. It was immaculate, a far cry from the inside of her own car.

He got in, eyes glimmering in the dark. 'Seat belt,' he reminded her.

She snapped the harness into place, and he maneuvered the stick shift. The engine gave a roar as they pulled away.

They drove right past Hooters. 'Hey, my car!' Lia cried, jolted out of her haze.

'I can't let you drive,' he pointed out calmly.

'I'm not drunk!'

He said nothing to that.

The memory of his muscle-hewn thighs made her realize how vulnerable she was right now. 'Where are you taking me?' she asked in a small voice.

'Home,' he replied, casting her a puzzled glance.

She was glad to hear it, though at the same time a little disappointed. What, no abduction in the middle of the night, being taken to his apartment, tied to his bed with silk handkerchiefs, ravished repeatedly? 'How'm I gonna get my car?'

'Friend of mine will help me bring it back.'

She stole a peek at him. Wow, for such a young guy, he sure was gallant. She'd never gone out with a guy who treated her like a piece of glass.

But then again, he'd gotten her fired. He was the reason she wouldn't be paying her rent anytime soon.

Scant minutes later, he pulled up in front of Penny's house. 'Cool pumpkins,' he said, admiring the neighbor's jack-o'-lanterns.

'Yeah,' Lia agreed. What now? Letting him kiss her would be a big mistake. On the other hand, she was curious. Just what was this young SEAL's kiss like, anyway?

Vinny rounded the car to escort her to the door. 'If you want to see me again, you need to find me first,' he said as they crossed the front lawn.

'What are you talking about?' she demanded as she concentrated on walking.

'Let's see how good of an investigative reporter you could be,' he challenged lightly. 'Which one of these keys gets you in?'

'Give me that.' She snatched the key ring from his hand and unlocked the door. 'My sister's probably sleeping,' she added, hinting heavily that he couldn't come in.

'So be quiet, then,' he told her.

'I am being quiet. God, you're annoying.'

'Yeah, but you like me. I need those keys back,' he reminded her. 'I'll leave them under the floor mat on the driver's side.'

'Okay.' She handed them over. 'You didn't have to bring me home, you know. I could have driven.'

'Maybe, but then I wouldn't have gotten to do this.'

In the next instant, he had her in a lip-lock.

She started to push him away, but his lips were so warm and skillful, her hand stopped pushing and went around his neck instead. She felt herself melting like a snow cone in the sun. God, the boy could kiss!

He kissed her like she'd never been kissed before.

Then it was over. Too soon.

With a cocky grin, he detached himself. 'Find me,' he said again, striding jauntily toward his Civic. Then the car roared and pulled away.

Ophelia watched until his taillights disappeared from view. She'd gotten fired tonight and let a twenty-year-old kiss her.

Could her life get any more screwed up?

9

Halloween night was different this year than last. Perhaps it was the fog rising off the pavement in the wake of a sultry afternoon. It crept over the curb and onto the grass, creating an otherworldly mist that was perfect for this spooky annual ritual, but it made Penny feel uneasy.

As was her custom, she'd donned her witch's costume, complete with a fake nose and a pointed hat, and mixed the batter for pumpkin bread. Still, she could not simulate the lighthearted anticipation she normally felt.

Ophelia had confessed this morning that she'd lost her waitressing job. Maybe that was getting Penny down. Her little sister was never going to move out. Tonight Lia'd taken herself, dressed as a belly dancer, to a party hosted by a former college roommate. To her credit, she did seem troubled by her financial woes.

Maybe Penny was depressed because she'd sworn last year that *next* year she'd be handing out candy with her husband-to-be. Yet she wasn't. She didn't even have a boyfriend. Steven Parks hadn't called at all lately, though he'd been as charming as ever at the hospital this week.

Shutting her pumpkin batter in the oven, Penny hurried to answer the ringing doorbell. She secured her fake nose as she went, and snatched up the candy bowl. The toddlers at the door had to be prompted by their escorts to utter the magic phrase.

'Trick or treat!'

'How about a treat, my dearies?' Penny answered in her nice-witch voice. She kneeled to be at eye level with the pink poodle and Tinkerbell and dropped candy in their plastic pumpkins.

With a smile, she straightened and eyed the fog inching toward her steps like a wicked tide. 'Creepy,' she said, glancing at Joe's leering jack-o'-lanterns. He appeared to be handing out treats himself tonight. She'd always pegged him as a sucker.

The ringing of her telephone drew her back inside.

She didn't recognize the number on her caller ID. 'Yes, hello,' she said, praying it wasn't Eric again.

'Hey, this is Steven,' came the warm male voice, relieving her fears. 'Did I catch you at a bad time?'

It was only seven-thirty. 'No, not at all.

Where are you?' The noises in the background suggested a party.

'I'm at a bar downtown. I was wondering if you'd like to join me. It's kind of a young scene, but the music's good.'

'Oh.' She was tempted, if only to say that she'd gone on a date, but . . . 'It's Halloween,' she pointed out. 'I have to hand out candy.'

'What, someone's holding a gun to your head?' he laughed.

'No, but I get a kick out of seeing all the kids dressed up.'

'Oh, I know what you mean.'

'Would you like to come over here?' she offered.

'Uh . . . ' He hesitated, and her hopes started to rise, but then he dashed them. 'No, I'd have to ditch some friends,' he admitted. 'They'd be mad at me.'

'I see.'

'How about later this week, though, like on Friday?'

'Friday's perfect.' She tried not to sound too eager.

'Okay. I'll probably see you at the hospital before then. We'll talk some more.'

'Sure. Thanks for calling.'

For the next forty minutes, every child in the neighborhood stopped by to soak up the attention Penny lavished on them. She treated a Dracula, two Batmen, a cheer-leader, twins dressed as Crayola Crayons, one Shrek, and a six-year-old firefighter.

At eight o'clock, the younger children disappeared. A definite lull followed. Penny checked on her bread and decided it needed twenty more minutes. The doorbell rang again, and she went to open the door.

Her smile froze in place. In lieu of a trick-or-treater, her stuffed scarecrow had been moved directly in front of her door. It sat there looking at her.

'Okay,' she said, putting the candy down. She stepped outside. Suspecting mischievous teenagers of pulling a prank, she scanned the bushes around the house, but the fog offered ideal concealment.

Lifting the chair, she put the scarecrow back in its original position. A movement in her peripheral vision had her whirling with a gasp. A man dressed in black and wearing a green goblin mask leaped onto the porch. Her heart jumped up her throat as he seized her arms, overpowered her, and dragged her back inside, slamming the door shut.

She couldn't believe this was happening. One minute she was thinking she was the brunt of a joke. The next, she was grappling with a stranger whose breath rasped through the slits of his rubber mask.

Joe was hoping the endless trickle of children had subsided when his doorbell rang. With a grunt of discomfort, he went to answer it. His back was hurting him again. Tuesday's session with Penny hadn't been long enough.

'Oh, my God,' one preteen was saying to another. 'He scared the crap out of me!'

'Do you think he's a friend of Miss Penny's?'

'I don't think so. I think he wants to scare her, too.'

'Who are you talking about?' Joe demanded, with a bowl of Hershey's chocolate under one arm.

'There's a man dressed as a goblin hiding in the bushes,' said the boy wearing a dress. 'He scared the crap out of us.'

Concern raked through Joe. 'Where? Next door?'

'Yeah.' The boy pointed. 'Right over there.'

'Take this.' Joe shoved the bowl of chocolate at the kids and pushed past them. He ran through knee-high fog to Penny's. His concern was probably unwarranted — a neighbor could be playing a hoax. But with Eric on the loose, he didn't want to take chances.

Her porch light was on. Her door was

closed. Not a goblin in sight.

But as he stepped up to the door, he saw through the beveled glass that Penny had company. A tall, dark figure was shaking her.

Joe pounded on the door.

A green goblin's face whipped in Joe's direction. The stranger wheeled away, fleeing toward the rear of the house.

It was all the invitation Joe needed to go after him. He pushed through the unlocked door, passing a stricken Penny as he gave chase.

But the man had already gone out the back door. That same French door that Joe had examined the other night stood open. Joe shot through it, into Penny's backyard. The sound of running feet had him chasing the goblin around the house.

The fog swirled in funnels before him, letting him know that he was close. Ignoring the twinges in his back, he sprinted toward the street and down the sidewalk, scarcely visible for the thickness of the mist.

The patter of footsteps ceased. Joe stopped and listened, stilling his breathing, but all he could hear was the chatter of children. Glow-in-the-dark night sticks bobbed here and there.

A car engine throttled suddenly, and Joe pivoted toward the sound. Brake lights flared as a car squealed away not twenty yards from him. It sped recklessly out of the neighborhood with the headlights extinguished. 'Damn!' Joe swore, watching helplessly as the car disappeared.

Ignoring the spasm in his back, he returned to Penny's and found her exactly where she was before, petrified by shock. 'You look like you've seen a ghost, not a goblin,' he teased to ease her fear. He went to close the French doors.

'You okay?' he added, coming back.

'I think so,' she whispered, removing the fake nose that had slipped to her chin.

'I take it that was Eric.'

She nodded. 'I've never been so scared in my life.'

He reached for her, rubbing her arms briskly. 'It's over,' he reassured her. 'I hate to admit it, but he got away from me.'

'How did you even know that he was here?' she asked.

'I heard some kids talking about a man in a mask. I thought I'd check it out.'

With a huge sigh, she fell against him. A tremor went through her, prompting him to put an arm around her and pull her closer. He was caught off guard by how soft and feminine she felt and by his impulse to rock her. She smelled of autumn spices — or

161

maybe it was the house that smelled like that. 'What did he say to you?' he asked.

She pulled back slightly, her brow puckered in thoughtful reflection. 'He didn't make a lot of sense. First he said he didn't kill my father. He said something about his wife being sick — he needed money to pay her doctor bills. But then he got violent and he started shaking me and calling me stupid. He said we're all going to die.' At this point, her own voice rose in panic.

A sharp-edged chill sliced through Joe. Shit, he thought. No wonder she'd been scared. 'You're not going to die,' he comforted. 'But we need to call the cops right now,' he decided, pulling her toward the kitchen with him.

'I'll call Hannah,' Penny decided, slipping from his grasp.

Wanting inexplicably to hold her some more, Joe watched her dial the agent's number with trembling fingers.

Listening to one end of the conversation, he was relieved to hear that both the agent and the state police were on their way.

'They'll want a statement from me, too,' Joe realized when she hung up. 'What's that smell?' he added, finding it too hard to ignore.

'My pumpkin bread!' She rushed to the

162

stove. 'Oh, I hope it's not burned.'

It didn't look burned. Joe's mouth watered as she set it on the stovetop.

'Would you like a slice?' she asked.

It seemed strange to eat at a time like this, but performing a mundane task like serving bread might soothe Penny's agitation. 'Sure, why not?'

She busied herself cutting them each a slice. 'Have a seat,' she offered, pouring two glasses of milk.

Joe eased down at the little dinette table, broke a corner off his bread, and popped it in his mouth. 'Oh, man,' he moaned, 'This is good.'

Her smile flickered briefly, but then her shoulders drooped.

'You know, my mom cooks stuff like this,' he added, determined to distract her from thinking of Eric's threat.

'Where does she live?' she asked.

'Right now, in a Winnebego somewhere in New Mexico. My folks are enjoying their retirement.'

'That's so nice.' She sighed with envy. 'Where are they from originally?'

'From Nevada. I grew up there.'

'Are they planning to drive this far east to see you?'

'I don't know.' He hadn't exactly invited them.

She gave him a penetrating look. 'Aren't you close to them?' she asked.

'Sure. Yeah. I'm an only child, and they're great parents, the best.' He loved the fact that they were still enamored with each other. At the same time, he was always reluctant to see them, to hear their concerns that he wasn't married. Like he could just grab the next woman to come along and he'd have the same perfect marriage they had.

'They're not used to seeing me all scrawny and scratched up,' he said, making excuses. 'I'm hoping to put some weight on before I see them at Thanksgiving.'

'They're coming out here?' she asked, looking pleased for him.

'No, I'm planning on going home.'

'Have another slice,' she urged, picking up his plate to fetch him one.

He had to smile as she handed it to him. 'Thanks.'

'I wish I had two parents,' she tossed in unexpectedly as she sat back down.

Her father was killed. 'What happened to your mother?' he wanted to know.

'Oh, she took off when I was six.' Penny shrugged. 'We never saw her again.'

He hadn't expected that. All he could do was look across the table at her and marvel that she'd turned out so squared away. From her mother's desertion to her father's death, she'd been dealt some tough blows, yet there she sat, composed and kind. Her spirit shone with a nurturing flame.

He realized suddenly that he'd never known a woman like her. His lovers had been, for the most part, spoiled, privileged, and unquestionably self-centered.

The doorbell rang, and Penny jumped like a squirrel on a high-voltage wire. 'That must be Hannah,' she said, getting up to answer it.

Joe trailed her to the door, in time to see a striking redhead step inside. As Penny made introductions, the FBI agent assessed Joe through frank green eyes. 'Nice to meet you,' she said.

'Same here.'

'Joe's a Navy SEAL,' Penny explained. 'He showed up in time to chase Eric out the back door and around the house.'

'Yeah, he got away from me, though,' Joe admitted with a grimace. 'Drove off in his car.'

'Sergeant McCaully should be here any minute,' Hannah said, slipping out of her trench coat. Her gaze swung back at Joe as she draped it over Penny's banister. 'My husband's a SEAL,' she said, surprising him. 'Maybe you've heard of him — Luther Lindstrom?'

'Oh, sure, the former football player. We met a couple of years ago.'

Her considering gaze focused on his scar. 'That's quite a battle wound,' she commented.

Joe didn't rise to the bait.

'Come on in the kitchen, Hannah,' Penny spoke up, steering her toward the back of the house. 'Have some pumpkin bread while we wait for the police.'

Joe followed somewhat reluctantly. He didn't know the extent of the rumors circulating the teams about the disaster in Afghanistan. Most likely, all the SEALs knew the survivor was a lieutenant commander. That would explain the speculative look in Hannah Lindstrom's eyes. He didn't want to go there with her, if she was bold enough to bring it up.

Fortunately, she fired other questions at him, as did Sergeant McCaully, who arrived in short order and requested that Joe retrace Eric's footsteps. They strobed the lawn with their flashlights, hunting for prints in the mist. They swabbed everything Eric had touched, looking for trace samples of DNA. Joe stood in the foyer watching Sergeant McCaully scribble in his notebook. He could hear Penny and Hannah in the kitchen.

'So, do you know what happened to your neighbor's face?' Hannah murmured, sotto voce. 'I'm just curious.'

'I'm not sure,' Penny hedged.

Joe stiffened as mistrust rose up in him. Would she betray him, after all?

'But I think it was a car accident,' she continued, and Joe's misgivings evaporated. 'I heard a rumor that the passengers in the car didn't make it.'

'That's terrible,' Hannah remarked after a shocked silence.

Joe scratched his head. Had Penny just made up a tale to throw Hannah off the scent? He found himself walking toward the kitchen.

Both women looked up guiltily.

'Is there anything else you need from me?' he asked both of them at once.

'No,' said Hannah brightly. 'But thank you. You've been very helpful. Unfortunately for Penny, the FBI has no real cause to get involved yet, so the police are still handling the investigation at this stage.' Her cell phone vibrated and she sneaked a peek at it. 'Excuse me just a see,' she said, heading for the patio.

Joe and Penny exchanged a long look. 'Why can't the FBI get involved?' he wanted to know.

'They can't convincingly prove that Eric stole the ricin or that he pushed my father off the road. This is a simple case of harassment and trespassing,' she added with defeat.

It was all Joe could do not to pull her into

his arms again. 'I'm sorry,' he said, jamming his fingers into his pockets. 'You gonna be okay tonight?'

'Sure,' she said, forcing a smile. 'Lia's on her way home now.'

'I overheard what you said to Agent Lindstrom about how I got this scar,' he heard himself admit.

She had the grace to look embarrassed. 'I wouldn't feel so bad about lying if I understood why you don't want anybody knowing. There's no shame in serving your country, is there?'

He looked down and away. 'Maybe I'll explain one day,' he answered.

She sent him one of her searching looks. 'It'd be good for you to talk about it,' she urged.

She was probably right, but he was cautious about sharing too much. Sometimes women took advantage of shared secrets.

'Here, take some bread with you,' Penny offered, turning toward the stove. 'You need to fatten up,' she reminded him. 'Thanksgiving isn't all that far away.'

He couldn't refuse that offer. As she handed him the warmed block of tinfoil, their fingers brushed and a pleasant feeling stole over him. That had to be because her massages were so soothing.

He turned away, envisioning the type of man

Penny would eventually secure. Someone tame and gentle, who was hopefully as caring and generous as she was. Envy spurted through him. Penny wasn't his to hold; she was just his physical therapist, a bit of a confidante. But he knew that he wanted the best for her, whoever that lucky man might be.

★ ★ ★

'Huh,' said Hannah, looking away from the television as she searched her mental archives.

'What?' Luther looked up from the opposite end of the couch, where he was reading a Tom Clancy novel.

'A deputy Chief of Staff member was found dead in his home,' she said, relaying the news she'd just heard on television.

'Did you know him?'

'No, never heard of him,' she muttered, drumming her fingers on the arm of the couch, 'but this is the fourth time in like five years that a military leader has died unexpectedly.'

'Five years is a long time, baby. People die.'

'Yeah, but this is weird,' she insisted. 'I mean, to find no cause of death on four separate men, all of whom serve or have served in the highest levels of the military?

That's stretching things.'

'So tell the FBI,' he teased.

But she took him seriously. 'I think I will.' Rolling to her feet, she padded to the kitchen to retrieve the cordless phone. She returned to the living room, dialing Special Agent Rafael Valentino's number, and flopped back on the couch.

Luther watched with tolerant interest as she greeted the man responsible for bringing her into the Bureau.

'Hi, sir, it's Hannah. Did I catch you at a bad time?'

'Not at all,' rasped the Italian American, a legendary peacekeeper who'd put the famed mob boss Tarantello in jail for life. 'Just a minute. Let me turn down the music.'

The opera music in the background dimmed abruptly. 'To what do I owe this pleasure?' His once-silky voice now sounded like a rock grinder, thanks to a bullet that punctured his vocal cords last year.

'Well, I just saw something on the news. I wondered if investigators had made any connections.'

'What was it?'

'About the deputy Chief of Staffer who died unexpectedly?'

'General Fripp,' the agent answered. 'I'm working that case right now.'

'Are you? Then maybe you've noticed that his death bears a striking resemblance to some others?'

A definite pause followed. 'I'm not surprised you connected the dots, Hannah, but we have no evidence to suggest that the murders are connected.'

'But you think they are,' she guessed, shooting a wide-eyed look at Luther.

'That's hard to say without a motive or a murder weapon.'

'What have you ruled out?' she wanted to know.

'Well, none of them died of the usual. Every autopsy test imaginable has been run without yielding the exact cause of death. Some of the victims died immediately; others appear to have been poisoned over time, but there's no consistent data.'

'Have you considered ricin poisoning?' Hannah asked, with a shiver of excitement.

'Ricin,' Valentino murmured thoughtfully.

'I don't believe it's routinely tested for in autopsies.'

'No, it's not,' he agreed.

'And it can be ingested or injected or even passed straight through the skin if it's mixed with DMSO.'

He was silent for some time.

'Or maybe I'm just grasping at straws,' she

added with belated self-doubt.

'No, I'll look into that. I don't suppose you've also thought of a motive?' Now he sounded amused.

'No, sir, I can't think of one.'

'So, what's new down at our Norfolk branch?' he asked, shifting to a more neutral topic.

'Oh, same old stuff.' *Luther's trying to get me pregnant*, she wanted to add, only she was terrified of the impact on her career. Besides, how would news like that affect Valentino, whose three children, not to mention his wife, had been killed by mob retaliation?

'I'm thinking of taking a break from the office,' volunteered the older agent.

'What do you mean, sir? Retirement?'

'No, no, just considering a step down to get back into the field.'

'That would be cool,' said Hannah, wondering why he'd chosen to park his butt behind a desk in the first place. 'Make sure you drop in if you come down this way.'

'I'll do that,' he promised. 'Thank you for calling.'

'You're welcome.' She hung up the phone wishing she called him more often. He never complained of his solitude, yet the loneliness that crept into his voice at times tugged at her heartstrings. 'Wouldn't that be something,' she said to Luther, who was giving her that warm stare that was the first indication of his intent.

'What?' he asked, pulling her into his powerful arms.

'Maybe terrorists stole ricin from a government lab in order to poison our military leaders.'

'I can think of more effective ways to kill the top brass than by poisoning them,' he pointed out.

'Hmmm, that's true,' she conceded. But with Luther nuzzling her neck and slipping a hand under her sweater, it was hard to come up with an alternative motive.

'You know what I want in my stocking this Christmas?' he murmured, finding her nipple and thumbing it into stiffness.

She hadn't given a single thought to Christmas except to hope that Luther would be back from his upcoming mission to Southeast Asia. 'What?'

'An EPT with a positive result sign.'

'You have a one-track mind,' she scolded, sliding a hand up his thigh.

'Yeah, but the train is headed in the right direction.'

'I sure hope so,' she replied.

Any more words of doubt she might have said were cut short by his deep, all-consuming kiss.

10

Lia frowned at her reflection in the antique mirror above the marble-top dresser in Penny's guest bedroom. 'To go or not to go?' she asked herself. The fact that she was still home at seven o'clock was a novelty.

Her beaded jeans, a turquoise camisole edged in black lace, and a cropped velvet jacket were suitable for a night at Peabody's. Her friends were probably already there, scoping out the guys.

But Lia didn't feel like going.

Her stomach wasn't settled. Eric was still on the loose, and after what he'd done to Penny the other night, leaving bruises on her arms, maybe it wasn't smart to leave the house. On the other hand, Penny had a date tonight; she'd probably like for Lia to go.

'So, I'll go,' said Lia, making up her mind.

But then she thought of Mark Minors, who'd groped her at Katie's Halloween party. He was a thirty-three-year-old stockbroker with a fast car. When he'd kissed her, she'd found herself wishing he was Vinny the SEAL.

Find me. The challenge that the SEAL had

tossed over his shoulder was taunting her. She couldn't forget it any more than she ould forget about that kiss. It was annoying to admit, but the boy SEAL had gotten underneath her skin in an alarmingly short amount of time. She couldn't get him out of her thoughts.

A knock downstairs pulled Lia back to the present. She left the room for her first glimpse of Penny's suitor.

Like Brad, Penny's former fiancé, the Navy surgeon was of average height, average build, with brown hair and blandly pleasant features. He bestowed a warm smile on Penny as he stepped through the front door. 'I've never seen you in civilian clothes,' he commented. 'You look nice.'

'Thanks,' said Penny, touching a self-conscious hand to her shiny hair.

Nice? thought Lia. Wearing a gold blouse, black skirt, and sheer, sexy stockings, Penny looked better than nice.

'This is for you,' he added, producing a long-stemmed rose, which he'd held behind his back. It was yellow — for friendship.

Good choice, Lia conceded.

'Oh, I love roses,' said Penny, putting it to her nose.

They both turned their heads as Lia descended the stairs.

'This is my little sister, Ophelia,' Penny said, introducing them.

'I've heard a lot about you,' said Steven, with annoying innuendo in his voice. His eyes performed a quick tour of Lia's body.

'I can only imagine,' she drawled, glancing at Penny to see if she'd noticed her boyfriend's wandering eye, but Penny was looking at her, not at Steven. 'Aren't you going out?' she inquired.

'I'm not sure,' said Lia.

'It's Friday night. When have you not gone out on a Friday night?'

'Don't worry. I'll stay out of your way.'

'You're not in the way,' her sister rushed to reassure her.

'I'm not sure if I want to go out with Eric on the loose,' Lia tried to explain.

'Oh,' said Penny. 'Well, good. I don't want to have to worry about you, either.'

'Eric?' Steven asked, looking between the two of them.

'I'll explain over dinner,' Penny promised. 'Take your jacket off and come on back. Do you like red wine or white?'

'Both,' he said, trailing after her with one last look at Lia.

She resisted the impulse to stick her tongue out at him.

Joe Montgomery had never ogled her like

that. In Lia's book, he got major points for rescuing her sister. She shuddered to think what might have happened if he hadn't chased Eric off. He was the man Penny deserved, not that whey-faced surgeon who looked like Brad.

Scowling, Lia plodded back upstairs. She threw herself across the guest bed feeling discontent, self-critical. It really bugged her that Penny had done so much for her, seeing her through college, cheering her on through rehab. She'd been Lia's lifeboat when reality had done its best to drown her. Nurturing and committed, Penny had put her future on hold for her sister and lost the man she loved.

Lia thought back. It was four years ago that Brad had left. She must have really, really loved him not to date any other man since. The realization made her feel like even more like a loser.

She needed to get a real job. She missed her candles and pillows, her wall art, and her collection of cut glass. She wanted Penny to get a life.

Vinny's words reverberated in Lia's head. *Prove it to yourself.*

He had a real job, the little twit. He probably had his own apartment, too. Maybe even a house.

Scowling, Lia rolled off the bed and stalked

out the door. She crossed to the third bedroom, which Penny used as an office. Maybe she'd work on her résumé instead of going out. What would it hurt? She had nothing to lose by trying. The world of news media demanded grit and tenacity, and she had both in spades.

An hour later, Lia sat back with a sense of accomplishment. The printer hummed as it spat out her résumé, a cut-and-pasted conglomeration of résumés found online. It was two-thirds fact and one-third fiction, but hopefully no one would question the shades of gray or call up the folks she'd listed as references.

Tomorrow she'd look up the local television stations and send in her résumés.

Enough for tonight. Lia stood and stretched.

That same itchy-under-the-skin feeling ambushed her. She wanted something — but what? Another kiss from that boy SEAL would be nice, if only to verify whether it was really as toe-curling as she recalled.

Find me.

Oh, she could find him, no problem, the same way she'd found Joe Montgomery's number, by performing an online search.

But what would she do once she found him? Her heart beat faster at the thought.

Maybe she'd have sex with him, just to see what a younger lover was like.

With a shimmer of excitement, she sat down again to execute an online search.

Vinny DeInnocentis had an unlisted number.

Lia crossed her arms and thought hard. After a moment, her frown cleared. She reached for the phone and dialed Penny's SEAL.

'Montgomery,' he answered with a faint western drawl.

'Hey, this is Lia next door.'

Silence answered her cheery greeting. She plowed ahead. 'I was wondering if you could do me a favor. You know that guy who was here the other day, the Navy SEAL? You think you could find out where he lives?' Adrenaline made her heart race.

'Why would I do that?' Joe asked.

'Well, because . . . I have information to give you in exchange.'

His silence was skeptical. 'Like what?'

'Tell me you'll find his address first. His name is Vincent DeInnocentis, all one word.'

'I'll do my best. What did you want to tell me?'

'Well, uh . . . ' God, was she really going to come right out and say it? Oh, why not? Men loved a challenge, and Penny wasn't getting any younger. 'Penny hasn't had sex in five years,' she blurted.

The silence was bottomless this time.

'Do we still have a deal?' Lia finally asked.

'I'll call you back,' he said, hanging up the phone.

She dropped the receiver in its cradle and came shakily to her feet. Now what?

Her grumbling stomach prompted her to pad downstairs, where she found that Penny and Steven had finished their dinner of grilled salmon. They sat on the couch with a yard between them, watching a movie on DVD.

Lia helped herself to leftovers and a glass of wine. The drama in the movie captivated her, prompting her to join the couple. She sat in the recliner, nursing her drink.

In her peripheral vision, she saw Steven Parks turning his head to study her. She ignored him, drawing her feet up in a visual cue for him to back off. But the retard didn't get it. And Penny, who was engrossed in the movie, didn't seem to notice.

For the next ten minutes Lia tolerated Steven's stares. How crass could a guy get, ogling his date's sister right in front of her? At last, she turned her head to send him a warning glare. *Back off*. To her horror, he winked at her.

That's it. Lia pushed to her feet. 'Penny,' she said, 'send this idiot home. You're wasting your time with him.'

Penny gaped at her. 'What?' she cried, looking horrified.

'I'm sorry, but I can't stand the fact that he's here on a date with you and he's checking me out!' Lia's face burned with indignation.

Penny swiveled a questioning look at her beau.

The Navy surgeon had the grace to look chagrined. 'I'm sorry,' he laughed. 'I'm just amazed by how different you two are.'

'Yes, we're different,' Lia retorted. 'But you're on a date with her, so stop looking at me.'

'Ophelia!' Penny cried, obviously mortified. 'Do you mind?'

'Obviously I do mind. He's not right for you.'

Penny put her hand over her eyes. 'Why don't you go out?' she moaned. 'I'm sorry,' she added to her date. 'She says what she thinks.'

'That's all right. Listen, uh, I think I'd better call it a night, anyway. I have to work tomorrow.'

'Oh, I thought you had the weekend off.'

'No, they need me to step in for

181

Commander Owens. He's got the flu or something.'

Lia, who had beat a quick retreat, paused where the stairs turned. She couldn't tell if Steven Parks was lying through his teeth or telling the truth. Either way, she'd scared him off, ruining Penny's date.

She tried to hide in her room, but her conscience wouldn't let her stay there. Creeping down the stairs again, she found Penny in the foyer, arms crossed, looking pale and taut. She waited for Lia to speak first.

'I'm sorry,' Lia apologized. 'But I swear to you, he was coming on to me. I did you a favor by pointing it out.'

'A favor?' Penny pounced on the word. 'If you do me any more favors, Ophelia, I'll be single for the rest of my life!'

'What's wrong with being single? You have everything you need. At least you have a job.'

'Is that what this is about? Are you feeling so sorry for yourself that you have to ruin *my* evening?'

'I'm not feeling sorry for myself,' Lia hotly denied. 'This has nothing to do with me. The guy's a worm. He's not good enough for you.'

'Well, thanks a lot,' said Penny caustically, 'but I don't need you to decide who is or isn't right for me. That's my decision. Just like this is my house and this is *my* life! Mine!' she

182

added, stabbing a finger at her chest.

A light knock sounded on the door behind her, causing Penny to gasp and whirl. The sisters peered anxiously outside, only to exhale in relief when they recognized their neighbor.

'Hi,' Penny greeted him, dredging up a ghastly smile.

Wearing a rust-colored flannel shirt, jeans, and boots, Joe looked just like the Marlboro Man, even with that scar on his face. 'Hey,' he said. His dark green eyes took in everything from Penny's heightened color to Ophelia's secret smile. 'Sorry to interrupt.'

'No problem,' Penny replied.

'Any word on Eric yet?'

'No, nothing. The police still can't find him.'

'Damn,' he said, shaking his head. He finally caught Lia's eye and handed her a Post-it note.

'Thanks.' She glanced down at it, feeling pleased with herself.

Penny divided a puzzled look between them, but before she could ask, Joe said, 'You look different.'

It wasn't a compliment, but Lia saw Penny blush.

'Did you change the lock on your back door yet?' he added matter-of-factly.

'Uh, I bought the right kind of deadbolt, but I haven't mounted it yet,' Penny admitted.

'You want me to do it for you? Right now?'

'Oh.' The offer seemed to catch Penny off guard. 'Well, sure, if you don't mind.'

He glanced at Lia as he shut the door and wiped his boots on the mat. She had trouble stifling a grin. *I knew that would get you stirred up, you naughty boy.*

'I'll get the new lock,' Penny volunteered. 'It's in the garage.'

As she disappeared into the laundry room, Lia murmured, 'Just don't tell her that I told you.' And then she beat a quick retreat, praying for her meddling to have the best possible outcome.

* * *

'Let me see that Phillips head,' Joe requested, pointing to where the screwdriver lay in Penny's modest toolbox.

Her gaze slid over his long, powerful finger as she bent to retrieve the screwdriver. Why was it that every part of his anatomy, from his ears to the size of his feet, was so immensely appealing to her?

As she passed him the tool, a crisp breeze sighed through the cracked French door, carrying his unique scent into her nostrils. It summoned memories of kneading the dense muscles of his back. Lord, if he knew how much enjoyment she got from touching him, he'd stop coming to his appointments!

'So, what happened to your date?' Joe inquired, going down on one knee to tighten the screw on the faceplate.

He must have seen Steven's car and assumed the rest. 'Ophelia scared him off,' she admitted, aware that her disappointment had flown.

'Your sister's a trip,' Joe commented.

'Yes, she is.' Penny lips firmed.

He glanced up at her disapproving tone. 'I heard you two arguing,' he volunteered.

She cringed. 'I'm sorry.'

'Don't know if you realize it,' he added, ignoring the apology, 'but she looks out for you, you know.'

'She does?' Had she missed something between Joe and Lia?

'Yep. She chewed me out good the other day for coming over here to dress you down.'

Penny gasped. 'No!'

'It's true. You may think she's in the way, but I like how she sticks up for you.'

With a hot face, Penny considered the words he must have overheard. 'You must think I'm such a bitch,' she lamented.

'A bitch?' he repeated, swinging an astonished look at her. 'I would never use that word to describe you,' he said, coming to his feet.

What words would he use?

'It's none of my business, so don't worry about it. Here, hold this side still while I tighten up the back.'

She had to step within inches of him to hold the lock in place while he tightened up the screws. Eying his long, muscle-corded neck, she savored this moment. A wave of desire rolled through her, making her want to lean into him. She had to get a hold of these feelings or she'd end up making a fool of herself.

'All set,' he said, disappointing her that it was over so quickly. 'Keep this handy but out of sight,' he recommended, dropping the key into her hand.

'Thank you,' Penny said. 'That would have taken me all morning. Can I interest you in a glass of wine?' she asked, almost desperate to keep him from leaving.

Trailing her, he cut a glance at the half-empty wine bottle as she hung the key on a peg in the kitchen. 'I'm trying not to drink at night,' he confessed with a shuttered expression.

'Oh.' She understood why. 'Well, how about some juice?' she offered.

'Sure, I'll take some juice.'

With a tremor that she couldn't quell, she poured two low-sugar fruit drinks.

'Hey, I buy the same brand,' he observed, practically in her ear.

Penny gasped. She hadn't heard him step up behind her. Trapped between him and the counter, she blurted the first thing to pop into her head. 'You want to help me with a jigsaw puzzle?' Immediately, she wanted to kick herself. Joe wasn't the type to sit around putting puzzles together.

'Puzzle?' he repeated, with a quizzical look.

'It's in here.' She shoved his glass at him and led him to the dining room. 'I've been working on it for weeks.'

As she snapped on the lights, the crystal chandelier shone down on the thousand-piece puzzle that was two-thirds complete and took up half the mahogany tabletop.

* * *

Joe took one look at the project and thought, *No wonder she hasn't been laid in five years.* But then he looked closer, and he couldn't believe his eyes. 'This is Red Rock Canyon. This is where I grew up.'

'Are you serious?' She smiled her amazement.

'I used to propel off this lip right here.' He touched the part of the puzzle that was put together, then dragged his gaze upward to look at her. 'You just happened to be putting this together.'

'Well, yes. I have a passion for canyons. I love the colors and the wild, almost other-earthly terrain.'

Alight with enthusiasm, her face struck him as beautiful.

'What?' Penny asked, looking suddenly self-conscious. 'Do I sound stupid?'

'No.' He was the stupid one, stupid for coming over here against his better judgment. Platonic friendship involved as much catlike balance as rock climbing. He didn't know if he was even capable of it. But he liked Penny too much not to try.

He dragged out a chair and surveyed the puzzle pieces, picking out those that complemented the section he wanted to work on.

Penny eased down beside him. Catching on to what he was looking for, she handed him several more pieces.

'One night I slept in a hammock, right here, two thousand feet in the air.'

'You're kidding me,' said Penny with a dubious look.

'Nope. Slept like a baby.'

'Why would anyone do that?' she wondered out loud.

Joe shrugged. 'I'm an adrenaline junkie, what can I say?' he confessed, mocking himself. Ah, the things he'd done in his youth to catch a natural high, to feel like he was really living life, not just going through the motions.

He reminisced over a few more daring adventures. Penny sat wide-eyed, listening to him. At last, he worked up the courage to share what he'd been wanting to share for a while now. 'You, uh, you wanted to know what really happened in Afghanistan,' he reminded her.

'I'd like that,' she admitted, on a soft, inviting note.

'Okay, then.' With a deep breath, he told her the story, pushing every painful detail through a tight throat. And when he was done, he looked up, dreading so much as a glimpse of Penny's disappointment. 'I don't know if I took Harley's place for the right reasons or if I was just being selfish,' he admitted, feeling his eyes sting. 'Maybe I just craved some excitement. I'd been away from the field for ten years. I was rusty. Harley might have done things differently. He might have kept our boys from dying.'

Penny's eyes were luminous with compassion. 'Oh, Joe. I'm sure your reasons weren't selfish. Remember how you helped out the vet who came back from Iraq paralyzed? That's the kind of man you are. You weren't thinking about yourself.'

Her faith in him lessened the weight on his chest. 'Ah, that was nothing,' he said, dismissing it.

'Have you talked to anyone else about this?' she asked, sounding concerned. 'A psychiatrist?'

'Are you saying I'm crazy?' he retorted, bristling slightly.

'No. No, I just thought the Navy supplied mandatory counseling, that's all.'

'They do,' he admitted. 'But the fastest way to sink your career is to tell the Navy shrinks too much.'

'I see,' she said, her shoulders slumping. 'Then I'm the only one you've talked to?'

'Yeah,' he admitted, feeling self-conscious.

She shook her head. 'Listen to me, Joe. No one in the world would blame you for what went wrong,' she told him. 'You need to forgive yourself.'

He nodded in agreement. 'I'm starting to,' he replied.

'Good,' she said.

He considered her gentle, caring countenance for a thoughtful moment. Her sister had to have been telling him a lie, probably just to lure him over, or for her own selfish reasons. 'How long's it been since you've been with a guy?' he worked up the courage to ask.

He watched in fascination as a pink tide rose from her neck to her cheeks and made her eyes water. 'That long?' he marveled when she remained mute.

'What did Ophelia tell you?' she demanded with sudden suspicion.

'Ophelia?' he repeated, shaking his head like she had nothing do with this. 'I've been your neighbor for a long time,' he explained, 'and tonight was the first time I ever saw a guy come over.'

'Oh.' She bought the lie. Her blush subsided. 'It's been a while,' she admitted, sticking a puzzle piece where it didn't belong and pulling it out again. 'I was engaged once.'

'What happened?' he asked, curious to know what kind of fool had let her go.

She moved the piece to another spot and got lucky. 'First my father died,' she admitted, looking somber. 'Ophelia was in college. She was on the verge of dropping out. She got sucked into a partying crowd and developed a habit. I guess I focused so much of my energies on rescuing her that Brad — my fiancé — became disgusted and walked out.'

'Well, fuck him,' said Joe. 'What were you

supposed to do? Turn your back on your sister?'

She sent him a look that was half astonishment, half gratitude.

'Sorry,' he apologized. 'I'm a bad influence.'

She waved a hand, dismissing his language as inconsequential.

'You know — ' He cut himself short.

'What?' she prompted when he hesitated.

'You're an amazing woman.' There, it was out. 'I'm surprised some guy hasn't snatched you up.'

'Well, I've been busy,' she explained. 'After Brad left, I went back to school and got a master's in physical therapy, but first I had to join the Navy so they'd pay for it.'

He nodded his understanding. 'Then you're a career woman.'

She shrugged. 'Not really,' she admitted sheepishly. 'Call me old-fashioned, but I've always just wanted to get married and have children.'

Which was why she was not for him, he reminded himself. 'So let me introduce you to some friends of mine.' Maybe if she was taken, it'd be easier to be a friend and not be tempted.

She concealed her thoughts behind the downward sweep of her lashes. 'Sure, why not?' she said lightly. She picked up two more pieces and tried to work them into the puzzle.

The silence that fell over them felt suddenly sticky.

'Maybe I've overstepped my bounds,' he suggested, seeking a reason for it.

'No, that's okay,' she assured him, but her smile was forced. 'I'm just sensitive about my old-maid status.'

A vision of her naked and lying in his bed offered an immediate solution, but he bit his tongue against suggesting it. That was not the direction he wanted to head with Penny. Her views on casual sex were probably far different than his.

'I think I better go,' he said, tossing down his drink and standing up.

The disappointment in her eyes caught him off guard. He realized with sudden alarm that she was lonely and needy enough to compromise her standards.

'Thanks for having me,' he said, retreating to the kitchen with his cup. 'I'll let myself out.'

'Joe?' she called as he headed for the foyer.

'Yeah.' He hesitated at the top of the hall.

'You're not a selfish person,' she reiterated, harking back to his self-doubts.

'You sure about that?' he drawled, raking her figure with a look she couldn't mistake for anything but sexual interest. At the widening of her eyes, he offered her a mocking smile and let himself out.

★ ★ ★

Though Eric was stunned by the force of the car crash, his instincts told him to get out of the incapacitated vehicle, but he could not remember why.

Get out. Get out.

Through his shattered windshield, he saw spumes of steam escape the sides of his crumpled hood, rising like ghostly spires toward the tree branches. The lonely pine forest was lit by the headlights of a car idling in the break-down lane behind him.

The driver of that car was his foe — he knew that much. As he scuttled across the seat toward the passenger door, Eric fumbled in the glove box for the loaded gun. It gleamed wickedly in his trembling hand. He pushed the groaning door open with his feet.

Panting with fear, disoriented, he rose from his battered vehicle on knees that quaked. Blood coursed warmly from his nose to his lips. He squinted at the car behind him. Unable to see the driver through the corona cast by the headlights, he raised a hand to block the streaming beams.

Suddenly, a powerful arm looped about his neck. Fingers clamped down over his, taking control of the gun. Eric struggled to free himself, but his attacker overpowered him, raising the 9mm pistol upward so that the barrel gouged Eric's ear.

'What did you tell the Price girl?' growled a familiar voice.

Eric fought to place the voice. Oddly, though he couldn't remember much, he knew that the man would kill him.

'Answer me!' snarled the voice as the barrel prodded him.

The Price girl, the Price girl.

A vision of Penelope Price formed in Eric's mind. What had he said to her the other day?

'Tell me or I'll blow your fucking head off,' growled his assailant.

Memories crystallized. Ah, yes, his nemesis was Buzz Ritter, the one who'd arranged to buy the ricin, then killed his partner, Danny Price, because he considered him a liability.

'I . . . I . . . I . . . ' Terrified, Eric could not control his stammer any more than he could stop the cold sweat from filming his limbs.

'Talk, you stupid fuck.' The grip about his neck tightened. 'What did you tell her?'

Eric clawed at the stricture tightening around his neck, but it was thickly powerful, squeezing like a boa constrictor. 'I just, just,

just . . . ' *told her why.* But he couldn't get the words out.

His attacker growled in frustration. 'Why can't you talk like everyone else? You want me to ask the girl myself — huh? Do I need to question her in person?'

'No! No, no, no, no!'

'Just forget it. You're wasting my time.'

A thick gloved finger slid over Eric's, putting pressure on the trigger.

With a whimper of acceptance, Eric closed his eyes. *I'm coming, Sonja.* A searing roar incinerated his last thought.

11

If Lia'd had the money, she would have bought seventy-three bottles of beer to dump on Vinny's doorstep, but she didn't. She had something even better to offer to compensate him — and then some — for having to replace his taillight.

Angling her rearview mirror, she glanced at her reflection. She'd made certain that the package was irresistible. He wouldn't turn it down.

Her hair was a cloud of copper ringlets. She wore a metallic gold sweater with a plunging neckline; stone-washed jeans with strategic holes patched by lace; golden, high-heeled ankle boots — she'd had to grab those out of a box in the trunk of her car; and beneath it all, the sexiest cream-colored satin-and-lace undergarments she owned.

He'd have to be gay to say no.

She glanced again at the Post-it note stuck to the center of her steering wheel. Number 1005 Shore Drive was along this strip of roadway somewhere. She hadn't realized yesterday that Vinny lived right on the oceanfront, north of the boardwalk. How cool was that?

A stiff November breeze rocked her car as she slowed before a row of beach houses. Granted, they were town-houses, but they were big and freshly painted in tones of peach, aqua, and pale yellow. She sought Vinny's Honda parked in the carport beneath the lofty first floor, but the sports car wasn't there.

Where else would he be on a Saturday morning?

Braced for disappointment, she parked along the curb, buttoned up her cream-colored jacket with the faux-fur collar, and approached the steps to 1005.

She punched the doorbell and waited, tingling with anticipation. Yes, she had a wild streak, but it wasn't her style to go chasing after a man, especially not a *younger* man. Although she wasn't exactly chasing him with a relationship in mind. This was all about sex.

A soft thud inside was all the warning she got before the door swung open. Lia regarded the pretty young black woman in mute surprise. She ought to have expected it, but she hadn't.

'Sorry,' she muttered, turning to leave. 'I think I have the wrong address.'

'Who are you looking for?' the girl inquired, not unkindly.

'Er . . . ' Lia turned around and caught

sight of a barrel-chested black man coming down the stairs. Relief washed over her. 'I thought Vinny DeInnocentis lived here.'

'He does,' said the woman, smiling at Lia's confusion. 'I think he's still out running on the beach, but why don't you come in and wait for him? He shouldn't be long.'

'Thank you.' She stepped gratefully into the warm, marble-tiled foyer.

'I'm Natalie,' the woman introduced herself. 'Call me Nate. And this is Teddy.'

The muscular black man smiled, revealing the whitest teeth Lia'd ever seen. 'Pleased to meet you,' he rumbled in a bass voice.

'Teddy and Vinny work together,' Nate explained.

'Oh,' said Lia. 'I'm . . . ' *Just some girl up the street that wants to sleep with Vinny and kick him to the curb.* 'I'm Lia,' she said, clasping her frigid hands together.

'Come into the kitchen, Lia. We have plenty of coffee and toast,' Nate invited.

Lia took her jacket off and draped it over the back of the dinette chair. The kitchen was light and bright, with a breathtaking view of the Atlantic Ocean. Today it looked tumultuous, with white-capped waves under a watery sun smothered by scudding clouds.

'Wow, this place is great,' Lia confessed, casting an envious eye around the generous

199

kitchen. 'Do you own it or . . . '

'No, we all rent it together,' said Nate, putting a familiar hand on Teddy's broad back. 'Pour Lia a coffee, will you, baby?' she requested.

'Sure. How do you take your coffee, ma'am? Cream and sugar?'

Ma'am? She'd never been called that before. 'Uh, yes, please,' Lia answered, humbled by the couple's hospitality and their obvious attachment.

As she gazed out the window, sipping her coffee, she wondered what kind of nut would run outside on a day like today. As if conjured by the question, a hooded figure bounded up the concrete steps that brought him to the first-story balcony. Vinny was back, cheeks ruddy with cold, hands lost inside the sleeves of his sweatshirt. She got to study him a second before he knew that she was there.

His watering eyes seemed especially bright in his wind-chapped face, a face that did justice to both his Italian and Irish ancestors. But then he chucked a wad of spit over the balcony, reminding her that he was flesh and blood and barely out of his teens.

In the next instant, he was slipping through the door. Catching sight of her, he drew up short, his chest rising and falling in the aftermath of his run. 'Well, well,' he murmured, looking pleased. 'Look who found me.'

'Tag,' she said, toasting him with her coffee mug. 'You're it.' She was pleased to sound utterly nonchalant.

'I'm it,' he repeated. He seemed to give the phrase some serious consideration. 'I'm *it*,' he said again, putting stress on the second word. 'Yeah, I like the sound of that. I'm *it*.'

Lia rolled her eyes. God, he was cocky. 'In your dreams,' she muttered, aware that Teddy and Nate were witnessing their childish exchange.

'Obviously, I got somethin' you want,' Vinny pointed out as he unzipped his sweatshirt. 'Otherwise you wouldn't have bothered looking for me.'

She scarcely heard what he was saying. Beneath that baggy sweatshirt, he was wearing a long-sleeved shirt of Under Armour. The newfangled material supposedly locked warmth in when it was cold and heat out when it was hot. It stuck to his torso like second skin, delineating every muscle in his shoulders, arms, and abs and making her head spin. Her blood heated at the thought that his body might soon become her playground.

'Why don't you come up to my room,' Vinny offered with a familiar crooked smile. 'So we can talk.'

Oh, sure. They were going to talk. In his

bedroom. While he got naked and took a shower. She sneaked a self-conscious peek at the other couple, who were suddenly preoccupied with dirty dishes.

This was going a little fast, even for Lia. Nonetheless, she stood up to follow Vinny. The sooner they got past the sex, the sooner she could forget him. She cringed at her crudeness, but honestly, it wasn't like something long-term could ever happen anyway.

His room was a retreat of vast potential. 'Holy shit,' Lia sighed, taking in the high ceilings, the reading alcove with a window overlooking the length of the beach.

At night he would have a view of the city, ablaze with neon lights. In the morning, the rising sun would wash this room in golds and oranges. If it were her room, she'd put a huge metallic sculpture of the sun on one wall and dangle wind chimes in the window. She'd break up the space with silk screens and throw bamboo rugs on the floor.

'I know, it's messy,' Vinny apologized, oblivious to the pictures in her mind.

It wasn't really. For a guy, it was a relatively neat, with just a simple queen-sized bed, navy sheets still rumpled and inviting, and serviceable furniture. Like any young man, he had a couple of posters tacked to the wall, but they were pictures of tropical beaches, not pop stars, thank God.

'So, why'd you bother to come looking for me?' he asked, locking the door surreptitiously behind him.

Lia's mouth went dry as he hung his sweatshirt on the back of his door. He proceeded to pull the Under Armour over his head, revealing a mat of black hair on his perfect chest. More hair than a boy his age ought to have, it narrowed to a line that disappeared into his low-slung sweatpants.

'Just to prove that I could,' she managed breathlessly.

Taking the situation in hand, Lia approached him with a slow, seductive walk. In her high-heeled boots, she could stare him straight in the eye. She did so now, catching a watchful gleam in his chocolate-brown eyes.

Lifting a hand to his shoulder, she found his skin hot and silky, softer than the skin of any man she'd ever touched. She let her palm stray downward over his bulging pectoral muscle. It flexed, thrilling her with the realization of her power.

'I need to shower,' he told her, preventing her from trailing that line of hair that bisected his abdomen.

She stepped back, dismissing him. 'Go ahead.'

He gathered a change of clothing, then disappeared into the adjoining bathroom and shut the door.

Lia listened for a click. There wasn't any. The door was wide open if she decided to join him.

But she'd spent hours this morning doing her hair, pampering her skin, putting on her makeup. She didn't want to wash all that work down the drain.

The bathroom was out of the question. She would have to seduce him when he came out. But how?

She'd never seduced a man in her life. The older men she'd been with had always been the aggressors. Granted, it was fun to wield a little power, but she was tad bit out of her element here.

Should she lie across his bed? Nah, that was overdoing it. She could seat herself in the cushioned alcove, strike a seductive pose, and wait. It seemed a safer bet.

She did so, gazing out the window to a view that captivated her.

When she was just a little girl, her father used to take them to the beach all summer long. She would sit at the edge of the sea, just sit and sink into the sand, becoming one with the ocean. How long had it been since she'd felt the surge and retreat of the waves, rocking her like a mother?

She closed her eyes, listening to the ocean's roar.

What she heard was Vinny turning the water off. Her heart beat faster. She assumed what she thought was a sultry position, legs slightly splayed, one foot up on the cushion and one on the floor.

She never heard the bathroom door open. Vinny's reflection drifted across the window-pane. Startled, she turned her head and found him sitting on the edge of his bed, looking at her. She thought she'd find him shirtless, or at least half-naked. But he was completely dressed, wearing jeans and a burgundy T-shirt. He slipped his feet into sneakers, all the while assessing her intently.

'How good are you at bowling?' he asked her.

The question was so random that it took Lia several seconds to understand it, yet alone supply an answer. 'I haven't bowled in years,' she admitted.

'You want to come? I have to be at the bowling alley in fifteen minutes.'

So, no wild monkey sex on his rumpled bed right now.

Relief swamped her, mingled with disap-pointment. 'Okay,' she answered, careful to conceal her mixed response.

'Great.' His smile was a hundred percent boy.

He stood up, and she came to her feet, a little miffed that he would rather go bowling than jump into bed with her. As she made to brush by him, he caught her with a quick hook of his arm and spun her around. His lips landed like a well-aimed missile right on her startled mouth.

And then he was kissing her with that same heady skill he'd used before. Actually, it had to be an innate talent rather than a skill, because it wasn't cold or practiced. It was hot and hungry and completely spontaneous.

And she couldn't get enough of it.

Lia's knees turned to water. She melted against him, forcing him to tighten his hold. That brought their hips flush, leaving no doubt in her mind that he'd rather have sex with her than go bowling any day.

The kiss ended as abruptly as it began. Keeping an arm around her waist — she would have collapsed otherwise — Vinny herded her to the door. 'Don't want to be late,' he gruffly explained.

That was when she had her first real inkling that getting Vinny out of her system wasn't going to be that easy.

★　★　★

'You're late!' barked a male voice, booming out of the confusing blend of multiple conversations, rumbling bowling balls, and crashing pins. 'You missed the warm-up. What part of eleven hundred hours didn't you understand, PO2?'

Lia realized that it was Vinny who was being yelled at, by a man in his late thirties with a streak of silver in his black hair and eyes of such a pale hue they were opalescent. She looked at Vinny to see how he would answer the charge. To her surprise, she found him grinning. 'Come on, Senior Chief, you know I don't need to warm up.'

'That's bullshit and you know it. Where the hell is Teddy?'

'Teddy's not coming.'

'What? This is a tournament, not a goddamn practice.' A V-shaped vein appeared on the senior chief's forehead.

'Easy, McGuire.' With affable authority in his voice, another man stood up to tower over everyone. Lia gaped, awed by his height and breadth and his all-American good looks. 'What's Teddy doing?' Mr. Sports Illustrated demanded.

'Nate's got him looking at houses,' Vinny explained with an inner-city shrug.

'Christ,' swore the senior chief, looking disgusted. 'I knew it was a woman.'

Lia raised an eyebrow at the misogynistic comment.

'But I brought someone to take his place,' Vinny added. 'This is Lia Price. Lia, meet Lieutenant Lindstrom and Senior Chief McGuire.'

'Nice to meet you,' she murmured. 'I haven't played in years,' she hissed in Vinny's ear. 'I can't be in a tournament!'

'We just want to play,' Vinny answered persuasively. 'We don't care if we lose.'

'The hell we don't,' the senior chief started to mutter, but Lieutenant Lindstrom cut him off.

'We need a fourth player or we have to forfeit,' he pointed out.

'So come on,' said Vinny, taking the man's observation as permission to proceed. 'Let's get our shoes.' He tugged her to the rental counter, where she grudgingly requested a pair of size sevens.

The atmosphere, complete with music from the fifties, made Vinny's eyes sparkle. His enthusiasm was contagious. Lia felt her pulse quicken.

She watched Senior Chief McGuire place a pitcher of beer and four plastic cups on the table behind them.

'His code name's Mako,' Vinny divulged, following her gaze.

'As in mako shark?' she asked. With the silver streak in his hair and his pale eyes, he looked just like one.

'Yeah, but don't worry. His bark's worse than his bite. Or rather, his bite isn't all that bad,' he amended to keep from mangling metaphors.

'You're up first, Vinny,' Lieutenant Lindstrom called. 'And then you, ma'am.' He nodded at Lia.

Ma'am again. Weren't there expectations of behavior that went with that word?

'Here's a ten-pound ball for you,' Vinny said, dropping one in her lap. 'Let me know if it's too heavy.' He hefted his own, heavier ball and stepped onto the wooden platform to launch it down the lane.

Lia watched, enjoying the way he cocked his hips and took aim. The ball whipped down the lane, arced at the last second, and slammed into the pins, landing him a strike.

The lieutenant high-fived him as Vinny returned to his seat, grinning. 'You're up.'

Lia's dismay rose along with her blood pressure. 'I'm going to suck at this.'

'Nah, just have some fun,' Vinny said.

Feeling tense and exposed, with a hundred pairs of male eyes pretending not to notice her, Lia gave it her best shot and landed a gutter ball.

'That's all right,' Vinny called out. 'Try again.'

Determined not to disgrace herself, she aimed her second ball with even more care, then tentatively released it. It rolled lazily down the lane and toppled a few measly pins.

Humiliated, she returned to her seat.

Before she could flop into her chair, Vinny grabbed her hand and pulled her up to their table. 'Have a beer,' he offered. 'It'll relax you.'

While Lieutenant Lindstrom and Senior Chief McGuire took their turns, Lia chugged down a beer.

'Your backside looks great in those jeans,' Vinny said with a grin. 'Could have heard a pin drop when you walked up to take your turn.'

She moaned. 'Please don't tell me that everyone's watching me make a fool of myself.'

'You'll do fine. Teddy's not all that good anyway.'

The screen over their area flashed a strike for Lieutenant Lindstrom.

'So, you work with these guys?' she asked Vinny.

'Yeah. LT's our operations officer, and Senior Chief's our top enlisted.'

'He's scary,' Lia confessed as the man in question hurled the ball toward the pins, knocking them all down but one.

'Naw. He's a pussycat with fins.'

An hour later, Lia realized that Vinny might be right. Maybe it was the beer they all imbibed, but the senior chief made a point to say that her score had improved with every turn, and she started liking him better.

And Lieutenant Lindstrom kept calling her ma'am, which she found dignifying. At the end of every turn, he held out a hand for her to slap.

She was feeling like one of the guys, a critical part of the team. Only Vinny's hot gaze kept reminding her that she was very much a woman — a woman he intended to possess, when the time suited him.

Here she was in a bowling alley when she thought she'd be in his bedroom — on the floor, on the bed, against the wall. Oh, my God, on the window seat where people on the beach could look up and see them!

She cursed the inhibitions that had kept her from taking Vinny in hand. This seduction thing was so not going according to plan.

★   ★   ★

'We're in second place,' divulged Senior Chief McGuire two hours later. 'We're three points behind Team Ten.' His opalescent gaze settled on Lia and narrowed.

She got the message: *If we lose, it'll be your fault, woman.*

She couldn't let her team down. Despite the pleasant buzz that came from drinking two beers, Lia summoned her determination. She'd played softball in high school. Bowling wasn't all that different from pitching. Maybe if she thought of the pins as home base and drove the ball straight across the plate . . .

'Your turn,' said Vinny, giving her knee a squeeze. 'Good luck.' He kissed her cheek.

He'd spent the last two hours making her feel like the queen of the bowling alley. He'd bought her nachos. He'd polished her bowling ball. He'd powdered her hand.

She caught herself thinking he would sure make a sweet boyfriend.

Are you crazy? said her pride. *He's four years younger than you are!*

Shut up and pitch to the plate, chimed in her competitive side. Stepping up to the platform, she hefted the ball, squeezed her biceps, and released it.

The ball remained airborne for a moment. But then it hit the lane screaming. To her astonishment, it flattened all ten pins. 'Ahhh!' she cried, throwing her hands in the air.

The senior chief and the lieutenant surged to their feet, roaring with surprise. Vinny rushed at her, picked her up, and whirled her in a circle.

Clutching his broad shoulders and laughing, she realized she was happy in a way she hadn't been in years.

'You get to go again,' he said excitedly. 'Do it the same way!'

'Phew, okay.' She shook off her happy jitters and went to collect her bonus points. *Don't think. Just throw.*

Vinny hushed the others into silence. Lia envisioned home plate again, reared back, and let go. The ball did exactly the same thing as last time. With a scream of delight, she jumped into Vinny's arms, legs locked around his hips, and kissed him.

His arms clamped her into place. Right there in front of God and everybody, he kissed her like he owned her.

Sex could not have been better than that one perfect kiss.

With reluctance, Lia let her legs slip to the floor. She gazed at Vinny, dazed, wondering what had just passed between them.

'Are you *Ophelia* Price?' Lieutenant Lindstrom called, jarring her from her dreamy haze. He had a cell phone tucked under one ear.

'Uh, yeah . . . ' *Who wants to know?*

'Your sister's trying to get in touch with

you,' he explained, handing her the phone.

'My sister?'

'Here, talk to my wife. Your sister said you were with Vinny today. Luckily, Hannah knew that Vinny was with me.'

Hannah Lindstrom, the FBI agent? Good grief, it was a small world!

As the lieutenant got up to earn a spare, Lia listened to the agent tell her that Eric Tomlinson was dead and that she and Penny might or might not be targeted by his killer.

'What?' she gasped, sinking into a seat. 'Why would someone kill Eric? I thought he was the bad guy.'

'We assumed he was the bad guy,' the agent corrected her, 'but it seems that your father, and now Eric, was killed by whoever purchased the ricin. You need to return to your home, where the police can keep an eye on you.'

The happiness that had buoyed her up was wrenched away. 'I'm on my way,' she said. Out the corner of her eye, she noted Vinny's grave regard.

Ending the call, she sat a moment processing the awful discovery that someone else, and not Eric, had killed their father. All this time, he'd probably been trying to warn them, not threaten them! *You'll be sorry,* he'd said, and he was right.

'Lia?' It was Vinny, sliding closer, putting his arm around her. 'What'sa matter?'

'I have to go home,' she told him, subdued by shock.

'Why?' he asked, taking the phone from her frozen hands.

She leaned briefly against him, needing his strength. 'It's just, um . . . ' She was just inebriated enough to make her thoughts muddy. 'I have to go.'

'Okay,' he said. 'Sir, I need to take her home,' he relayed to the lieutenant as he passed him back the phone.

'The game's pretty much over,' Luther Lindstrom pointed out. 'Feel free to leave. And thanks for helping us out, ma'am,' he added to Lia.

'Oh, sure,' she said distractedly.

They turned in her shoes and made their way to the parking lot. Lia couldn't summon a word of small talk. Vinny kept quiet, too. He put her into his passenger seat and started driving.

She was halfway home when she roused from shock enough to realize that her car was parked at his condo. 'Oh, not again! I could have driven myself this time.'

'It's not a problem,' he reassured her.

'But you have to bother your friend to help you, and I hate it when I inconvenience people. He's going to think I'm some kind of irresponsible — '

'Listen to me,' Vinny cut in. He had a quiet authority about him that made her stop talking. 'It's not a problem,' he repeated. 'Now tell me what's going on that's got you talking to an FBI agent.'

She wasn't sure she wanted him to know. For a guy she'd intended to seduce and walk away from, he was managing to make himself look and sound more like a boyfriend, and she was not — repeat, was *not* — going to let that happen. 'Don't worry about it.' She looked out the window to keep from seeing the effect of her words on his face.

The car got dangerously quiet.

As Vinny approached the next intersection, he down-shifted, his muffler roaring, and then he executed a U-turn.

Lia's heart beat faster. She sneaked a glance at him and found his jaw muscles jumping. 'Where are we going now?' she asked. It occurred to her that she really didn't know this man at all. Somehow she wasn't surprised to discover that he had a temper.

'Back to your car,' he said on a cold note.

Okay. She'd wanted that, but not when he made it sound like it would be over the minute she stepped out of his vehicle. The thought of not seeing him again made her feel

216

like her innards had been ripped out and thrown out the window.

As they screamed along an empty four-lane road, bypassing a school and a playground, Lia struggled for something to say that would keep him dangling. Nothing witty or alluring came to mind.

Vinny hooked a right and they were bearing down on his oceanfront condo. He whipped in behind her car and turned his engine off. 'When you're ready to share your life with me, let me know,' he said. With that, he stepped out of the vehicle, rounded it like a true gentleman, and pulled her door open.

She got out on leaden legs.

He stood intentionally in her way, forcing her to brush by him. Every nerve in her body flexed with awareness. The air seemed to crackle as memories of their last kiss shortened her breath.

Can't we just have sex and go our separate ways?

She didn't dare articulate the question. Not only did it belittle their attraction, but it made her seem like a slut. She was beginning to glean that Vinny didn't do one-night stands. For whatever reason, he wasn't your typical twenty-year-old opportunist.

On the other hand, how naive could he be, asking her to share her life with him? Young love rarely lasted, and she wasn't about to invest the best years of her life in a relationship that was doomed to fail.

Hence, it was up to her to do the mature thing and walk away.

'Goodbye, Vinny.' She kissed his cheek, feeling the tension in his jaw. He jammed his hands into his pockets as he watched her get into her own car and take off.

She tried not to look back, but a quick glance in her rearview mirror showed him standing where she'd left him, looking like the rug had been ripped out from under his feet.

'Shit!' Lia swore, striking the steering wheel with her palm. Her body ached with unfulfilled desire, her heart throbbed with the morning's unexpected happiness, and her conscience swelled with the guilt of how badly she'd treated Vinny in the face of his concern. But Lia couldn't let herself dwell on any of that.

She had weightier matters to consume her, like whether she and Penny were next on a killer's hit list.

12

Joe wasn't so drunk that he couldn't walk home. Beneath a moonless sky, the invisible sidewalk felt as treacherous as the mountain pass where his reconnaissance team had run into insurgents. He stumbled over cracks in the cement. Cars sped by him, headlights blinding him, tail-lights streaming.

The air was clear and cold. It nipped at his ears and went straight through his jeans and sweatshirt. He was in Virginia Beach, right? Not wandering through the Hindu Kush in a delirious haze.

The tang of the ocean and the smell of exhaust reassured him.

Shit, he never should have hit the sports bar after working out at the gym! But the call he'd received from Millington, Tennessee, informing of his new orders, had gotten him so agitated that he'd pushed himself at the gym. Then, instead of going home, he'd showered and driven to the nearest pub.

On his third shot of whiskey, he realized that even with a Saturday-night crowd pressing in on him, he was drinking alone, wallowing in self-doubt, thinking, *What if I get more men killed?*

He'd looked around the bar, wanting consolation, an easy stranger to help him forget the awful responsibilities looming before him. Eye contact and a receptive smile would get him what they always had — the company of a beautiful woman. If anything, his disfiguring scar got him more notice than ever from the opposite sex.

It would take very little effort to pick a woman up and take her home. Usually just three words did the trick: Navy SEAL officer. But come morning, nothing would be different. He'd still have this crushing sense of doom weighting him down. The only person in the world who could make him feel better by bolstering his confidence, soothing his self-doubts, was Penny.

The realization had had him pushing aside his drink with relief. He'd paid his tab and left.

But then he'd had to walk the three miles to his house because he was too drunk to drive.

As he turned down the street that led to his subdivision, Joe began to jog. He turned in to his neighborhood at a run, sprinting past his home and through Penny's yard to the lights shining warmly in her windows.

Twin beams of bright light leaped out of

the darkness, accompanied by voices that caught Joe completely by surprise. 'Halt! Police! This is the police! Get your hands up! Hands up now! Get your hands up and keep them up!'

Joe tried to stop, but his body was slow to respond as commanding voices closed in on him. Through the glare of blinding lights, he made out two uniformed officers. Their guns were drawn and pointed specifically at him. Joe checked the impulse to launch a counterattack. 'What the hell?' he demanded, even as one of them continued to bark orders at him.

'Put your hands behind your head and get down on your knees.'

It dawned on Joe that the police must have set a watch in hopes of catching Eric. 'Stupid fuckers,' he muttered, including himself in that number. He couldn't believe he hadn't seen them. He kneeled on the frost-covered grass, his jeans going instantly damp. Every household in the vicinity was witness to what was going on. Son of a bitch.

'Wait!' With relief, Joe looked up to see Penny flying toward him in her slippers and bathrobe. Lia stood at the door with a hand over her mouth.

'Ma'am, stay back! He could be armed!'

'This is not who you're looking for!' Penny

snapped furiously. 'This is my neighbor. For God's sake, stop yelling and waking the entire neighborhood!'

That's my girl, thought Joe as she rushed over and helped him to his feet.

'Your neighbor?' repeated the cop. Joe flinched as the man's flashlight plumbed his eyes.

'Yes, he's my neighbor,' Penny insisted. 'I called him and asked him to come over.'

She secured an arm around Joe's waist, keeping him steady.

'He was running at your house like he was going to break the door down,' the officer insisted.

'He was out jogging. Weren't you, Joe?'

'Yep,' he said.

'He's a Navy SEAL,' she added, throwing out the fact like it was a badge of honor. 'He has to keep in shape.'

'Navy SEAL, huh,' said the second cop. 'Could I see some ID, please, sir?'

Joe fished out his wallet and handed him his military ID. He detested falling back on rank to pull him out of trouble, but it did the job, every time.

'Oh, sir,' said the first cop, who paled when he noted Joe's pay grade. 'We're — ah — very sorry to bother you, sir. You have a good night sir. Good night.'

They handed the ID back and beat a hasty retreat to their patrol car. 'Huh,' said Penny, clearly confused by the change in their demeanor. 'Come on in, Joe. It's freezing out here.'

He couldn't wait to step into the warm, cozy house of a woman who hadn't had sex in five years. Whoa, he wasn't even supposed to think about that. But was she horny all the time, or had she gotten to the point where she didn't need it anymore?

Penny shut the door behind them, pulling back to send Joe a searching look. Ophelia had magically disappeared. 'You've been drinking again,' Penny accused. 'And you've been in the cold so long your cheeks are chapped. That is just awful for your burn. How do you expect it to heal?'

Damned if he didn't love being scolded by her! With a quick step forward, Joe pulled her back into his arms and hugged her for warmth and reassurance. Filling his head with her roselike scent, he felt the stress slip right out of him.

'Are you okay?' she asked, tipping her head back to give him a worried look. 'Joe?'

'Better now,' he replied.

'Come on in the family room,' she urged. 'I've got a fire going.'

He loved fires, especially the outdoor kind,

under a star-spangled sky in the desert. Squatting before the hearth, he held his fingers to the heat, lost his balance, and landed on his butt. The flames mesmerized him, beating back the self-doubt he'd been wrestling with since the detailer's call.

'Drink this,' said Penny, reappearing with two mugs. She handed him one, then eased down beside him.

It was fragrant, scalding tea. As he blew on it, he took closer note of her cotton nightgown and blue velour bath-robe. 'You were going to bed,' he observed.

'I wouldn't have been able to sleep anyway.'

There was something in her voice. 'Why not? What's going on?'

'Eric's dead.'

His synapses backfired. 'Dead? How'd he die?'

'He was shot in the head. It was supposed to look like a suicide, but his car was run off the road, and another set of footprints was found on the scene.'

The hairs on Joe's nape prickled. In other words, *murder*. 'The terrorist who bought the ricin,' he guessed.

'Most likely,' she agreed.

'That's why the cops are out front. They're protecting you.' *Jesus*. He ran a hand through his hair, then searched her face for the fear she had to be feeling.

There it was, in the tremulous smile she gave him. He wanted to hug her for being so brave.

'So, what has you running up to my door at midnight?' she inquired, lifting her chin.

It took him a second to remember. 'Oh, yeah. I got new orders today.'

Her eyes flew wide. 'To where?' she gasped.

'Right down the road. Dam Neck Naval Annex. I'm going to take command of Team Twelve.'

She seemed to breathe a sigh of relief. But then she gave him that look that made him feel transparent. 'And that made you drink tonight,' she realized out loud. 'Why, aren't you happy with your orders?'

He had to look into the fire. 'It's a lot of responsibility,' he hedged.

She waited for more. Her silence wrapped around him, giving him time to voice what he'd felt all afternoon since the detailer's call.

'I think about what happened when I took command of a four-man squad. This time I'll be in charge of forty guys. I'm . . . scared I'm gonna make a call that gets more guys killed.' His voice shook.

'Oh, Joe.' And there she was, slipping an arm around him, resting her cheek briefly on his shoulder. 'You're going to do fine, better than fine. You were born to lead others, and you know it. What happened in Afghanistan was not your fault, but it will make you a better leader, Joe. You, more than anyone, will understand what you're asking of your men.'

He'd known she would reawaken his self-confidence without lying or flattering him. He sent her a grateful smile, and their gazes locked. Without a trace of forethought, Joe kissed her, lightly, on the lips.

Her indrawn breath had him realizing his mistake. 'Sorry,' he said. But he wasn't really, because her mouth had been soft and sweet, just like he vaguely remembered from the night he'd passed out. He just had to kiss her one more time.

She didn't resist. In fact, she parted her lips in welcome, moaning faintly as he rubbed his tongue with hers.

The room started to spin again. 'Whoa,' Joe laughed, pulling back. 'I'm still drunk,' he added as a means of excusing his behavior, covering up his astonishment that she could taste so good.

The hurt he glimpsed in her face made his gut wrench. He wanted to explain that he didn't trust himself not to hurt her. Their burgeoning friendship was special. He didn't want to ruin it. 'I should go,' he said.

'You don't have to,' she whispered softly.

'Call me,' he added, ignoring her scarcely uttered invitation. 'If anything happens and you need me, I'm right next door, you know.'

'Oh, I know,' she said, looking down at her hands.

He got to his feet, careful not to touch her again. Her vulnerability had a powerful pull on him. He wanted to give her what she'd been missing all these years, except she had expectations of sex that he didn't have.

''Night,' he said, heading straight for the door. 'Sweet dreams.'

★ ★ ★

Penny shut the door and turned the deadbolt. She drew the edges of her gown closer and sighed at the throbbing emptiness inside her. The only way her dreams would be sweet was if Joe had stayed and . . .

What? she asked herself. *Slept with you? Kept you up all night?*

Yes! After five years of celibacy, she deserved a night of abandonment.

And what would you expect after that? argued her reason.

'I don't know,' she conceded. She'd always expected to marry and raise a family. But with Joe, those expectations would get her nothing but heartache. Maybe she could harness them.

If he even wants you, mocked the inner voice. He'd walked away pretty damn fast.

Shaking her head in confusion, she turned and plodded up the stairs to retire alone, again.

★ ★ ★

Lia pushed through the exit at Wavy Television Studios with confidence in her stride. *I got the job!* she marveled, tamping down the urge to do a happy dance.

Slidel and Holmes, her police escorts, watched her waltz into the sunshine. She drew herself up to walk like the professional she was, briefcase in hand, to her car.

The human-resources office had called her for an interview on the same day they'd received her résumé. They were looking for a field reporter — articulate, tenacious, with a nose for news.

'I'm your girl,' she'd told her interviewers, a former news anchor and his male secretary. She'd folded her legs just so, flashing her cream-colored stockings and drawing their attention to her slim calves, proving — once again — that it's not what you know but how you use it that gets the job done.

All those years of taking drama back in high school had paid off. Not once did they realize that beneath her woolen charcoal suit, she was suffering through cold sweats.

'We'll call you this afternoon with an official offer,' Mr. Grady promised her. 'But I can tell you right now that you will love working for this station. I've been happy here for twenty years.' He'd pumped her hand enthusiastically, his gaze dipping toward the satin ribbon that peeked over the lapels of her jacket.

She wasn't certain she was all that qualified for the position, but what did it matter? They were going to pay her a decent salary, *with* benefits. Not only could she afford her rent again, she might even buy a new car!

Best of all, Vinny might just see her on the news.

She envisioned him slapping his forehead. *Oh, man, I could have had that woman!* He could have. She'd been right there in his bedroom with the alcove overlooking the ocean, all hot for him, praying he would rip her clothes off. Instead, he'd taken her bowling.

Okay, maybe he had his act together. Maybe he looked like the responsible adult, with a thing or two to teach her about growing up. But those days were over. Ophelia Price was getting her shit together now.

And she couldn't wait for him to realize it, either.

Hell, she could rub his nose in it this very minute — without having to *share her life* with him.

Slipping into her car, she reached for Penny's cell phone and snatched up the Post-it with Vinny's contact information on it. She dialed his number, then gazed out the window at the fountain in the manmade pond, hoping to leave a message.

'Yo, this is Vinny.' He sounded full of energy and impossibly young. And he was there in the flesh in the middle of a weekday.

'It's Lia,' she said, caught off guard by that. 'I just wanted you to know that I got a job. I'm a field reporter for Channel Ten.'

'Well, well,' he said, with more warmth than she could've hoped for. 'Congratulations.'

'Thank you. I'm surprised you're home. It's two in the afternoon.'

'I get off early on Wednesday so I can go to class,' he explained.

'Oh. Well, I don't want to make you late.' At the same time, she didn't want to hang up yet.

'Actually, I was thinkin' of skipping class today and taking my Harley for a ride.'

'You do not have a Harley,' she countered,

suddenly breathless.

'Yeah, true, but Westy does, and he said I could borrow his whenever I wanted.'

She had no idea who Westy was, but, 'Oh, my God.'

'Wanna go for a ride?'

'Uh . . . ' Yes, but she had a slight problem. Her police escorts would pitch a fit if she tried to hop on a bike with a total stranger. 'I need you to pick me up somewhere,' she said, tingling with sudden excitement.

'Sure. Like where?'

She gave directions to a boutique on the oceanfront. 'Meet me in the alley in the back, by the employee exit,' she instructed.

'Okay.' His tone was suspicious, but he didn't ask.

'I'm still in Portsmouth,' she added, hurrying now to start her engine and back out of the parking lot. 'I'll need twenty minutes to get there.'

'See you in twenty,' he said, and the phone clicked in her ear.

★　★　★

Vinny knew trouble when he smelled it, and when Lia slipped out the back door of the jewelry boutique smelling like a million dollars, he knew he was going to find himself in a pile of shit eventually, and he honestly didn't care.

Wearing a gray suit with cream-colored stockings and pearl earrings, she looked chic and sexy. Her golden-red hair was twisted up into a knot. The spikes on her high heels qualified them as weapons.

She took his breath away, and that was before he even noticed the coy satin string that cinched up whatever she was wearing underneath. God have mercy, because he knew that Ophelia Price wouldn't.

He wanted her in his life, forever.

'Who are you hiding from?' he demanded, handing her a spare helmet.

'Don't worry about it.' Her turquoise eyes glimmered like gemstones as she hiked her skirt to leap on board behind him. Whatever she was up to, she was enjoying the hell out of her herself. 'Just get me out of here, fast.'

Calculated risks were an everyday affair for Vinny, but there wasn't much calculating going on in his brain as he squealed out of the alleyway with Lia plastered to his back.

She wanted a onetime deal, he reminded himself. And she was still keeping secrets. Since once would never be enough for him, he had to find a way to keep her coming back.

It was Joe's last physical-therapy session. As Penny eased her thumb into the serratus posterior inferior to the right of Joe's spine, she savored the velvety texture of his skin and the density of his muscles, wishing she could touch him this way forever, wishing he was hers.

In the same breath, she berated herself for her continuing obsession with him. And he should not have kissed her the other night — not if he didn't mean it. She hadn't been able to think straight since then. Her body ached for more. This business of caressing him, inhaling his unique scent, listening for his groans of pleasure was just slow torture.

'How's — ah — how's the turnover period going?' she asked him in a desperate bid to get her brain functioning at a higher level.

He grunted, betraying reluctance to talk. 'It's good. I decided to meet the men at the top of the wall, sort of catch 'em off guard during their PT time.'

'The wall?'

'It's part of the obstacle course.'

'Oh.' His low, sleepy voice sounded so sensual. It made her want to touch him in other, quite specific, places. Last night, as she'd lain in bed, that had been her fantasy

— touching Joe's body with her lips, tasting him with her tongue. Her imagination had fast-forwarded, and he'd flipped her over and done the same for her. Lost in the yearnings evoked by her fantasy, she'd had to sate her body's needs, her climax so ferocious that she shed a tear, crying out, 'Oh, Joe!'

The memory made her palms hot now, made her breathing quicken. She hoped he didn't notice.

'You want to come to my change-of-command ceremony?' he asked, oblivious to her heightened state.

'Sure, when is it?' Was this like a date? Was he inviting her in the place of a spouse?

'This Friday,' he murmured. 'Please don't stop.'

The sensual plea made her pulse speed up.

'That's an awfully quick turnover,' she commented.

'Mmmm. The outgoing commander has cancer. He can't work right now.'

She paused. 'Oh, that's awful.'

'He'll beat it,' said Joe with conviction. 'I'm having a party Friday night, too, if you can come. Remember, I said I'd introduce you to some friends.'

He might as well have slapped her hands off his back. Penny stopped what she was doing. 'I'll try to come,' she said, bringing their session to an abrupt end. 'The muscles in your back have healed, Joe. As long as you keep up the stretching exercises and limit heavy lifting, you'll be fine from now on. If you feel any spasms, alternate with hot and cold compresses.'

She stepped down off her stool.

Joe lay there motionless. 'If I paid you, would you still give me massages?' he asked with unguarded longing.

A pang went through Penny's heart. 'I don't think so,' she said, hurt by his offer to pay.

He lifted his head and looked at her. 'I didn't mean that like it sounded,' he told her gently.

She drew a deep breath, fighting back the impulse to burst into tears. 'I know.'

A rapping at the door saved her from the emotional roller coaster. 'Yes?' Penny called out.

The receptionist peered through the cracked door. 'You have an urgent call on line three from an Officer Slidel,' she told Penny.

The walls in the small space did a slow turn. 'I'll take it in my office,' Penny said, hurrying from the room.

She was gripping the receiver in consternation when Joe sidled up to her office door. 'What's wrong?' he demanded.

Tears pressured her eyes. 'Lia's missing,' she admitted. 'She disappeared out of a boutique on Atlantic Avenue.' She fumbled the receiver as she replaced it.

Joe stepped into the office wearing the battle dress cammies he'd worn to work. 'Don't jump to conclusions, Pen,' he soothed, shortening her name for the first time. 'Check your messages. She might have pulled a fast one on her watchdogs.'

'You're right,' she agreed, grateful for his level head. It was just like Ophelia to give the cops a slip. She snatched up the phone again, entered her password, and listened to her voice mail. The second message was from Ophelia. 'Hey, sis, it's me. Listen don't worry about me, okay? I just need a break from these clowns who're getting on my nerves. I'll be with Vinny. He's a SEAL, remember. You know he can take care of me. Oh, and by the way, I got the job! Wahoo, time to celebrate, huh? I'll be out of your hair in no time.'

Penny slumped with relief and put the phone down. 'She's fine,' she said to Joe, who'd probably overheard every last word of Lia's exuberant message.

He squeezed her shoulder. 'Told you. Lia's tougher than you think she is. No one's going to catch her by surprise.' He started for the door.

'What do you know about this Vinny?' Penny asked. 'Isn't he on your team?'

'You have nothing to worry about,' he reassured her, pausing at the door. 'The kid's squared away.'

'The kid? How old is he?'

'Like twenty.'

'What? Lia's never gone out with a younger man.'

'There's a first time for everything,' Joe replied. His gaze dropped toward the front of her blouse.

Penny's nipples peaked as if he'd physically caressed them. 'I guess so,' she said, wondering what he meant by that.

'As soon as I know more, I'll get you the details about the change-of-command ceremony.'

'Okay,' she said with a genuine smile. 'I look forward to that.'

'You know, I'm going to miss coming here,' he admitted, glancing at her tidy desktop. 'I get jealous thinking of all those soldiers getting your attention.' His dark eyes were inscrutable as they looked back at her.

He actually felt jealous? Penny's cheeks heated at the admission.

She was scrounging for the courage to offer her services — free of charge — when he grimaced and patted the door frame. 'Well, see you.'

''Bye.'

And then it was too late. She sat alone in her office, more empty and unfulfilled than ever. 'First time for what?' she wondered out loud.

13

By the time Vinny pointed the Harley toward the water-front, they were miles up shore, following the curve of the beach toward his townhouse. The chill breeze billowing up Lia's skirt couldn't cool her simmering anticipation.

Body heat radiated through his black leather jacket, keeping her warm in the crisp November air. Her hands, locked around his waist, strayed downward, and Lia grinned. Those jeans couldn't get much tighter at the moment.

But then he drove right past his town-house.

She gaped over her shoulder at it, her expectations taking a free fall. 'Where are we going?' she shouted.

'Somewhere private,' he called back. He turned onto a pocked street, flanked by motley beach houses. It dead-ended at a gate, complete with chain-link fence and guards toting M15 rifles.

As Vinny flashed his military ID, Lia read the plaque pegged to the guardhouse: 'Fort Story.' Wasn't this an Army-run facility, site of the two Cape Henry lighthouses, the old and the new?

Oh, Lord, he wasn't going to take her sightseeing, was he? After their bowling date last weekend, she didn't know what to expect.

As they proceeded through the gate, moving more sedately, she was relieved to see that the base was indeed private. They were surrounded by gnarled bayberry trees and grass-covered sand dunes. The two lighthouses jutting up beyond them looked like something off a postcard.

Vinny took them past the newer lighthouse with its white and black checkered design to the older structure, less than a hundred feet high and made of brick. 'It's just been closed to the public,' he divulged.

Sure enough, a chain had been drawn across the entrance. But Vinny drove around it, onto the soft shoulder. The rear tire fishtailed, and Lia's adrenaline raced. *Whoa, hey, we could get into trouble for this.*

He drove past the concrete steps that led up from the parking lot. Up a narrow footpath they bumped, forcing Lia to hang on tight. He nosed the bike into a grove and killed the engine. 'Shhh,' he said, turning profile to whisper to her. 'Listen.'

She listened, but all she could hear was the roar of the surf, the sound of the wind whistling around the lighthouse, and the call of seagulls wheeling overhead.

'All clear,' he decided. Getting off the bike, he helped her to dismount, his chocolate-brown eyes alight with mischief.

'What are we doing here?' she asked him.

'You'll see.' He glanced down at her spiked heels. 'I think I'd better carry you, though.'

That was all the warning she got before he hefted her in his arms, so high that she flopped over him like a rucksack.

'Hush,' he said as she voiced her concerns.

'Put me down.'

'I will.' But he didn't. He ran out from the cover of the dunes with her bouncing on his shoulder, jogged up several steps, and put her down before a wooden door with a padlock on it. She watched in amazement as he pulled a pin from his pocket and worked the lock open.

'Awesome,' Lia breathed, casting a worried glance around them. But they were still alone.

Vinny pulled her into the cool, dank stairwell. 'Having fun yet?' he asked, shutting the door.

She giggled uncertainly. 'I think so.'

'Good. Start climbing.'

A hint of sensual intent in his voice quickened her pulse.

'There'd better be a reason for this,' she

huffed. Narrow windows illumined the steel steps that wound up and up, seeming never to end.

'Just don't twist an ankle,' Vinny cautioned. He was right behind her to catch her if she fell.

They climbed for what seemed like half an hour but was more like five minutes. By the time she arrived at the top, Lia was perspiring in her woolen suit. Vinny didn't look the least bit winded.

The view startled an exclamation from her. The top of the tower was enclosed by a cylinder of glass, offering a panoramic vista of the cape. The new lighthouse loomed nearby, with a cluster of outbuildings at its base.

'Have a seat.' Vinny drew her over to one side and patted the cement ledge.

Lia collapsed. Contrary to how modest the structure appeared from below, she felt like she was miles up in the air. The ocean cast a blanket as far as the eye could see, moving through a spectrum of blues and grays as it mingled with the waters of the Chesapeake Bay. 'So beautiful,' she sighed, leaning her cheek against the glass to take it in.

Vinny sat beside her, his cheek close to hers as he peered straight down.

Her gaze slid to his powerful neck and the

sensual curve of his lower lip, and she forgot about the view.

He caught her staring, and in the next instant, he was kissing her.

Oh, yes. Lia moaned. Desire rolled through her like the waves pounding the shoreline below. But every time she reached for his zipper, he restrained her questing fingers.

This was happening his way, but that was fine by her. What a thrill to make love at the top of a lighthouse!

He released the buttons of her jacket, easing it off her shoulders to reveal the corset-style bustier beneath it. 'No wonder you got the job,' he stated with a leer.

She tried to cuff him, but he caught her wrist, holding it captive as he tugged the satin bow that kept her tightly bound. The two halves of the garment parted, exposing her full, pale breasts.

'You are so fuckin' sexy,' Vinny exclaimed, his dialect especially thick.

She hooked a heel over the smooth edge of concrete, exposing her cream-colored garters. *You think that's sexy, try this on for size.* The heat in Vinny's eyes sent a delicious thrill through her.

'You dress like this every day?' he asked hoarsely.

'A girl never gives away her secrets.'

With flared nostrils and a taut jaw, Vinny went down on his knees. He nudged her legs apart and leaned between them to nuzzle the edges of her bustier.

Lia caught his head in her hands, humming her encouragement as his warm mouth sought and teased the sensitive tips of her breasts. His hands, meanwhile, moved possessively up her silk-clad thighs.

He could have taken her right then; she was more than ready. Instead, he nibbled, licked, and sucked until she wanted to scream.

She fisted his T-shirt, dragging it upward on a quest for bare skin. His was impossibly silky and stretched taut over rock-hard muscles. She furrowed her fingers in his chest hair, felt his heart race beneath her palm. 'Please,' she urged, trembling with the desire to be overcome.

His slow-moving fingers were tracing the straps of her garters. *Oh, please.* She quivered with anticipation. Finally, finally, he eased a thumb beneath her thong and caressed her in slow, maddening circles. *Oh, my God.* Lia's head fell back as she surrendered to his touch.

At last he shifted, and she nearly sobbed with relief. But instead of unzipping his jeans, he pulled her hips closer, lowered his head, and put his mouth where his hands had been.

Lia couldn't slow herself. She climaxed the instant his tongue touched her. Before her pleasure even ebbed, he pushed two fingers inside her and stroked her from within. 'Do it again,' he ordered gruffly.

His tongue resumed its dance, and unbelievably, in just seconds, she did.

She cried out her amazement, then collapsed like she'd run a marathon.

The first thing she saw when she blinked her eyes open was Vinny's small, triumphant smile.

With chagrin, she realized how slutty she looked — legs splayed, her skirt hiked to her waist, breasts, exposed. She started to cover herself.

'Don't. I like looking at you.'

She blurted the first thought to enter her head. 'Is there something wrong with you?' She darted a meaningful glance downward.

He sent her a pained smile. 'No.'

'Then, why didn't you . . . ' She trailed off, heat rising like a geyser from her neck to her hairline.

'I didn't bring a condom,' he said, standing up.

Oh. 'You should have told me,' she lamented. 'I would have brought one with me.'

Vinny just looked at her, and she felt a little trashy letting him know that she was all about self-protection while having her fun.

'I can . . . return the favor if you want,' she suggested, flicking another glance downward. If she couldn't get the horse out of the gate, how was she ever going to get him to the races?

'That's okay.'

She smoothed her skirt down, confused, not understanding. Didn't he want her? Why refuse the release she offered him?

'When you're ready to share your life with me, your heart, your head, everything, *cara mia*,' he said, reaching out to caress her cheek and the tops of her breasts, 'then I'll be ready to give you what you really need. You can start by explaining why you had to meet me in an alley earlier.'

Lia gasped at the ultimatum. 'You think you're going to coerce me into having a relationship with you?' She sat up straighter, jerking the edges of her bodice together.

'Think of it as encouragement, not coercion. No one's forcing you to have sex,' he pointed out mildly.

She was furious. 'This is ridiculous,' she snapped. 'I don't want to 'go out' with you like we're in middle school or something. I just want to have some fun and a little sex and go our separate ways. That's how it's going to end up anyway.'

'You think?' he said quietly, but she could tell by his sudden stillness that his own temper was igniting.

'Oh, grow up!' She snatched her jacket off the sill and jammed her arms into the sleeves. 'What do you think is going to happen after we date for a while? You're going to get tired of me, or I'm going to get tired of you. Neither one of us is ready for a long-term commitment, so why complicate things?'

He leaned over her with a hand braced on either side of the ledge, arm muscles straining to support his weight, and Lia was reminded of his deadly training. 'It's already complicated,' he told her in a soft but intense voice. 'I don't want to just fuck you, Ophelia.'

He let the crude word hang between them for a sizzling moment. 'I want to live inside your head, in your heart. I want to taste what you taste and feel what you feel. And I won't settle for anything less.'

In the midst of his ultimatum, Lia forgot how to breathe. She felt submerged within herself, clawing for the surface, desperate for oxygen. 'I can't,' she choked, suffocated by the fear of loss.

The light in Vinny's eyes slowly dimmed. 'You can't,' he repeated.

'No,' she said, but she wasn't so sure this time. She could feel him retreating, taking his warmth and passion with him.

He pushed himself upright and looked down his nose at her. The grooves that edged his mouth made him look older than his twenty years. 'It's time to go,' he said quietly.

Lia felt chilled. She stood up slowly and buttoned her jacket all the way up. Her heart sat in her throat like a pill she couldn't swallow.

She felt cheap now, cheap and mean for using him. But what did he expect? She wasn't naively romantic like he was. She didn't believe in young love's ability to endure.

With the reminder that she was older and therefore called the shots, Lia headed for the stairs. She'd gotten what she wanted — well, not really. Her traitorous body clamored for the real deal, but she'd never tell Vinny that.

'Wait,' he said, squeezing past her. 'Put your other hand on my shoulder.'

She wanted to refuse him, but the steps were way too treacherous to descend in heels.

Touching him, even lightly, filled her with remorse.

Forget him, she commanded herself. Anything more than a fling with the young SEAL was asking for heartache. She'd suffered enough heartache in her short life never to want to feel that way again.

★ ★ ★

'Well, hello.'

Penny glanced up from the program she'd been reading to find Hannah Lindstrom towering over her in a violet pantsuit. 'Oh, hi,' she countered, pleased to see a familiar face at Joe's change-of-command ceremony. Ophelia'd had to work and couldn't come.

'Is anyone sitting here?'

'No, please join me. I'd forgotten that your husband was a member of Team Twelve. Which one is he?'

'He's not here, actually,' Hannah admitted, taking the seat beside her. 'He and two others are on assignment in Southeast Asia. I'm here to represent him, though.'

'How long will he be gone?' Penny asked, marveling at Hannah's easy acceptance of her husband's dangerous work.

'About a month.' She hushed herself as she realized that the ceremony was beginning. The color guard marched onto the small stage in front of them and placed the flags in their holders. Joe stood in the company of two other men, the departing commander and the base admiral.

Admiral Johansen approached the mike to address the crowd. 'Family, friends, and guests, and members of SEAL Team Twelve, welcome.'

The procedure was standard. Penny, along with other guests, sat before the stage, flanked by Team Twelve's senior enlisted standing on one side and officers on the other. At the rear of the room, more than twenty junior enlisted stood elbow to elbow, wearing their service blues.

As Admiral Johansen launched into his speech praising the accomplishments of the outgoing commander, Penny caught Joe's eye. He'd cut his hair the other day. The shorter style gave him a harder edge, as did his dead-serious demeanor. This was not the playboy neighbor she'd known for years. His biography, printed on the back of the program, had nudged her respect to an unprecedented level. Not only was he leader of his ROTC program at USC, but he'd been the honor graduate at BUDS/SEAL training, Class 180.

There was no question in Penny's mind that Joe had earned the right to lead this team of commandos. She was proud enough to pop the buttons off her work khakis.

As the outgoing commander made his way to the podium, Penny remembered what Joe had said about his health, and she sent up a quick prayer for him. He kept his comments short and simple, imparting confidence that his men were being placed in the most capable hands imaginable.

Penny noted Joe's indrawn breath. She could tell that beneath his stoic expression, the tragedy in Afghanistan was still fresh in his mind.

But his posture was impeccable as he joined the admiral and outgoing commander at the podium. In minutes, the burden of responsibility was passed from one man to the next, sealed with a handshake and a two-way salute.

As Joe addressed the assembly, Penny gripped her hands in her lap. The murmured words of a teenage girl pricked her ears.

'What happened to his face?'

'Shhh,' hushed her mother. 'It was a car accident.'

Penny almost shook her head. Had she done Joe a disservice with that rumor? He deserved recognition and respect for surviving the disaster.

'I've always believed,' he said, sweeping a brooding gaze over the crowd, 'that actions speak louder than words.' She knew him well enough to sense that he held powerful emotions in check as he spoke. 'So, I'm not going to waste your time by talking. Follow me,' he commanded, his gaze compelling and powerful.

Penny could sense by the tense silence of the men around her that his words had exactly the impact intended.

'Hooyah!' he added, and the room echoed with a resounding 'Hooyah!' from all the SEALs assembled.

Penny smiled. Joe had innate charisma. It wouldn't take long at all for his men to follow him unquestioningly.

Commander Goodwin led Joe offstage for a Pass in Review, in which Joe was formally introduced to the men he'd already met under less formal circumstances. Guests were invited to rise and partake of the cake and punch.

'I'd better get back to the office,' said Hannah, reaching for her briefcase. 'I'm sorry there's been no break-through on your case yet,' she added, looking pained.

'How much longer will the police guard our house?' Penny wanted to know.

'Not much longer,' the agent confessed. 'I'm working on a new angle, though. If Eric sold the ricin to pay for his wife's medical treatment, then maybe the payoff went directly to a hospital or to a doctor and never touched his hands.'

'That's a great idea,' said Penny.

'I think so, but it's tougher than it sounds. Sonja Tomlinson was treated by at least a dozen different doctors, some of whom have moved over the past five years. I'll call you the minute I learn anything new. And don't hesitate to call me,' she added, turning to leave.

Penny wandered to the punch bowl, where she helped herself to a full paper cup. She admired the enormous sheet cake but, having eaten lunch just a short while ago, abstained from taking a slice and stepped outside onto the balcony.

The change-of-command ceremony took place in the officers' club on Dam Neck, a building that stood some distance back from the beach. The wind was blustery and cold, but the sunshine kept Penny from freezing.

An offshore wind rocked her as she reached for the balcony rail. The wind wreaked havoc with the bun at the back of her head. The fitful ocean tossed and bucked beyond the dunes. It failed to offer her the consolation she was looking for.

Feeling eyes on her, Penny turned, hoping that Joe had joined her. She recognized the interloper as one of the senior enlisted who'd stood to her left during the ceremony. As he circled her, he pinned her with his light-colored eyes. Amazingly, the combination cap that covered his dark hair remained on his head, in spite of the wind.

She sent him a small smile and looked away.

He drew to within a yard of her. 'Do you swim?' he asked. The question came out in a gruff voice that held a hint of a quaint dialect.

'Of course.' She darted him a curious look.

He hadn't introduced himself. But his name and rank were readily apparent: 'McGuire, Senior Chief.' Service pins vied for space above his left breast pocket. He looked about a decade older than she was, with a handsome, weathered face, a black moustache, and eyes of such a pale hue that they seemed almost colorless.

Those weird eyes took inventory of her figure. Penny suffered the impression that he could see straight through her linen uniform.

'Women have an easier time treading water than men,' he stated.

'That's because they have more body fat,' Penny countered.

'Exactly.' The gleam in his eyes made it clear that he appreciated the difference. A shiver of awareness went through Penny. Why couldn't Joe look at her like that?

'Take a look out there,' he invited, turning

his gaze at the ocean. 'Y'see that column of water that looks sandy? The waves are lower there.'

Following the trajectory of his finger, she nodded. 'I see it,' she said, finding his conversation bizarre.

'That's a riptide.' He pinned her with those eyes. 'One minute you're swimming near the beach, the next you're being sucked out to sea.'

Something about the way he said that made her shiver. Of course, it was mid-November, and the weather was a far cry from tropical.

'Do you know what to do,' he quizzed her, 'when that happens?'

Were they talking about something more than riptides? If so, she had no idea what. 'Uh, stay calm,' she suggested, accessing her mental archives, 'and swim parallel to the shore?'

He didn't smile, but she got the impression he was laughing at her. 'What if you're not strong enough to escape the ocean's pull?' His gaze was mesmerizing.

'I don't know,' she admitted. 'I don't swim in the ocean all that much.'

'Afraid of sharks?'

'Not necessarily. I don't like getting sand in my suit.'

His gaze flickered downward. This time, he did smile, though just barely. 'My name's

Solomon,' he said.

'I'm Penny.' She stuck out a hand to cover up her confusion.

His hand came up slowly and swallowed hers whole.

Penny's knees went weak.

God, he was intense, but at the same time his hand was firm and strong, and by hanging on to hers, he made it obvious that, yes, he was coming on to her. He wasn't Joe, but he was a man — apparently single, good-looking, and interested in her.

And she could use a little male attention to keep from obsessing about Joe.

'Water's a little cold or I'd take you for a swim right now,' Solomon said, stroking his thumb across her palm.

With a self-conscious laugh, Penny tugged her hand free. The man was too much.

To her relief, she heard the door squeak open. She turned, and there was Joe strolling toward them, his face expressionless.

Solomon dropped his hands to his sides. 'Sir,' he said, acknowledging Joe's approach.

Joe gave him a hard look. 'Senior Chief.' His gaze slid to Penny, lingering long enough to notice heightened color. 'Did you get some cake?' he asked her.

'I had to pass,' she explained. 'Thank you for inviting me, though. The ceremony was well done. Not too long, not too short. And your speech was perfect.'

'Are you heading home now?'

Home? He made it sound like they lived together.

'No, I have to go back to work.'

'But you'll be over tonight, right?'

'Of course.' She couldn't wait to be in the midst of one of Joe's famous parties, her first time ever to be invited.

'Why don't you drop by, Senior Chief?' Joe asked, but his invitation lacked warmth. 'You should've received an invitation.'

'I did, sir,' said Solomon. 'I'll do my best.'

Joe reached for Penny's elbow. 'Come back in. It's cold out here.'

Was he rescuing her?

As he held the door for her, she took a peek at his face. He looked tense and moody.

A suspicion stitched through Penny's consciousness that Joe was jealous. Hope floated like a bubble, then burst. Jealous of what? Joe could have any woman he wanted, and he didn't want her. He'd made that clear the other night.

He'd also just invited Solomon to his party along with all the other male friends he wanted her to meet.

No, in his eyes, she would always be the girl next door.

14

'Whoa,' Lia gasped, halting in her tracks. 'I didn't see you there.'

Of course she didn't. Vinny was dressed in jungle-green fatigues that kept him hidden in the shadows by Joe's front step. She hadn't known he was there until he stepped into the light and blocked her way. The throb of techno music, indiscernible from Lia's pounding heartbeat, carried through the closed windows, letting her know that the party was well under way.

'Sorry,' Vinny said, his crooked smile notably absent. 'Didn't mean to frighten you.' He raked her with an incinerating gaze. 'You look beautiful.'

'Thanks.' Her red-silk dress, reminiscent of a traditional Chinese qipao, seemed to glow in the moonlight. Tonight she intended to cut loose, to forget the new story she was putting together and to forget her lingering regrets over letting Vinny slip through her fingers.

But here he was, reawakening the yearning she'd tried to put to rest. 'I didn't know you were invited,' she said in a shaky voice.

'I wasn't. I came to tell you that I'm going wheels up.'

She shivered in the night air. 'I don't know what that means.'

'It means I'll be gone. Can't say where, can't say why, can't say how long.'

The agitation she'd been suffering all week morphed into nerve-snapping tension. 'Why does that sound so dangerous?' she asked.

His cocky smile made a brief appearance. 'What do you think I do for a living? Shoot pea shooters at Boy Scouts?'

She felt an overwhelming urge to cry. She'd worked so hard to convince herself she didn't want him — didn't need him. Here he was, telling her that he was going away. But rather than relieve the struggle inside her, the news devastated her.

'I saw your sister at the change-of-command ceremony today,' he volunteered.

'I was invited, but I couldn't get off work.' She shivered again, wishing now she'd brought a coat.

'How's the new job?' Vinny asked.

'Fine.' Her voice sounded strangled, far away. 'I'll be moving back into my apartment soon.' As soon as it was safe to move back.

With the small talk used up, silence coiled around them, redolent with unarticulated desires. 'I came because I needed to say goodbye to you,' Vinny explained. *Just in case I don't come back.*

He didn't say the words aloud, but Lia's heart heard them loud and clear. It was wartime, after all. Soldiers didn't always make it home. The realization struck her like a bolt of lightning: *Vinny could die.*

Her eyes pooled with tears.

'Hey, life doesn't come with guarantees,' he soothed, sounding older than his years.

And wasn't that the truth? One day she'd been kissing her daddy goodbye, sending him off on a business trip. The next, they'd been lowering his coffin into the ground. She didn't want to go through that despair again or lose control by trying to numb the pain by any means possible.

With a cry of fear, Lia threw her arms around Vinny's neck and hugged him hard. He pulled her into him, infusing her with his warmth, his scent, his energy. She could feel his heart beating through his camouflage jacket. Despite all the reasons she'd come up with to avoid him, it felt so right to be in his arms again.

She envisioned him parachuting into a desert filled with rebels or into a jungle rife with drug runners, and she clutched him closer still. 'How long do you have?' she asked, determined to seize happiness while she could.

'Tonight?' She felt him consult his watch. 'Bout an hour.'

She drew back, just far enough to see his face in the shadows. 'Come back to my house with me,' she begged. Desperation mingled with anticipation.

He stood very still, searching her face in the moonlight. 'You have to make me a promise first,' he said.

Feeling his arousal thicken against her pelvis, she would have promised him anything. 'What?'

'Tell me you'll be mine when I get back.'

The words slipped over her like a noose, closing off her airway. But the need to get a fix of joy before he left was too intense. 'I'm already yours.' Even as she said those words, she realized with a sense of shock that they were true. She was addicted to him — to the warmth and laughter he offered her. No wonder she'd been miserable without him.

He kissed her then, with all the toe-curling passion that he'd branded into her memories. She realized that this was what she'd wanted all along, to truly love again, holding nothing back, the way she'd loved her father — only with benefits.

'Come on.' He flashed his grin, and together they raced toward Penny's house.

Too late, Lia forgot that her watchdogs

were ever vigilant, keeping an eye out for intruders. She and Vinny were impaled by their spotlight as it shot out from across the street at them.

'Jesus!' Vinny swore, flinching from it.

'Just ignore them,' Lia advised, and they ran like a pair of jailbreakers for the door.

'Those are the cops you ditched the other day,' he guessed.

'I'll explain another time,' she promised. They weren't going to talk tonight. She had better things to do with her mouth, and only one hour in which to do it.

★ ★ ★

'What are you doing?'

With a guilty start, Penny looked up from the cutting board. She hadn't heard anyone approach the kitchen, but there stood Joe, the affable host, in his champagne-colored button-up shirt, beer bottle in hand. He'd hadn't been ignoring her, but he'd been working the crowd, introducing the latest guest to arrive, his new executive officer, Lieutenant Gabe Renault.

'Just refreshing the cheese plate. The Cheddar was almost out.'

He put his bottle down. 'I didn't invite you over to play hostess,' he chided. 'Here, give me the knife; I'll do that.'

Thinking she'd overstepped her bounds, Penny relinquished the knife without protest. 'Sorry.'

He cut her a funny look. 'Why don't you come upstairs and play pool with us?' he suggested. He'd already introduced her to his buddies — four guys from Team Three — and as she'd expected, they'd obliged her with small talk, but not one of them found her interesting. Lieutenant Renault had watched her with detached gold-green eyes that made him look like a cat. Going by the gold band on his left hand, he was taken.

'I was thinking of trying the hot tub,' she confessed. In addition to Joe's male guests, there were women in the game room upstairs, including one of Joe's longtime playmates. Leslie was everything Penny wasn't — tall, vivacious, and blessed with big breasts. Penny didn't enjoy watching her fawn over Joe.

She would rather climb into the hot tub alone, or go home, for that matter. Only Vinny's car was parked outside, and Lia hadn't made it to the party, which meant that those two were likely having a party of their own at Penny's house. Everyone was getting it on but her. And she was getting damn tired of it.

'Did you bring your swimsuit?' Joe asked her.

'What, I can't get in naked?' Penny quipped with an edge to her tone.

That brought his gaze up. A shiver ran through her as he assessed her figure under the aqua-blue sheath dress she wore. Lia had suggested the push-up bra. Joe's lingering look told her that he'd noticed, and Penny flushed self-consciously.

'You'd be taking your chances getting in naked,' he warned in a soft voice.

Penny's mouth went dry. Flustered by the comment, she turned to pour herself a second margarita. Was he serious? Nah, he couldn't be. He had Leslie here to keep him entertained.

As if to prove it, he hefted the cheese plate and reached into the fridge for another beer. 'Why don't you come up?' he urged again as he headed for the stairs.

The doorbell rang. He looked down at his full hands.

'Go ahead. I'll get it,' she offered. 'Whoever it is, I'll bring them up.'

'Thanks, sweetheart,' he said, in the tone of a man shackled to his wife. With that, he carried his beer and the cheese plate up the stairs to the bonus room.

Penny headed to the door. Was that a subtle

putdown? Maybe her helpfulness left him feeling obligated, trapped? Perhaps he preferred a woman who wasn't observant enough to notice that the hors d'oeuvres were disappearing. Who cared about munchies anyway, as long as the sex was good?

She yanked open the door with more force than necessary, nearly spilling the margarita in her other hand. Her breath congealed at the sight of Solomon McGuire standing on Joe's doorstep with his hands plunged into his pockets. He wore a black turtleneck, no coat. His eyes seemed to slice straight through her.

'You made it,' she said, with a sudden case of jitters.

'I wanted to see you,' he replied.

A thought occurred to Penny that made her knees wobble and her heart race. She didn't have to be the only person not getting a piece of the action tonight. For whatever reason, Senior Chief McGuire was pursuing her. And he was handsome in a rugged, intense sort of way. After five long years of celibacy, she'd be an idiot to turn him down.

★ ★ ★

Vinny had to break for air. He could hold his breath underwater for nearly two minutes, but he couldn't kiss Lia against the front door and feed his starving lungs at the same time, because his heart was galloping. 'Shit,' he muttered, a little alarmed by how badly he was shaking. He'd thought himself sexually experienced, but he'd never wanted a woman the way he wanted Ophelia Price. Her name was like a litany in his brain.

'Take me upstairs,' Lia hinted.

He scooped her into his arms, eliciting a squeal of surprise. Opting to keep the lights off, he took the steps two at a time. 'Which way?' he asked as they neared the second floor. She was kissing his neck with hot, openmouthed kisses that utterly distracted him.

'Across the hall.'

He kicked the door open, stalked across the moonlit room, and tossed her onto the four-poster bed. Lia's scream of laughter thrilled him. He stood there, struck by the depth of his need for her. Every inch of her inflamed him, from the dainty sandals that she kicked off her feet, to the opaque stockings encasing her slim legs, to the china-red silk that sheathed her from shoulder to thighs.

With a sense of desperation, he knew that one hour would never be enough. Not even one year.

Maybe not a lifetime.

He clawed at his uniform, fumbling to release the buttons. He flung his jacket on the floor and yanked his T-shirt over his head. With eyes that glimmered in the moonlight, she watched him, heightening his urgency.

He scrabbled with the laces of his boots, kicked them off, shucked off his pants and boxers, and then he was naked, praying that the planes of his body and the proud, flushed proof of his desire would be pleasing to her.

She sat up to look at him. 'Oh, my God,' she breathed, reaching out to touch him. 'You're so . . . ' Her soft hands slid from his pectorals to his hips. She brushed her fingers lightly over the head of his cock. 'Unbelievably beautiful.'

He'd never been called beautiful before, but the compliment bolstered his confidence. If he could be the youngest SEAL to make the teams, he could make Ophelia his.

The thought fragmented into a thousand pieces when she bent her head and put her lips around him.

Jesus, Joseph, and Mary, he did not want to think about how she'd gotten so good at that. Swear to God, he could feel her tonsils.

It was fear that made him pull away. He wanted this to be unlike any experience she'd ever had.

Slow down.

But the textures that greeted him — the silk of her dress, the satin heat of her skin, the coyness of her darting tongue — brought on sensory overload. Taking the dress off her proved impossible. He managed to unzip it, to pull the sleeves down her arms, so that it bunched just below her belly button ring. Groping under her skirt, he encountered pantyhose and shredded them. 'Sorry,' he said, but he wasn't, especially when he realized she wore nothing underneath. 'You are so damn naughty,' he muttered.

The scent of her, the memory of her responsiveness the last time, was just too much. He jerked her to the edge of the bed, and like a fifteen-year-old behind a car steering wheel, put the pedal to the metal, pressing all the way to the floor.

She let out a cry that managed to penetrate his haze of lust. 'Did I hurt you?' he asked with remorse.

'No!' She writhed against him. 'Do it again!'

Those were the words he'd used on her in the light-house. His lust doubled. 'Don't worry.' He intended to do it again. And again. And again.

Only he needed to put on a condom first. 'Oh, shit! Wait,' he begged. Somehow he found the willpower to pull out of her.

It took several seconds to get his pants right-side-out in order to find the pocket that the condom was in. He covered himself with hands that shook, distracted by Lia's impatient little noises.

Finally, he was protected. Vinny threw himself on top of her. She was already spreading her thighs, lifting her hips. He was buried inside her in less than a second, lust pounding through him, making him less than gentle.

The antique bed creaked. Lia was louder, urging him to go harder, faster, deeper. He clung to his composure by a thread.

She whispered something in his ear, and the thread completely snapped.

Oh, no. Vinny fought to keep a lid on the geyser that rushed up to overtake him. *Not yet.* But he couldn't stop himself. She was just too hot, too eager, too fucking beautiful.

The minute the waves of ecstasy ceased their crashing, he lifted his head to apologize. But instead of looking dismayed, he found her wearing the dreamiest smile imaginable. 'That was amazing,' she murmured. 'Fast, but amazing.'

Vinny tingled. Her words had an instantaneous effect on him. He gave an experimental thrust. Oh, yes, he was still plenty geared up and good to go. 'Let's do it again,' he suggested, 'only slower this time.'

Her eyes flew open. 'Are you serious?'

'Do I feel serious?'

'Oh, my God.' She gaped at him in wonder. 'You can really do it more than once?'

'With you, I could do it all night,' he swore. And he knew it was true, except he had only one hour.

She seemed to remember that fact in the same instant he did. A look of regret replaced her wonder, and then she was reaching for him, pulling him down for a soul-searching kiss.

If I die tonight, Vinny thought, surrendering to bliss, *I will surely die a happy man.*

★ ★ ★

Lounging in Joe's hot tub under a string of colorful lanterns, Penny thought of the time her father'd taken her fishing out in the Chesapeake Bay. The bluefish she'd hooked weighed almost as much as she did. She'd needed her father's help to reel it in.

Daddy wasn't alive to help her right now. And the fish she'd snagged on her latest lure was the size of a shark.

Oh, help, cried the part of her that was still sober. Solomon McGuire was showing her how long he could hold his breath underwater, but that wasn't the only thing he was doing.

He was nibbling his way up her bare legs, starting with her toes. She wasn't ordinarily ticklish, but the rasp of his moustache had her clutching the sides of the hot tub to keep from jumping out of her skin. She felt especially susceptible in the itty-bitty hot-pink bikini Ophelia had insisted she borrow.

Why was Solomon moving this fast? One minute they'd been talking about constellations, bringing back memories of an astronomy course she'd taken in college, and the next he was telling her he could breathe underwater.

Of course, she'd scoffed at that, and he'd had to prove it. Before she knew it, he was nibbling her toes under the water, making her giggle and squirm. He'd held her fast. He'd moved to her ankles, then her calves. Now he was licking the undersides of her knees, which at first made her laugh. But then laughter subsided into panting, because the message was absolutely clear. He intended to devour her.

She wanted that, too, didn't she?

Half of her insisted that she did. If she couldn't learn to be more spontaneous and sensual, like her sister was, she might never find a man to share her life with. The stimulating jets of water and the memory of Joe's kiss both compelled her to release her inhibitions.

Okay, Solomon wasn't Joe. But he was a man, and he knew just what to do to get her worked up. Every nerve in her legs, from her toes up, was tingling. His brand of foreplay was as unique as the man was himself, but she wanted the experience of being desired, pursued, completed in the most elemental way.

If Joe wouldn't give her that, then Solomon would.

Thankfully, he came up for air, breaching the water's surface with stealth that made her feel more like his prey than a prospective lover.

'I guess you can breathe underwater,' she marveled, her voice sounding thin and high.

'I cheated,' he admitted. 'I sucked air out of the jets.' He moved in closer, closer, closer. Unable to sustain the force of his unblinking gaze, Penny shut her eyes and submitted to his kiss.

Oh, dear. It was more of an invasion than a kiss. He locked his mouth over hers and dove in, demanding acquiescence, stealing her solitude.

With a gasp of astonishment, she hung on

tight. His shoulders were made for that. She marveled how she could feel utterly secure and so vulnerable at the same time.

He pulled her toward the center of the tub, forcing her to relinquish her hold on the sides. She had nothing now to cling to but his dense body. Like a giant octopus, he wrapped his arms around her. The sensations washing through her were unsettling but intoxicating. He pinched her nipples, and she gasped at the sparks that shot toward her womb. Her thighs quivered. She could sense his tumescence, close but not quite touching. It both intimidated and enthralled her.

A flicker at the windows caught her eye. With a self-conscious gasp, Penny realized Joe was watching. Regret collided with recklessness, and it was a heady combination, given the alcohol she'd imbibed earlier.

Unsure and unwilling to question her motivations, she rose partway out of the water, just enough to put her breasts even with Solomon's mouth. He nipped her, as she knew he would, through the fabric of her swimsuit.

Joe turned abruptly from the window.

With a stab of regret, Penny realized that what she really wanted was to be rescued, before it was too late.

15

'Party's over,' Joe said to his former teammate, Todd Hadley. 'Help me get everyone out of the house.'

Todd shot him a disbelieving look. 'Are you kidding me?'

'No,' said Joe. The scar on his cheek felt like it was burning. His face was hot. His temper was raging.

The lens of inebriation fell from Todd's eyes. 'What's going on?' he demanded.

'It's personal,' said Joe, who had not the slightest clue as to why he was furious. Penny was enjoying herself in his hot tub with his new senior chief. So what? Big deal. He'd introduced her to four or five guys himself tonight.

But his blood pressure soared. 'I need everyone out of here in two minutes.' Because, from what he'd seen, Penny was going to be eaten alive in under five. He didn't need anyone witnessing a potentially ugly scene between him and his new most senior enlisted.

Todd gestured toward Leslie, who was showing off her best side while pretending to shoot pool. 'What about her?'

'Everyone,' Joe repeated. Thankfully his new XO, Lieutenant Renault, had left half an hour ago, or he'd think Joe was crazy.

'Whatever, man,' said Todd with a look of deep concern. 'But you owe me an explanation. Listen up, people,' he added, raising his voice to be heard over the techno music. 'The party's moving to my house. Joe just got a call from the office. He's gotta go to work.'

Perfect, thought Joe, grateful for Todd's ability to mobilize and direct. 'Thanks for coming,' he called, backing toward the stairs. 'I gotta change and go.'

'Let's move,' he heard Todd call out.

'Joe, wait!' Leslie cried.

Pausing on the bottom step, Joe watched her breasts jiggle as she hurried to catch up to him. Professing profoundest disappointment, she clung to his collar and pouted.

Joe muttered a cliché about success and responsibility. Dodging her kiss, he gave her a quick hug and retreated to his bedroom, where he paced back and forth, waiting for his guests to leave.

Am I drunk? he wondered, thinking back on the number of beers he'd had. Only three. So he wasn't drunk. Not enough to explain the urge to pummel McGuire into the ground

— not that such a feat was even possible. The man wasn't as tall as Joe, but he was built like a bull, with a hard edge to his character that made him a dangerous enemy.

Joe paused at the window. Perverse curiosity got the better of him. He bent the blinds to peer out on his deck. What he saw made his temples throb. Senior Chief McGuire's hands were underneath the water. Penny's arms were wrapped around his shoulders. Her eyes were closed; she was biting her lower lip.

The blind snapped back into place. Joe clenched his hands and then unfurled them. He wondered what was so wrong with the scene outside that he'd had to chase his guests out of his house. He could hear the last few leaving now.

'Clear!' Todd shouted, shutting the door.

Joe counted to twenty. Digging deep for a semblance of clam, he left his bedroom, went straight to the back door, and stepped out onto the patio, slamming the door shut to announce his presence.

Penny sprang out of Solomon's arms like a clown out of a jack-in-the-box. The senior chief turned his silvery gaze on Joe, noted his rigid stance, and smiled cynically.

'Everyone's gone home,' said Joe, stepping close enough to see the scrap of a swimsuit

Penny wore beneath the water. Her face was the same hot pink.

He depressed the buttons on the side of the tub, silencing the jets and extinguishing the lights to afford her some belated modesty. Still, the lanterns strung overhead kept her chagrin illuminated. Her gaze darted from him to Solomon and back again as she picked up on the tension between the two men.

'It's time for you to leave,' Joe said to his senior chief.

'As you wish, sir.' Solomon rose from the tub like Poseidon, still shamelessly aroused. Water streamed over his powerful torso, glinting like rivers of mercury as he swung his feet to the deck. He reached for the towel and briskly rubbed himself. All the while, his mouth remained quirked in that sardonic smile.

Tossing the towel aside, he scooped up his carefully folded clothing. 'Is there a back gate?' he asked

'Yes, there is,' said Joe, tipping his head. 'That way.'

'Good night, sir. Ma'am.'

'Good night,' Penny murmured. Her eyes followed him as he marched off the deck into Joe's yard wearing nothing but the black briefs he'd gone into the tub with.

Not a word was spoken until the gate clicked shut.

Penny whipped her head around. 'I can't believe you were so rude to him!' she cried, pushing to her feet to stand up. Even in the shadows, Joe could make out her nipples. Stiff from the cold or from the senior chief's fondling? he wondered.

'Having sex in my hot tub is rude,' he countered.

His words kept her mute for a full three seconds. 'And why is that?' she demanded on a saucy note, 'Because you weren't the one doing it?'

'What the hell were you thinking?' he shot back, ignoring her argument. He tossed her a dry towel as she clambered out of the tub, but not before glimpsing her sleek bare thighs. Solomon had been caressing them, he thought with a pang of regret.

'I can't believe you are lecturing me,' Penny marveled, tossing the towel over her shoulders. 'Isn't that the pot calling the kettle black?'

He put a hand to his scar, which was still burning him. 'Come on, Penny. Can't you see that the man's just using you for sex?' he snapped.

She gave a short laugh, looked at him, and then threw back her head and guffawed.

Infuriated, Joe stood there, grinding his teeth.

'Perfect,' Penny added, her laughter curtailing abruptly. She sent him a fulminating look. 'You don't want me, but you don't want anyone else to have me, either. Thanks a lot.'

She marched into the cabana and slammed the door behind her, locking it intentionally. The light came on, followed by the shower. Steam poured out of the vents up by the ceiling.

What the hell? Had she just accused him of not wanting her?

Stunned, Joe mulled over the accusation. It might have been true at one time, but now that he'd gotten to know her better, of course he wanted her. She was amazing. The only reason he hadn't stolen more than a kiss the other night was because he respected her, obviously more than she respected herself.

He stalked to the shower house door and pounded on it.

'What?' she demanded, obviously still spitting mad.

'Who the hell said I didn't want you?' he demanded.

'I can't hear you,' she called back.

That had to be a lie. She could hear him just fine. Too bad for her, a locked door was not a deterrent, not when the key was sitting on the lintel right over his head. He snatched it up and let himself in.

Startled by his abrupt entrance, Penny backed to the far side of the shower spray. Given the dimensions of the cabana, she was just out of arm's reach.

The single bulb overhead revealed that she'd removed the bikini she'd been wearing. She stood there, back to the wall, perfectly naked, her female form flecked in water droplets, cringing from the cold air he'd let in.

Joe shut the door. The pressure in his head rushed straight to his groin, making him suddenly, painfully aroused. She looked beautiful.

'The problem with the senior chief,' he articulated gutturally, 'is that the man doesn't respect women.'

'Oh, and you do,' she retorted, pushing off the wall to prop her hands on her hips. She looked magnificent like that.

'Yes, I do,' he growled, distracted by her pert little breasts. His palms itched to touch them.

'Well, thank you very much, but respect isn't what I wanted tonight.'

Her words snatched his gaze upward. With a sense of shock, he realized that his proper little neighbor was as human as he was. The itch in his palms spread elsewhere. 'You want to be disrespected?' he asked, reaching for the buttons on his shirt. 'I can arrange that.'

Penny's eyes widened, but she didn't utter a word to stop him. Joe kept undressing, yanking his shirt out of his jeans and tossing it onto the bench along with his undershirt. He kicked off his shoes and shucked his jeans, not caring that he dragged them through the water pooling on the floor.

At last, he was as naked as she was. They stood on opposite sides of the steam-filled cabana, staring at each other. Then, in the next instant, through some unspoken form of agreement, they met under the shower spray, a collision of desire.

Joe tangled his fingers into Penny's hair. Picturing her in the senior chief's arms, his temper surged, and he tugged her head back to deliver a punishing kiss. She returned it in equal measure. Unable to grab hold of his shorter hair, she seized his ears and speared her tongue into his mouth. She had to stand tiptoe deliver that retribution.

She was as hot and feisty as any woman he'd ever been with. He wanted to think that it was him and not Senior Chief McGuire who'd turned her heat up. A possessive shudder went through him as he splayed his hands over every inch of her slippery-wet

281

body. He'd been raised an only child. He did not like to share.

But he couldn't get enough, either. Frustrated by their height difference, Joe cupped her bottom and lifted her off her feet. At the same time, she practically climbed him, coiling her legs around him, seeking purchase.

Oh, yeah, now they fit, and it felt incredible. Her soft, wet skin rubbed against his. Anchoring her against the wall, he freed one hand to twist the showerhead so that water rained between them. She glanced at it, smiled, and offered herself to the wet massage.

God damn, she was hotter than he'd ever imagined. The glazed look in her heavy-lidded eyes, the flush in her cheeks, it excited the hell out of him. He wanted to watch her come.

Aligning her spread thighs beneath the water's spray, he watched it lick at her. She was beautiful down there, so pink and full, like a lush flower soaking up a heavy rain. She moaned and touched her breasts, and it made his knees tremble. When her tongue darted out to lick the water off her lips, he couldn't stand it anymore. He had to kiss her mouth, to be the recipient of her passion, not just a spectator.

He groped along the ledge for the condoms he kept handy. Lifting his lips from hers, he tore the foil package open with his teeth.

'I've gotta put you down,' he warned, letting her slip to her feet.

She looked dazed, like she'd lost track of where she was. 'Where'd you get that?' she asked, eyeing the prophylactic.

'Up there.'

She glanced at the ledge. She looked back at him. And the disillusionment in her eyes was like a slap in the face. 'So this is a regular thing for you?' she asked. 'Nail the girl in the cabana, which is conveniently located right beside the hot tub?'

'Uh . . . ' Her dismay — not to mention the explicit way she said it — left him momentarily without words. He fell back on honesty. 'Come on, Penny. I've been your neighbor for three years. You know I'm not exactly celibate.'

Her eyes took slow measure of him as she contemplated her decision. His erection gave a throb of denial that she was going to put an end to this now.

He needed this. He really, really needed this for reasons he didn't want to think about. 'Look, it's up to you,' he ground out, 'but it's pretty damn obvious what I want.' His face was on fire.

283

'Just tell me something,' she demanded, a vulnerable look on her shadowy face. 'Are you doing this because you feel obligated to me?'

Joe tried to follow her line of thought. 'What? No. Of course not.'

He tried to nudge her chin up to better see her in the scant light, but she pushed his hand away.

'Then maybe you feel sorry for me or something,' she suggested.

'Penny!' he exclaimed in frustration. 'Look at me. This is not the result of pity — or obligation.'

As she took him in, visibly swallowing at the sight he presented, his desire surged to new heights. 'I've wanted you for a while now,' he heard himself admitting. 'Ever since I saw you naked at your bathroom window.' At her shocked expression, he continued, 'Yeah. I was checking the security of your home and you were up in your bathroom, getting ready to shower or something. I liked what I saw, Penny. Every time you massage my back, I have to fight my body's response to you. And your eyes, they hit me right here.' He put a fist on his stomach. 'And that's not all,' he added. 'I came back from duty an emotional wreck and you marched right up to me and made me talk. You forced me to deal

284

with my issues. So don't try and tell me that this is a pity fuck, because if it is, it has to be you who is taking pity on me.'

At his words, a strangled cry came out of Penny and she launched herself into his arms. He caught her face and kissed her, shuddering with relief and a renewed surge of desire.

It was all he could do get the condom on now, he was shaking so badly. He needed to get her legs around him, to bury himself inside her *now* before she changed her mind. He grabbed her bottom and lifted her, pleased by how tenaciously she wrapped her legs around him. Then he kissed her, gauging her response to the invasion of his body by the way her tongue played against his.

The sensation of Joe taking of her body brought a moan of wonder to Penny's lips. Oh, my God, she'd forgotten how elemental sex could be. After Brad abandoned her, she'd turned her needs off, shut them down completely. It had been her best defense against disillusionment. But with desire riding on a hot tide of pleasure, she wondered how she'd ever lived without this. The sounds of repletion issuing from her throat sounded oddly familiar, like the voice of a long-lost friend.

She clung to Joe's broad shoulders, reveling

in the restrained power of his much bigger body. She could sense him holding back. For her sake, he was being so gentle with her. She ground herself down on him, urging him to just let go.

'Penny,' Joe muttered against her lips. 'This feels so damn good.' He sounded shaken. 'Tell me you're okay,' he requested.

'I'm better than okay,' she reassured him. Ecstasy was winding itself around her womb, drawing her tighter and tighter. Every deep stroke brought her closer to the edge of release. 'Oh, Joe!' she cried, riding the climax that exploded suddenly within her. To her delight, she felt him shudder and groan. How amazing it was that she — plain Penny — could have this effect on him!

In the wake of the storm, they clung to each other, dazed and shaken. The only sound was that of their ragged breathing.

'I have to sit down,' Joe finally confessed. He found the bench and collapsed, keeping her in his lap. 'My knees are knocking,' he said with a self-directed laugh. He caught her face in his hands and kissed her. 'You were incredible.'

'You don't have to say that,' she told him.

His smile fled. 'Damn it, Penny, I'm not flattering you. I'm serious. That was . . . ' he groped for the right word. 'Thrilling,' he added.

She could tell he was serious, as well as puzzled by their sexual compatibility. 'It was,' she agreed, wondering what had made it so special.

They exchanged a long look, as if reassessing each other, shifting preconceptions.

'You don't have to worry that I have all kinds of expectations now,' she felt compelled to assure him.

He looked suddenly nonplussed. 'Penny,' he protested.

'I know you're not exactly . . . a one-woman man,' she interrupted, aware that the condom was probably leaking — didn't he care? 'And I'm okay with that. I want us always to be honest with each other. I just needed to feel . . . sexy again.'

'I'm happy to oblige,' he said lightly, a little remotely. But then his head came up alertly. 'Someone's ringing the doorbell,' he announced.

Penny groaned. 'Maybe they'll go away if you don't answer,' she suggested. She wasn't ready for this moment to end.

'Good idea,' said Joe. His gaze returned to her face, and he leaned forward and kissed her, slowly, thoroughly. She could feel him quickening inside her.

The distant ringing of the doorbell ceased.

Penny privately rejoiced. From what she could tell, Joe intended to do what they just did all over again.

'Stand up a sec,' he suggested with a wicked little smile.

She never found out what exactly he had in mind, because the sound of Lia calling her carried over running water. 'Damn,' Penny swore, hearing desperation in her sister's voice.

Joe turned the water off. 'Tell her you're in here with me,' he suggested.

'I'm in here, Lia, next to Joe's hot tub. What do you want?' She couldn't bring herself to say that Joe was with her.

A mutter and a sniffle preceded the sound of footsteps on Joe's deck. 'Do you know what time it is?' Lia inquired. 'It's half past midnight. Aren't you coming home?'

'She sounds upset,' Penny whispered, accepting the towel Joe pushed into her hands.

'Talk to her,' he said, shaking out his own towel.

'Are you all right, Ophelia?' Penny called, wrapping herself for warmth. Cold air was pouring in through the slits at the top of the cabana's walls.

'I don't know, I . . . ' She broke off with a

muffled sob. 'I'm just confused. I just wanted to talk, but you never came home.'

Penny sent Joe a torn look.

'She needs you,' he mouthed. 'Go.'

Penny clutched the towel regretfully. She'd wanted so badly to stay with Joe tonight, to make all her fantasies come true.

'Are you with Joe in there?' Lia suddenly asked, on an incredulous note.

'I'll be right out,' Penny promised.

'No! No, I'm all right. Please.' She retreated quickly. 'Stay. I didn't mean to interrupt.'

With a sigh, Penny glanced back at Joe. Now *she* wanted to cry because the moment was gone, the spell broken.

'She needs you,' Joe repeated. 'It's okay. I know where to find you,' he said with a wolfish grin.

'Thanks. Can you reach my clothes for me?' She pointed to a shelf behind him.

'Sure. Don't forget these,' he added, bending to scoop up the two dripping halves of Lia's bikini.

Penny put them aside as she wriggled quickly into the push-up bra and panties, then the dress. 'Do you have to watch me?' she demanded self-consciously.

Joe stood there with a towel around his hips, unmindful of the cold. 'I'm getting my adrenaline rush,' he explained.

'Yeah, right.' She couldn't believe they'd just become lovers, that she'd calculated the risks and decided to embrace them, but she'd needed to feel sexy and alluring again. She was lucky Joe had been willing to go along with it. Even if all he ever gave her was a romp in the cabana, then so be it. She wasn't going to try to tame him.

'Thank you,' she said, giving his damp torso a quick hug. Before words complicated their recent intimacy, she scooped up the wet bathing suit and left.

★ ★ ★

'Go back to Joe,' Ophelia wailed. 'I'm fine. I should never have come looking for you.'

'I'm not going back,' Penny insisted. She'd found her sister lying face down on the couch, crying noisily into a pillow. 'Tell me what's wrong. You're obviously upset.' She sat down next to her and squeezed the water out of her damp hair.

'I'm such a pain in the ass,' Lia lamented, with a sniff.

'Well, yeah, but I still love you, Lia. I didn't want to overstay my welcome anyway.' She wasn't one of Joe's girlfriends. She refused to categorize herself that way.

Lia rolled onto her hip and looked at her. 'Did you have fun?' she asked. Her eyes were puffy, her mascara running, her dress crumpled.

'Yes,' said Penny, honestly. 'What happened to you?'

Lia's chin trembled. 'Vinny came by. That's why I didn't show up at the party.'

'I know, hon. I saw his car.'

'I'd sworn to myself I was never going to see him again.'

'Because he's too young?' Penny guessed. Empathy welled within her; she knew exactly where Lia was coming from, except that Joe wasn't too young, he was too wild.

'He's twenty years old!' Lia cried. 'And a Navy SEAL! What, am I stupid? That's just asking for heartache.' Her turquoise eyes pleaded for Penny's reassurance. 'He's gone on some freaky mission somewhere that he can't even talk about,' she added, her tears overflowing. 'He could be shot or killed.'

'Oh, honey,' Penny crooned, understanding her fears. 'Vinny's going to be just fine, you'll see. SEALs train day in and day out. They're prepared for just about anything.'

'I know,' said Lia, accepting her comfort. 'It's just so scary. Why couldn't he be an accountant or a dentist or something?'

Penny gave a wistful laugh. Why, indeed?

'I always thought I could choose who I fall in love with,' her sister added, on a thoughtful note. 'But it's not like that, is it?'

The truth stitched through Penny's consciousness like a darning needle. Dear God, Ophelia was right. 'No,' she agreed with a sinking heart. 'It's not.'

She had thought she could stay emotionally aloof while awakening her body's dormant responses. Sex and love were supposedly separate entities — to Joe, maybe, but not to her. Having shared that moment with him, her heart was in serious, serious peril.

Truth was, she loved him already; she had for a while.

Only Joe wasn't going to settle down with her and start a family. That had never been in the cards for him.

Doubt nipped belatedly at Penny's heels.

'I think we're both in trouble,' she confessed, giving her sister a hug.

16

Hannah hurried toward the elevator at FBI Headquarters, hoping to grab it before it closed shut. She was troubled by cramps this morning and dismayed by the sign that her cycle was coming, regardless of Luther's determination to get her pregnant. He would be so disappointed.

She didn't notice who had held the elevator for her until he spoke. 'Not awake yet?' he asked her.

She blinked in surprise. 'Rafe — I mean, sir! What are you doing here?'

He bestowed on her the barest suggestion of a smile. As was his custom, he wore a dark silk suit, paired with a snowy white collared shirt and no tie, which left him looking like a priest. Or maybe it was the sad but serene look in his black-as-night eyes. 'It appears,' he said, 'that we might be working on the same case.'

She gasped as the elevator lurched upward. 'You mean those four officers were poisoned with ricin — all of them?'

He gave a faint shrug. 'That's what the tests indicated.'

'Oh, my God.' The doors swooshed open on the second level, and they stepped out, walking past several partitions to Hannah's cubicle. 'I thought my idea was a shot in the dark,' she marveled.

'You have amazing instincts,' Valentino countered. 'That's why I hired you.'

She stopped at her office space. 'I'm sorry it's such a mess,' she apologized. 'I've been running in circles trying to make headway on this case. Here, draw up a chair. Make yourself at home. I'm going to run and get us coffee.' She dropped her briefcase inside the door.

'Hannah?'

'Yes, sir.'

'First of all,' he said placing a settling hand on her shoulder, 'You make me feel so old when you call me 'sir.' ' He wasn't a day over forty. 'Second, I've opted to step down the promotion ladder, so please do call me Rafe.'

'Okay. Rafe.'

'That's better. Now take a deep breath. I'm coming with you to get coffee.'

She drew a deep breath and nodded. 'I'm good now.'

His ghost of a smile was almost real. 'I'm going to enjoy working with you.'

★ ★ ★

Three hours later, Hannah pushed her chair from her desk and rubbed her stiff neck. 'I'm hungry and restless,' she admitted. 'How can you sit that still for so long?'

Rafe dragged his dark gaze from the monitor and looked at her in surprise. 'I don't know,' he said.

'We've pored through hundreds of documents. We've cross-referenced every aspect of the victims' lives, and we still don't have a motive,' she lamented.

'Perhaps we should talk about it over lunch,' he suggested.

'You're only saying that because I said I was hungry,' she accused.

'I'll never tell,' he retorted, rolling to his feet.

While Hannah stretched, he stood there like an undisturbed pond.

She gasped. 'I have an idea.'

'On an empty stomach?'

'Bear with me. It's probably not a good one. Who knows about the ricin poisoning besides you and me?'

'The three techs at Quantico who ran the tests,' he replied.

'What if we were to leak this to the press?' she suggested.

'And we would do this because . . . '

'Number one, so that high-ranking officers

know to be vigilant. This guy might be trying to poison someone else right now. We could save a life. Two, chances are that someone out there knows something we don't, like what these victims all had in common.'

Rafe regarded her thoughtfully. 'I'll think about it,' he promised.

'Fair enough,' said Hannah. 'Let's chow.'

★ ★ ★

Joe rounded his desk to gently close his office door.

His impulse was to slam it. Immediately, the noises that had been distracting him all afternoon were muted, and he heaved a sigh of relief.

Maintaining an open-door policy was an intentional leadership decision, but it was giving him a headache. The buzz of voices, punctuated by laughter in the break room or Senior Chief McGuire's bark, was making Joe as edgy as a Gerber blade.

He returned to his desk and thumped down into his wheeled chair. He found where he'd left off in the manual he was perusing, but after reading the same line three times, he accepted that he'd lost focus.

Joe slapped the book shut. He rubbed his aching eyes. Behind closed lids, he envisioned

Penny the way she'd looked with her legs wrapped around him, her head thrown back, lost in ecstasy. Longing surged through him. He wanted her again, and not just physically. He hadn't spoken to her in days. He missed the sound of her voice.

Glancing at his watch, he wondered if she was home from work yet.

But he needed a reason to call.

While leaving his house at dawn this morning, he'd noticed that the police who were supposed to be guarding Penny were gone. He could inquire into that.

Butterflies swarmed Joe's stomach as he punched an outside line. A minute later, her cell phone was ringing and his heart was doing an inexplicable jog.

'Hello?'

Pleasure broke over him. 'Hey, it's Joe,' he said, as casually as he could manage.

'Oh, hello.' She sounded startled.

'Are you home from work already?' he inquired.

'No, I'm sitting in my office doing paperwork. I usually keep my phone off at work. I guess I forgot to.'

'I'm at the office, too,' he said.

'You've been putting in long hours,' she observed. 'I hardly ever see your Jeep in the driveway.'

Did that mean she'd been looking for him? 'I'm still trying to get my bearings,' he admitted.

'So how's it going?'

He gave a grunt. 'My XO's been great — you met Lieutenant Renault at the party.'

'Oh, yes.'

'He's taught me a lot. The dynamics are different from what I'm used to, though — kind of laid-back. At the same time, we're short-handed with men in the field and the rest of us scrambling to get the paperwork done.'

She hummed sympathetically. 'How's Senior Chief McGuire?'

A sensation similar to jealousy snaked through him. 'Fine,' he said shortly.

'There's no tension between you two?'

Joe hesitated. 'We're professionals,' he said finally. 'We don't let personal stuff drive our working relationship.'

'Well, that's good,' she said.

Silence filled the phone lines before Joe remembered the purpose of his call. 'I noticed your watchdogs weren't out front this morning.'

'Oh, yeah, they got tired of watching the house and tailing Ophelia. Nothing's happened, so they've left us to our own devices.'

'Does Hannah Lindstrom know that?'

'I assume so.'

'But Eric's killer is still on the loose,' Joe pointed out.

'I know,' said Penny. 'They left us a number to call if something happens. At least we've made headway in another area. Get this, you know the military men who've died without any visible cause over the past few years?'

'Uh . . . '

'A deputy Chief of Staff member was the latest one,' she added helpfully.

'It rings a bell,' Joe admitted.

'Hannah told me last Monday that they were poisoned by ricin,' Penny said excitedly, 'in different ways, though, so that the cause wasn't noticed until recently. She thinks it's the same ricin that Eric sold five years ago.'

'Damn,' said Joe, growing more concerned by the moment. 'Obviously the victims had something in common, besides how they were killed, I mean.'

'Yeah, Hannah hasn't figured that out yet. But she's working with a bigwig from D.C. headquarters. I'm sure they'll catch this nut sooner or later.'

'Yeah, but in the meantime, no one's guarding you,' Joe pointed out. Uneasiness gnawed at him.

'I'm thinking of installing an alarm system,' she said, sounding only halfway serious.

'I could, uh, camp out at your place,' Joe suggested, 'if you want some protection.'

'Oh . . . ' That obviously caught her off guard. 'You're busy enough, don't you think?' she hedged.

Did she want him or not? He couldn't tell. 'Look,' he said, opening himself to rejection, 'I wasn't expecting what happened the other night to be a onetime thing,' he confessed. 'I want some more, Penny,' he added in a voice that betrayed his eagerness.

She was silent for way too long. 'Come over tonight,' she finally agreed.

Anticipation flared like a Bunsen burner. 'What time?'

'Whenever you get home. I'll cook dinner for you. Ophelia's working late,' she added.

He grinned at the underlying message that they would be alone. 'Great. I'll be there around six.'

'Okay. See you then,' she said, sounding breathless.

Yeah, she was trying to sound nonchalant, but she wanted the same thing he did.

Joe hung up the phone and glanced at his watch. It showed bad form when a commander left work before his men. He punched the interoffice button connecting him to his XO's office. 'Gabe,' he said.

'Sir.'

'What's it going to take to get everyone out of here by seventeen hundred?'

'Not a problem, sir. When do you want the halls cleared?'

★ ★ ★

'Holy shit! Change the channel back,' Vinny commanded, forgetting the Diet Coke that was stuck in the vending machine.

The two men watching TV in the lounge at Guantanamo Bay's airstrip ignored him. They'd found a comedy show instead.

Vinny lunged for the remote control, snatching it out of Haiku's hands. 'I said change the fucking channel,' he repeated, flicking through the stations.

He groaned out loud. There she was. The woman who occupied his every waking thought was clutching a microphone and reporting the news.

'Hey, come on!' Haiku protested. 'We're watching TV here.'

'You come on. That's my girlfriend,' Vinny boasted, nodding at the TV.

The other two SEALs eyed Ophelia with skepticism. Wearing a snug yellow sweater, her copper hair cascading over her shoulders, she looked hot enough to make Vinny break into a sweat. He focused his hungry gaze on her berry-colored lips and let her husky voice wash over him.

' — from this laboratory at Bio Tech five years ago,' she was saying. 'Ricin is listed on Homeland Security's National Terror Alert as a toxin attractive to terrorists. It is a stable but lethal substance, deadly if inhaled, ingested, or injected into the bloodstream. This is exactly what happened to Sergeant Master Ernest Aimes, U.S. Marine Corps; Colonel Luis Powell of the U.S. Army; Navy Commander Jonathan Pruitt; and most recently General Casey Fripp of the U.S. Joint Chiefs of Staff, four men who for reasons unknown were poisoned, possibly by the very ricin that disappeared from BioTech in 2002.

'Whoever murdered these four men is also believed to have killed two of BioTech's technicians. Danny Price died in a hit-and-run in 2002, soon after the ricin's disappearance.' The photo of Danny Price made Vinny's nape prickle. Was it his imagination, or did Ophelia look exactly like the man?

Danny *Price*. He even had the same last name as her.

Stunned by the possibility, he processed little about the murder of the second lab tech, other than the fact that it'd happened just recently. The conviction that Lia was invested in this news story kept him from hearing another word. He could read it in her body language, in the way she clutched the mike.

She'd never indicated to him that her father had been murdered. But apparently he had, by some freak who was now targeting military officers.

'Oh, man,' Haiku exclaimed, oblivious to Vinny's racing thoughts. 'She is on fire, brother! You go!' He turned to give Vinny a high five, but Vinny was digging for change in his pocket. He needed to call Ophelia and find out what this was all about.

Fuck! Here he was, ass-deep in a mission that would take him back to Haiti shortly, and his woman was stateside embroiled in a murder scandal. He looked down at his hand. He had twenty-six cents.

'Let's go, Echo Platoon!' shouted a voice from the end of the hallway. 'Helo's waiting.'

Vinny swore out loud. He glanced longingly at the pay phone even as he snatched up his rucksack.

There were times that he really hated being a SEAL, and this was one of them.

Damn it to hell, he hadn't even gotten his soda out of the vending machine!

★   ★   ★

Buzz Ritter had known this moment was coming. He was counting on it, calculating how much he could get away with asking for this time.

His cell phone vibrated within five minutes of the news broadcast. He smirked as he recognized the number. 'Ritter here,' he purred.

'Did you watch the news — Channel Ten?'

'Yes, I did,' said Ritter. Nor was he the least bit concerned. By terminating Tomlinson, he'd tied off what he considered to be the last loose string. Should've happened five years ago, as far as he was concerned.

But the caller sounded panic-stricken. 'I thought you had contacts at the Bureau. Are you going to tell me you didn't know about this earlier? They've made the connection, damn it!'

'I guess they have,' Ritter agreed, knowing that as yet they knew very little. 'They must have stumbled onto something.'

'Like what?' the caller demanded. 'You said that lab tech you just took out told you nothing. I want answers, damn it!'

'It won't be easy,' Ritter mused, priming his request. 'I'll have to question more people.'

'Don't hurt them,' the caller pleaded. 'That reporter implied that I'd killed those two lab techs. I don't like that, Ritter. You know I don't.'

'Sometimes that's the only way,' Buzz retorted.

'Just ... question people! Get some answers but leave them alive, for God's sake. How hard can that be?'

'Fifty thousand,' said Ritter, throwing out a number.

'Jesus,' the caller complained. 'What do you think I'm made of?'

'Take it or leave it.'

'If they catch me, Ritter,' the caller blustered, 'I'll make damn sure that you go down with me.'

Ritter smiled. 'I don't think so,' he said, cracking his knuckles.

An uncomfortable silence elapsed. 'Fifty thousand dollars,' the caller agreed with defeat. 'I'll wire it as before.'

★ ★ ★

Joe had beat her home, as revealed by the Jeep parked in his driveway. Penny let herself into her own house, eager to spruce up before he came over. To her astonishment, she found him sitting in her living room.

'How did you get in?' she asked, startled, a little taken aback that he would do such a thing.

His gaze was somber. 'Penny, your back door was unlocked,' he said with disapproval and concern.

'Are you sure?' she asked, crossing to the door to check it. 'Oh, it is.'

Joe stood up. He wore a checkered flannel shirt and familiar cowboy boots. Her heart beat faster as he joined her at the door. 'I thought maybe somebody'd broken in, but I don't see any sign of tampering.'

'Did you . . . check upstairs?' she asked, distracted by how good he smelled. He'd gotten to take a shower — not fair.

'No,' he admitted. 'But I haven't heard anything.'

'Maybe we should check upstairs.'

'Of course.' He sent her a suggestive smile, and her concerns faded at the realization that they weren't going to make it downstairs to eat for a while yet.

'I wanted to change first and fix my makeup,' she pleaded.

'You look good just like that.'

'In this old uniform?' She broke away, hoping for a head start. Joe chased her. Laughter erupted from her throat as she raced ahead of him, carefree in a way she hadn't ever been.

A glance into the office had her stumbling to a halt. She switched direction, approaching the open door in amazement and growing horror. The room was a mess, with file cabinets left open and papers and folders scattered all over. 'Oh, my,' she murmured.

Joe's hands settled on her shoulders, and she sagged against him. 'I don't think Ophelia did this,' she decided.

'We need to call Hannah,' Joe agreed.

★ ★ ★

They were not alone again until ten o'clock that night. The house had been dusted for fingerprints and swabbed for trace DNA. But the intruder, whoever he was, was more than just a master picklock. He'd left little behind him to suggest his identity. Whether he'd found what he was looking for was entirely up to speculation.

Hannah, who hadn't known that the state police had pulled the plug, made a furious phone call to McCaully, only to be told that his men were too tied up to guard the Price sisters. They would need to hire bodyguards.

Penny had reassured the FBI agent that she'd be fine. Joe was going to spend the nights at her house. And she'd managed to announce that without blushing, even when Hannah murmured a considering, 'Oh, really?'

But then, Joe wasn't there. He'd popped next door to retrieve an MP5 semiautomatic rifle, which he'd then tucked under Penny's bed. Even without police escorts and with her home recently broken into, Penny had never felt safer in her life.

Although when she emerged from the shower in a silk teddy to find Joe nestled among her pillows without a stitch of clothing on, she had to admit to a sudden sense of vulnerability. Surrounded by flowery pillow shams, he struck her as ruthlessly masculine and potent, like a bad-girl's dream come true.

He smiled wryly at her attire. 'Let me guess. Ophelia loaned you that.'

'Look, don't ruin this,' she warned him. 'I'm a novice at seduction, so bear with me.' She crossed to her bureau to light the rose-scented candles, a feat that almost proved impossible, given her trembling fingers.

He sat up as she approached the bed. Without warning, he pounced.

Penny found herself flat on her back, his hard, warm body pressing her into clean sheets. 'You don't need to seduce me,' he informed her gruffly. 'I've obsessed about you all week. Tonight,' he added with a wicked glint in his deep green eyes, 'I get to take my time.'

A warm shiver went through Penny. His magnetic pull on her was visceral — she could feel it deep within her womb. But he was just obsessed, she reminded herself, and obsession was temporary.

His breath was warm and sweet. He kissed her cheek, her chin, her nose, and finally her lips, with unhurried undulations of his tongue that went on and on, making her heart race, heating her from the inside out so that she melted like the candles on her bureau.

He savored her, making her feel special, unique, the only woman in the world. Half an hour later, he grinned with predatory satisfaction as she moaned, thrashed, panted, and gleamed with desire-induced sweat. 'Joe!' she cried, catching his head in her hands to stop him as he made to push her to the edge yet one more time. 'Please!' she begged.

'What?' he demanded. 'This is payback for all those deep-tissue massages. I had to lie there hard as a rock and not make a sound. You can scream if you want to. That's hardly fair.'

Penny laughed. Joe had turned her bed into a playground. 'You can't make me scream,' she scoffed. 'I'm not that kind of girl.'

'Oh, I can't?' That was all the warning she got before he hooked an arm around her waist, flipped her onto her stomach, and buried himself inside her in a single thrust.

Penny screamed.

'I hope I didn't hurt you,' he said, instantly contrite.

'Oh, no,' she said. 'And don't you dare stop, either.'

He didn't stop. He started and he kept on going until Penny screamed several more times.

Why not? It was just the two of them. Joe was in her bed, doing all those things she'd imagined for so many lonely nights. Except Joe in the flesh was even more inventive than the Joe of her fantasies.

He was magnificent. No wonder women flocked to him in droves.

At last, they lay face to face, limbs tangled, and Joe still wasn't done. Penny felt dreamy, sated, stretched, but content to keep this up all night. He lifted his lips from her neck and fixed her with a heavy-lidded gaze. 'Hey,' he said, smoothing a lock of damp hair off her cheek.

'Hey, what?' she murmured.

'I want us to stay friends,' he said gruffly, 'always.'

After this is over. He didn't say that, but she heard the words all the same. She blinked as reality overshadowed her joy.

'I don't want to hurt you, Penny,' he

added, looking remorseful for something he hadn't done yet.

'It's okay, Joe. I went into this with my eyes wide open,' she reassured him. But her heart still constricted. Just the thought of Joe with another woman shredded her emotionally.

He loosed a sigh and dropped his forehead onto hers. 'See, I am a selfish person,' he reiterated, harking back to a conversation they'd had weeks ago. 'Even when this is over, I'll want to keep you for myself.'

Her heart performed a funny flip. That almost sounded like monogamy; of course, he hadn't meant it that way. Fortunately, Penny was a realist. Expecting Joe to go from bachelor extraordinaire to faithful lover overnight was just plain naive. If being Joe's friend was all she could expect in the long run, then so be it. It was still more than she'd ever expected. 'I promise,' she agreed, 'that we'll still be friends.' *When this is over.*

He braced his weight on his elbows and gathered her closer. Putting his lips to hers, he thrust gently but with intent. Penny felt the difference right away. He wasn't playing anymore.

She clutched his neck and shoulders, driven by a desire that was as much emotional as physical. She could feel Joe's pleasure overtaking him. With an indrawn breath and a muffled roar, it flowed out of him and into her. She cried out as it crashed over her, pulling them both into a perfect, timeless undertow.

17

Penny pushed through her front door at the end of a tedious Monday and paused in surprise. Ophelia was bearing an armload of clothing down the stairs. 'What's going on?' Penny demanded.

'I'm moving back into my apartment,' her sister happily announced. 'Jenny and John have found a place of their own.' She tossed Penny a grin as she sauntered into the laundry room. 'So, I'll finally be out of your hair,' she called. 'Besides, three's a crowd, don't you think?'

Penny squelched the blush heating her cheeks. She trailed Ophelia into the garage to note that her sister had already filled the trunk of her car to capacity.

'And,' Lia added, slamming it shut, 'Vinny's going to be home eventually. When that happens, you'll be glad I'm gone.' The smile she sent her sister struck Penny as forced. Waiting and not knowing was taking a toll on Lia.

'I don't think it's a good time to move out,' Penny argued. 'Hannah says the FBI's been swarmed with calls since you aired the ricin story. Can't you wait until the murderer is caught?'

'That could take months,' Lia pointed out. 'I'm paying rent on an empty apartment.'

'So sublet it again.'

'I can't. The management is furious with me for subletting in the first place. Besides, I miss my things, Pen. I need wind chimes and suncatchers and the flowing water. I need good chi.'

Penny rolled her eyes at the impractical but impassioned argument. 'You need to be careful,' she advised her sister. 'You've got no one to watch over you at your apartment.'

'Are you kidding? No one could get by Mrs. Vatter.'

'The woman across the courtyard?'

'Exactly.'

Penny sighed. 'I want you to get a cell phone,' she insisted, 'and carry it with you at all times, and put that number the state police gave us on speed dial.'

'I will, Mother, I promise,' said Ophelia, giving her sister's cheek a peck. 'Thanks for putting up with me,' she added, her voice growing husky, 'and not just for these past few weeks, either. I know I've taken you for granted all these years. I never realized how much you did for me. It seems so lame just to say thank you.'

Lia's words summoned a rush of tenderness. 'Oh, honey,' Penny cried, giving her sister a fierce hug. 'I'm going to miss you.'

'It's not like I'm moving to Timbuktu,' Lia protested. 'I'll just be ten miles down the road. You won't even know I'm gone.'

That, Penny thought, was the understatement of the year.

★　★　★

Buzz Ritter glared at the intruder through his night vision goggles. *Who the hell is that?*

Wedged between a hedge of boxwoods and a cinder-block foundation, Buzz had waited hours for the right moment to slip unseen into Ophelia Price's apartment. At ten minutes to midnight, the complex stood quiet. He was just about to squeeze out of the bushes when a stranger drifted from the shadows.

Buzz squinted through his NVGs, astonished to discover that the third party not only wore camouflage, he was armed with a blade and a pistol. The young man knocked on Ophelia Price's door and waited. He knocked again. When it still didn't open, he reached into his pants pocket and pulled out a key. Or maybe it was a pick, since it took him a while to work the lock open. He let himself in.

Buzz grumbled with contempt. Obviously, this was a horny boyfriend, dropping in for a quick one. There went his plans to abduct Ophelia tonight, to question her and — he rolled his eyes at the stupidity of his boss — to let her go.

But then the crack of a gunshot split the quiet. It'd come from inside the apartment. 'What the fuck!' Buzz breathed, utterly perplexed.

He waited for someone to retreat, but then the door closest to his head opened, and a middle-aged woman poked her head out. 'Ophelia!' the woman cried, covering her mouth with a hand.

A dry leaf crinkled under Buzz's elbow, and the woman whipped her head around. 'Who's there?'

When he didn't answer, she pulled back, slamming her door shut. He heard her running through the apartment, no doubt headed straight for a phone.

Damnation, Buzz seethed, scuttling out of his hiding place. He would not be grabbing Ophelia Price now. And it was risking too much to stick around in hopes of grabbing her later tonight.

There was more than one way to skin a cat, he comforted himself. The other Price girl was just as likely to have answers. As long as he got his money, what did it matter where he got his information?

★ ★ ★

Lia slept with earplugs. Not even the gurgle of her wall fountain made enough white noise to disguise the shouts and thuds that went with living in an apartment complex. She'd forgotten how bad it was. Sleeping at Penny's had spoiled her.

The drawback of wearing earplugs was — ironically — that she couldn't hear *anything*, and that made her nervous with Eric's killer on the loose. A working woman had to get her beauty sleep, though, so she'd bought a handgun at a pawnshop, trusting her accuracy with a gun over a 911 call any day.

Tonight, something roused Lia from a deep sleep. What had wakened her? she wondered, lifting her head from the pillow to crack a bleary eye.

With an impatient mutter, she pulled the wax plug from one ear and listened.

There it was. A strange sound within her apartment!

With a stab of fear, she slid a hand beneath the adjacent pillow and grasped the Colt Commander she'd taken costly lessons to learn how to shoot. As she swung the barrel toward the door, she pushed up higher on the pillow, suddenly wide awake, her heart thumping earnestly.

The dying flame of a fragrance candle cast eerie shadows on the four walls of her room. The sound didn't come again, but Lia's instincts told her that someone was approaching her cracked door. With a tremor in her fingers, she disengaged the gun's safety.

Maybe she should have stayed with Penny, after all.

The slow opening of her door caused a sudden rash of goose bumps to spike up on her skin. The door yawned open, revealing the silhouette of a man — dark hair, broad shoulders.

Lia squeezed her eyes shut and pulled the trigger.

Bang!

'Holy shit!' the stranger yelped as he dove for cover.

For a shocked moment, she refused to believe that she'd fired a gun at the man she loved.

'Vinny!' she screamed, tossing the Colt aside to throw herself at the foot of her bed. She found him face down on the floor with his hands over his head. At the sound of his name, he peered up at her. Even in the darkness, she could see the disbelief in his eyes.

'Are you fucking crazy?' he yelled.

She cringed at the fury in his voice. 'I thought you were someone else. Did I hit you?'

'No.' He surged to his knees and crawled for the bed. Lia scuttled backward. 'It went whistling past my ear,' he snarled, climbing over the footboard. 'Why didn't you answer when I knocked on your door? I was afraid I was going to find you dead. Jesus! You tried to kill me!'

She lay flat on her back with him looming over her, rigid and outraged. 'You're the last person in the world I would want to kill,' she protested. 'I wear earplugs. I didn't hear you knocking.'

'So you're deaf *and* you own a handgun!'

'Look, you don't know what's going on — '

'Actually, I do,' he corrected her. 'I just came from your sister's house, where we had a nice long chat. What the hell are you trying to prove by living all alone — that you can wind up dead like any other helpless woman?'

'I am not helpless!' She took immediate affront. 'I've been taking shooting lessons.'

'Prove it,' he said, grabbing her wrists and pulling them over her head. At the same time, he pinned her legs beneath her. Lia squirmed, unable to escape. 'Where's your gun now?' he taunted.

'On the floor.' She struggled more earnestly, and he responded by increasing the pressure in her wrists. Tears stung Lia's eyes. 'Stop,' she pleaded. 'Why are you so angry?'

The pressure eased immediately. 'Fuck.' Vinny expelled a sharp breath and released her. He sat back, straddling her hips, sitting on his heels. 'Why didn't you tell me that those cops were for your protection?' he demanded, still irate.

'Because I trusted you to protect me.'

'Bullshit. You didn't want me in your life, remember?'

'That's not true. I mean, it was true then, but it's not now.'

His sudden silence demanded answers. It was time to be honest with him, honest with herself.

'I was so afraid of falling in love with you,' Lia admitted, holding nothing back. 'I still am. Things happen, Vinny. People outgrow each other. People die, like my father died. I'm so afraid of the kind of pain that comes with that.'

She broke off as he caught her face between his hands, his touch now infinitely gentle. 'Listen, Lia,' he demanded, 'I know you're afraid. I am, too — not because I'm younger and I might outgrow you. I'm afraid of losing you to some psycho. I'm freaked out by the way you put yourself on television like a soldier putting himself on the front lines. Jesus!'

'Did you see me?' she asked, pleased to discover that he hadn't missed her first report.

'You were awesome. Whose fuckin' idea was it to have you give that report anyway?'

'The FBI's,' she admitted quietly.

'Why, because your dad was a victim?'

'Because my sister and I gave them information that got the ball rolling in the first place. Did you realize Danny Price was my father?' she added. 'Or did Penny tell you?'

'I figured it out. You look just like him.'

The observation made her eyes sting. 'I loved him so much,' she admitted, her voice breaking. 'When he died, I wanted to die, too. It messed me up so bad. But now we have the chance to catch the bastard who killed him,' she added fiercely. 'And I'll do anything to make that happen.'

Vinny closed his eyes. 'Oh, God. Okay,' he said, opening them again. 'I can understand that. When my mom got cancer, I worked my ass off to take care of her and my sister. So I get how you feel. But it's not your job to catch your father's killer. How do you know he won't come after you for tryin' to expose him? You lock your door and you get a gun and you think you're safe. It's not that simple, *cara mia*. You could be dead right now.'

She had to admit he had a point. 'I'm sorry,' she said in a small voice.

He slipped his fingers through her hair, combing out the silky tangles. 'You're so beautiful in the candlelight. I can't stand the thought of something happening to you.'

Lia hummed at the compliment, tipped her head back, and shrugged the spaghetti strap of her nightie off one shoulder. 'Show me,' she whispered.

Vinny groaned. He stroked his thumbs over the twin points pushing out the fabric.

'When did you get back?' she asked, reaching for the buttons on his jacket. They melted apart beneath her quick fingers.

'Tonight. I came straight from the landing field.' He shook off the jacket and yanked his T-shirt off.

Passion rose like a storm surge, sweeping them both up in its relentless path. They lunged for each other, mouths locking together, making further speech impossible.

Stay with me, Lia thought. *Always and forever, stay with me.*

Vinny tore his mouth from hers to taste the column of her neck, her earlobe, her collarbone. 'You smell so fucking good, I could eat you up.'

'Do it,' she commanded, spreading her limbs in symbolic surrender and ultimate trust.

He growled low in his throat, tickling her bare flesh with the rasp of his five-o'clock shadow. 'The whole time I was gone,' he said, his words broken by kisses as he roamed her body, bunching the silk of her gown, 'I thought about you and . . . what I wanted to do with you. It's gonna . . . take years an' years . . . to get it all done.'

'I'm in no hurry,' she said, breathless, quivering with anticipation.

'Yeah, we'll see about that,' he laughed.

She cried out her gratification when he placed his open mouth against her thigh. This was Vinny. He could make her come in under ten seconds.

As if to prove just that, he dove straight for home base.

The rumble of his laughter as she climaxed added a whole new dimension to her pleasure.

'I thought you weren't in a hurry,' he mocked as she fluttered down from heaven.

'I'm not the one who's fast,' she insisted.

'You're like a vibrator on high speed.'

'Go ahead and blame me,' he said. 'I don't mind.' Somehow, his pants were still on but he was wearing a condom and pushing inside of her.

Lia gasped her amazement. She locked her legs around him, loving the feel of his desperate bid to get closer, deeper. Yet no matter how earnestly they strained, it was never enough. 'More!' she cried, lifting herself to him.

Within minutes, they collapsed, overcome by the devastating proportions of the storm that ripped through them both.

A pounding at the door startled them from their lassitude. 'Police!' shouted a voice. The blue light of a squad car flickered on the walls of her living room, visible through the half-open door. 'Is anyone home?'

Vinny grinned as Lia gasped her consternation. 'Did you think you could shoot me and get away with it?' he asked her, rolling to his feet. 'Cover yourself, and I'll answer it.'

As he headed for the door, discarding the condom and buttoning up his pants, it occurred to Lia that he'd figured the law would descend any minute. No wonder he'd made love to her at the speed of light. That struck her as hilarious.

She was laughing her head off when Vinny answered the door.

★ ★ ★

At seven in the evening, Penny slapped shut the file in her hands. She was done reviewing treatment on her longtime patients, including Admiral Jacobs, whose knees were resistant to therapy and would soon require surgery. She put the folder in the surgery tray for Dr. Huxley to look at.

Snatching up her coat and purse, Penny bade good night to the petty officer at the reception desk and headed for the elevator. The hospital was quiet, with only inpatient and emergency care ongoing past regular hours.

She was halfway across the flyover that conveyed patrons to the parking garage when the lights in the garage ahead of her suddenly blinked off. Penny slowed to a halt. Thanks to the early dusk, the garage, which was usually well illuminated, was utterly dark. She wasn't sure if she could even find her car in the shadowy interior.

But then a figure bearing a flashlight appeared at the threshold ahead of her. 'Sorry, ma'am,' he called out. 'We've got a breaker problem. Can I help you find your car?'

He wore the uniform of a security officer. Relieved to have his help, Penny hurried toward him. She could make out his broad shoulders and a square face, but that was all, as he kept his flashlight pointed toward the cement floor. 'Watch that step, ma'am.'

'Thank you. I parked along the left, inner wall over there.'

He struck out with an efficient stride that had her hurrying to keep up. Their footsteps echoed loudly in the quiet space. Penny dug in her purse for her cell phone. Joe would probably work until seven-thirty, as was his custom. She wanted to ask him if he would prefer pork or chicken tonight. *Let's be honest, here*, Penny, her conscience scolded. *You just want to hear his voice.*

'I'm right over here,' she said to the security guard, catching sight of her Matrix. With the cell phone under one ear, she fished for her keys. 'Thank you,' she said, unlocking her door remotely. She turned her back on him.

'You're welcome.'

Something cold and wet hit Penny's face and clamped down hard over her nose and mouth. The cell phone fell from her shoulder and clattered to the concrete floor. Struggling to remove the hand that impeded her breathing, Penny struck the phone with her

326

heel and sent it sliding under the adjacent car.

Oh, my God! Confusion congealed into dread. Chloroform scalded her sinus passages and clouded her thoughts, but it could not block out her utter disbelief that this was happening, here, at this high-security hospital.

She had to remain conscious.

But snow drifted in front of her eyes. A noise like the clatter of a train roared through her head. Her knees hit the ground, and she knew she'd lost.

* * *

Joe picked up his ringing office phone. 'Commander Montgomery,' he clipped out, preoccupied by the proposal he was wading through. 'Hello,' he added, when the caller failed to speak.

Strange noises arrested Joe from his work. He listened, frowning at what sounded like a scuffle, complete with a woman's muffled cries.

What the hell?

It had to be a prank call. He was about to drop the receiver in its cradle when the sound of heavy breathing reached his ears. 'Bitch,' he heard a man mutter. 'Where'd you drop the fucking phone?' Many more seconds of heavy breathing followed, and then a swear word. 'Damn it.' The line crackled and clicked as if someone had grabbed the phone and dragged it closer. Then the line went dead.

Joe gently lowered the receiver. His heart beat uncomfortably fast. It was a prank call, had to be. He glanced at the wall clock and uncertainty lanced him. Penny sometimes called around this time, when she was working the late shift.

He picked up the phone again and tapped out her cell number, telling himself that he was worrying for nothing.

Her phone rang and rang until her voice mail picked up. He didn't leave a message. He buzzed his secretary instead.

'Veronica, get the Physical Therapy Clinic at Portsmouth Naval Medical Center on the line, ASAP.'

'Yes, sir,' she replied with a question in her voice.

He tried to refocus his thoughts on the proposal in front of him while he waited. But worry spun a web that kept his thought suspended.

'Line three, sir,' said Veronica, letting her efficiency show. That wasn't all she liked to show around the halls of Spec Ops, but she kept her dealings with Joe strictly professional. 'I have Petty Officer Davis for you.'

'Davis,' said Joe. 'Can you tell me if Lieutenant Price has left the hospital yet?'

'Oh, yes, sir. She left about ten minutes ago.'

Shit. That wasn't what Joe wanted to hear. 'Thank you.' He hung up and dialed Penny's cell again and got her voice mail . . . again.

She always turned her phone on the minute she left work.

Joe set the proposal aside, snatched up his car keys, and left the office.

Veronica regarded him inquiringly as he marched through the outer office. 'I have a personal emergency,' he told her. 'Tell the XO and senior chief that I had to leave.'

'Is something wrong?' she called after him.

Some questions didn't merit answers, and that was one of them. He breezed by her, riddled with doubts and fears.

★ ★ ★

'Well, I'll be,' Hannah marveled, glancing from the computer monitor into Rafe's glowing eyes. 'The caller is right.'

At four o'clock that afternoon, the FBI had received a tip from an officer at Central Command who claimed to know what the four victims of the ricin murders had in common. They had all been investigated by CENTCOM for incidences involving friendly fire. It had taken Hannah and Rafe only two hours of research to verify that the claim was true.

Rafe stroked his chin, and Hannah waited, struggling for the kind of patience he exhibited. 'Perhaps we have our motive,' he suggested carefully.

Hannah struggled to chase his thoughts. 'As in . . . somebody thought these four men were guilty, even though three of them were found innocent of any negligence?'

'Exactly.'

'So, we're looking for someone in Central Command, maybe, who thought that these four officers got off too lightly?'

'Perhaps,' Rafe conceded. 'It's a question of accountability. If our killer believes that leaders should be held accountable for errors made on the field of battle, then we have a motive. In that case, the killer is probably a military figure himself, someone with access to the investigations and the information coming out of them.'

'An insider,' Hannah agreed, fighting to contain her excitement. 'But he's got to be emotionally invested in this issue to actually kill someone.'

'Perhaps he's a veteran who was a victim of negligent leadership,' Rafe suggested.

'Or he lost a loved one in a friendly-fire incident.'

'Ah,' said Rafe with a wag of his finger. 'If that's the case, then the killer was probably vocal before he became vindictive. His protests would have found their way into the news, prior to the date of the first murder.'

Hannah turned to formulate a request for information from their analysts when the phone rang. When it was after hours, she ordinarily let her voice mail pick up. Something prompted her to take the call. 'Special Agent Lindstrom.'

'This is Joe Montgomery,' said a grim male voice. As she pictured Luther's commander, the blood drained from her face. If something had happened to Luther . . .

'Penny Price is missing.'

Penny, not Luther. 'Where — where was she last seen?' Hannah stammered, feeling guilty for her relief.

'At the hospital when she left work an hour ago. She tried to call me from her cell phone. I heard a scuffle in the background and then a man's voice.'

'Where are you?'

'Standing next to her car in the hospital's

parking garage.' He spoke with gunfire urgency.

'We'll be right there,' Hannah promised, sensing his desperation.

As she hung up the phone, Rafe rolled wordlessly to his feet and reached for his coat.

18

Penny awoke in a room as cold as a tomb and scarcely more comfortable. The musty scent reminded her of a basement, but she couldn't tell for sure, as her eyes were tightly blindfolded. She lurched upright, hearing the squeak of a metal bed, feeling the thin mattress beneath her. The coppery taste in her mouth brought back the memory of being chloroformed.

The blindfold, which was knotted tightly at the back of her head, blocked out even a suggestion of sunlight. The strips that bound her wrists behind her elicited waves of panic that intensified as she struggled to free herself.

She had to pee. Penny mastered the urge, crossed her legs, and forced herself to calm down.

What's going to happen to me? The terrifying question overrode her self-imposed calm. She rolled into a ball, shivering with bone-deep vulnerability.

At last, the sound she dreaded reached her ears: the slow, calculating step of a heavyset man.

A key scraped into a lock, which gave with a click. The door creaked open. Behind the blindfold, Penny detected a beam of light. Her captor shut the door and relocked it.

For a nerve-fraying moment, he regarded her wordlessly. 'Penelope Price,' he finally said, in a voice so devoid of emotion that it made her bones feel brittle.

'Yes.' It would gain her nothing to deny the truth. He had her purse, her identification. Perhaps if she was cooperative, uncomplaining, he would let her live. But then she remembered the fate of her father and Eric, and panic spiked anew.

At his approach, she shrank against the wall. She could sense him standing in front of her, close enough to kill her with his bare hands. 'What do you know about the ricin taken from BioTech in July of 2002?'

Was that all he wanted, information? 'Eric Tomlinson sold it to pay his sick wife's medical bills,' she divulged.

'Sold it to whom?'

'I don't know.'

The blow came out of nowhere. She landed facedown on the mattress with her left ear ringing. To her utter chagrin, she felt a wet warmth dampen the mattress under her hip. *Oh, God.*

'Does that awaken any memories?' the steel-cold voice taunted. It sounded as if he reveled in her humiliation.

Don't cry. Don't! She sensed that pleading and crying would gain her nothing. 'No,' she answered, pushing herself upright. She was only human. 'I'm telling the truth. I don't know who bought the ricin.'

'What does the FBI know?'

Penny hesitated. How much allegiance did she owe the Bureau? 'They think whoever bought the ricin is responsible for poisoning four military officers. It was in the news,' she added. 'I don't know anything more than that.'

'What about Eric Tomlinson?'

She licked her dry lips. 'What about him?'

'What did he tell you when he entered your home?'

How did he know about that? 'All he said was that he hadn't killed my father.'

'Who did, then?' She could tell by the tone of his voice that he was mocking her.

'You,' she said with sudden insight. A sharp-pronged rage rose up in her unexpectedly, too swiftly and fiercely to tamp down. She lurched to her knees, encountered a broad chest, opened her mouth, and bit her assailant as hard as she could.

Yelping in surprise, he gripped her hair by the scalp and yanked her head back. 'Fucking bitch!' he growled, flinging her backward so that her skull struck the wall and stars twinkled behind her blindfold.

Penny collapsed, heart pounding, terrified that he would kill her now. What had she done? It took every ounce of self-control to keep from curling into a defensive posture. Better to play possum in the hopes that he left her alone.

'Bitch!' he said again. 'Shit!' With more mutterings, he wheeled away, presumably to stanch the blood she'd drawn and now tasted in her mouth. Before he was out the door, there came a buzzing noise.

It took Penny a second to realize that the man's cell phone was ringing. 'What do you want?' he snarled.

The faintest thread of a man's voice reached Penny's ears.

'I told you, I've got it in hand.'

The caller made some type of request.

'What do you care?' the abductor demanded. 'It's Penelope,' he added, startling Penny by mentioning her name. 'Penelope Price.'

The caller's incredulity was obvious, though Penny couldn't hear his words. Whatever he said caused her abductor to return to the bed. She fought the instinct to cringe.

'So what if she is?' her captor retorted.

' — me, Ritter.' The caller's voice was suddenly audible.

Penny had a name now — Ritter. Why did

that sound familiar?

' — make the connection,' the caller continued. 'You'll need to get rid of her.'

Oh, God! Penny gasped in horror. There was only one way to interpret his words.

Ritter didn't hear her gasp. He was busy bickering. 'I thought you didn't want me offing anyone; now you want me to?' he growled in disbelief. 'You owe me another ten grand.'

The caller responded in outrage.

'Until I get the money wired to me,' Ritter countered, 'she remains alive. If you piss me off enough, I'll expose you myself.'

'Damn you to hell, Ritter . . . wire it as soon as I can.'

'I'll be waiting,' Ritter sneered. He swiveled from the bed and walked away, slamming and locking the door behind him.

Oh, God. Penny lay on her side, quivering in terror. Ritter had been ordered to kill her. But why? Unless the caller considered her a serious threat. Nausea roiled up suddenly, making her heave and spit up bile. Her stomach was empty.

She fell back and gripped the mattress, thrashing her head in denial. What would Lia do without her? And what about Joe? Would he ever realize how much she'd come to love him?

★ ★ ★

'Would you like more coffee?' inquired Special Agent Valentino.

'No, thanks,' Joe demurred.

Both FBI agents and Joe sat at Penny's dinette table while Ophelia paced from the kitchen to the living room and back again. Vinny stood against the pantry door, watching her with concern in his eyes. It was well past midnight.

'How do we even know the kidnapper is going to call?' Lia wailed, her eyes puffy, her chin trembling. 'How do we know he's not just going to kill her, like he killed Eric?' Her voice broke on the word *killed*. Joe gritted his teeth.

'Eric knew more than Penny does,' said Hannah, even as she scanned the security video from the parking garage. 'She has limited liability.'

Joe envied the agent's ability to remain cerebral in this moment of crisis. She and her watchful sidekick had descended on the parking garage with the forensics team. They'd swarmed Penny's car, commandeered the security video, and canvassed potential witnesses.

But no one had seen anything suspicious.

Like Hannah, Joe was trained to reason in

desperate situations, to keep emotion from clouding his reason. But tonight, he couldn't think, period.

He rubbed his forehead, desperate to erase the unbearable thought that Penny could meet the same fate as Eric and her father. Penny, who'd overcome so many odds and still brimmed with optimism. Capable and generous Penny, who'd refused to pity him or even allow him to pity himself. If something happened to her . . .

When had she stopped being just Penny, his kind and friendly neighbor? Flashes of memories, special moments spent with her since his return from Afghanistan, ran through his mind, but for the life of him, he couldn't identify the exact moment he started caring for her.

Penny had changed him, without ever once asking him to change. She had taken root in his life, and in the process, she'd made herself vital to him. How had that happened? He'd never found a woman he couldn't replace. Forever was a concept he'd thought he'd embrace when he was done with the teams, when the most beautiful, intelligent, and witty woman strolled into his middle years and took his breath away. Penny hadn't had that kind of effect on him. She'd stolen into his being with plain and gentle stealth. So how could he think of her and forever in the same breath?

'Excuse me.' Joe pushed back his chair and headed for the door. He needed fresh air to clear his thoughts.

'Joe!' Lia cried running after him. She caught him by the arm, forcing him to halt. 'I'm sorry. I'm sorry I said anything about Penny being killed.' She hugged him hard, and he found his arms going around her. She was petite like Penny, with the same copper-colored hair. Oh, Jesus. What if he never held Penny in his arms again? His knees went weak as he broke out in a cold sweat.

'She's going to be okay, Joe.' Lia looked up at him with faith in her eyes and in her voice. 'I know Penny. She's tough. She can survive anything.'

'Yeah,' Joe rasped, agreeing because the alternative was just too awful to consider.

'Found it!' Hannah announced. 'Here's when the lights go out.'

With a resurgence of hope, Joe released Lia. The two of them hurried to the kitchen to watch over Hannah's shoulder. The video player was attached to her laptop. 'Okay, look at this.'

They held a collective breath as the second level of the brightly lit parking garage went absolutely dark. The camera panned the broad space, alighting on the flyover from the hospital. A woman crossing the flyover slowed her step. 'Is that Penny?' Hannah asked.

'Yes,' said Joe and Ophelia at the same time.

A dot of light appeared from the left and bobbed toward her. The camera panned away, frustrating their view.

'Someone approached her with a flashlight,' Hannah interpreted.

Joe's heartbeat bounced off his eardrums as the camera swung back. A shadowy couple moved across the screen, preceded by the beam of light. It illumined Penny's car and then Penny herself. She had held her right shoulder to her ear as she reached into her purse for her car keys. The camera swung away again.

'Damn it!' Joe cursed, shuddering with frustration.

They waited again for the camera to turn. The beam of a flashlight did not come back. There was only a faint bluish glow and a single silhouette. The foursome leaned in.

'What are we looking at?' Hannah tapped a key to magnify the image. Suddenly, in the glow of a phone's display, a man's face came into focus.

Lia gasped.

'Gotcha,' said Hannah, depressing a button

to capture the image.

An ice-cold shiver gripped Joe's spine as he looked at the face of Penny's abductor — the man who'd killed Eric and possibly her father, too. With his blunt features and short, silver hair, he struck Joe as utterly ruthless. 'Who is he?' he demanded as Lia turned away to fling herself into Vinny's arms.

'I don't know,' Hannah admitted. 'But if he's got a record, we'll get an ID in no time.'

'He looks familiar,' mused Valentino with a narrowing of his dark eyes. 'I've seen that face before.'

Joe's hopes latched on to that statement. He dragged out a chair to sit down before his legs gave out.

*   *   *

The creaking of the door jarred Penny from a shallow sleep. Adrenaline spurted through her bloodstream, making it impossible to play possum a second time. She wriggled into the corner of the bed. *No, I'm not ready to die.*

Ritter said nothing. Over the awful silence, she thought she detected the chirping of a cricket. Was it still night? She'd lost all sense of time.

As his heavy tread approached, she cringed, expecting the worst. He fisted her hair, yanking her head closer. To her astonishment, she felt him loosen the knot that kept her blindfold in place. As it slipped free, he shoved her back. She blinked, catching sight of his silhouette but little else.

The room was black, with just the faintest suggestion of light framing the single window. Something metal gleamed in Ritter's hand. Penny was blinded by a flash of light. In the next instant, he grabbed her hair again and tied the blindfold back in place.

'What was that for?' she dared to ask.

'A memento,' he answered cryptically.

'What? You mean you take pictures of the people you kill? You are one sick bastard, you know that?'

'Shut the fuck up.'

She knew it wasn't wise to incite his anger, but she was in a fighting mood. She would not be snuffed out without exhausting every option for survival.

'Your pictures are going to get you caught one day,' she taunted.

Her reward was a blow forceful enough to knock her senseless.

★ ★ ★

Joe lifted his head off the table and wiped drool surreptitiously from the corner of his mouth. He realized he'd fallen asleep while Special Agent Valentino sat beside him, typing on Hannah's laptop. 'It's morning,' said the agent without looking at him.

A glance out the bay window revealed that it was dawn. The sky was the color of charcoal. Tiny flakes of snow pattered the windowpane.

'How long did I sleep?' Joe asked, chagrined. Navy SEALs weren't supposed to sleep while someone else did the work.

'Just an hour or so. Hannah's resting on the couch,' he added, hinting that they ought to keep their voices down. 'Ophelia and Vinny have left for Portsmouth. She's going to broadcast Penny's disappearance on the morning news and plead for the public's assistance.'

Joe rubbed his scratchy eyes. 'Any developments?' he asked wearily.

'Actually, we've heard from our analysts,' the agent admitted with enough reluctance to make Joe's heart stop.

'And?'

'We have an ID on the kidnapper.' He met Joe's gaze at last, his midnight eyes inscrutable.

'Tell me,' Joe demanded, bracing himself.

'He's Buzz Ritter, former state police officer turned mercenary. He's wanted in fourteen states for assault, murder, theft, and embezzlement.'

Joe swallowed against his suddenly dry throat. 'How many people has he killed?'

Valentino shook his head to convey the silent message *You don't want to know*.

'You think he's going to kill Penny.' It wasn't a question, because Joe already knew the answer, could feel it twisting his gut into knots. 'Lia won't be able to live without her.' He jammed trembling fingers through his hair. 'Hell, I don't know if I can,' he admitted with a humorless laugh.

He would never have said as much to anyone but Penny. But the agent's patient gaze made him confess, 'When I came home from my last mission, I was a wreck. I wanted to crawl into the bottom of a bottle and stay there.' He shook his head. 'Penny . . . I don't know how she did it, but she dragged me out of that hole. She doesn't deserve to have this happen to her,' he choked out.

Valentino looked away. 'It's intolerable when the innocent are victimized,' he concurred, his voice gravelly with despair.

The words turned Joe cold. It didn't sound as if the agent harbored any hope. 'We can't just sit here,' Joe bit out.

'We have an all-points alert out for Ritter,' Valentino soothed. 'We're waiting to hear what Ophelia's broadcast might turn up.'

Joe scraped back his chair. He headed for

the bathroom. Splashing water on his face, he avoided contact with the red-eyed stranger in the mirror.

Penny was his best friend, his lover. He didn't want to learn the hard way that she'd become something more: the woman he'd grown to love — and lost.

★ ★ ★

'Let's go.' The grip on Penny's arm jarred her awake.

In a semiconscious state, she hadn't even heard the door open or her captor approach her.

Go where? she wondered, her adrenal glands taxed by the rude awakening and the sudden presence of danger. Her aching head made it hard to respond.

Ritter yanked her to her feet and shoved her before him, propelling her blindly toward the door. She realized she was barefoot.

He's going to kill me now. The realization made her knees buckle.

Ritter hauled her onto her feet again. 'Walk!' he commanded.

She felt especially vulnerable without shoes.

The smell of fresh, cold air helped to sharpen her senses. He prodded her to climb a run of steps. They walked through a room with creaky floorboards and out another door. Hope fluttered momentarily as she detected a hint of sunlight creeping beneath her blindfold. Was it possible his boss hadn't paid him, after all, and he was going to let her go?

She stumbled down three steps and out into a yard where something cold and wet struck her face. It was snowing, and he'd taken her coat as well as her shoes. Hope expired with the realization.

Ritter pulled her to a stop. She heard him open a car door. 'Get in.' He sent her sprawling across a cold leather seat.

She vaguely recollected being transported this way before. At least he hadn't chloroformed her this time. Perhaps her wits could save her.

'Where are you taking me?' she demanded as he got into the front seat and started to drive.

He didn't answer.

Lying on her left side, with her arms bound behind her, Penny struggled to sit up. Her legs were free, she realized, but without shoes she was defenseless. Or was she? She could still run.

But then, he probably wanted her to do that. He would drive her to some deserted place and release her. She would run until a bullet tagged her skull.

No! Her muscles cramped in protest. She refused to die like that — a victim. She had to abort this awful mission before it was too late.

But how? Her freedom was limited.

The squeaking of the windshield wipers suggested an answer. It was snowing. The roads were slick. If Ritter lost control of the vehicle, he might never get her to his remote destination.

With her heart thundering, Penny slunk low in the seat. Slowly, stealthily, she moved her knees up the back of the front seat. Her legs felt weak, sluggish.

She would have only one chance to do this right. If she messed up, Ritter would secure her feet, and then she'd be truly helpless.

On the count of three, she told herself.

One.

Two.

Three! She pulled her knees to her chest and extended her legs suddenly, heels connecting solidly with Ritter's head. But he was built like an ox. 'What the fuck?' he roared, seemingly unfazed. Penny cringed. She'd failed. But the car was swerving, spilling her all over the back seat. Ritter fumbled with the steering wheel, seeking to bring the vehicle under control.

'Son of a bitch!' he growled. Tires skidded

over the slick pavement. Gravity held them in thrall. They were going fast. Too fast to elude the laws of physics.

The left tires dropped onto the shoulder. Ritter pulled a hard right and sent them into a spin. Penny braced herself.

Crash! They hit something unyielding. She was flung against the door, hard enough to knock the wind from her lungs. With a shattering of glass, the vehicle came to a sudden, shuddering halt. But then it started to tip, groaning as if in agony. Penny fought to stay where she was.

Whoosh! The car keeled all the way over, bouncing as it landed on its hood. Penny found herself lying in a puddle of broken glass on the car's ceiling.

Have to get out! her brain commanded, but she was too stunned to move. She listened, hearing a strange warbling coming from the front.

In the crash, her blindfold had slipped a little higher. Lifting her head, she encountered the back of a headrest, which she used to scrape the blindfold all the way off.

Suddenly she could see. The mangled interior of the vehicle prompted a whimper of fright. She looked down at herself. Her wrists were still bound, but she didn't appear hurt.

She dared a peek over the seat and got her

first good look at Ritter. He was trapped underneath the dashboard. Blood bubbled from his mouth as he sought to breathe and talk at the same time, giving rise to that hideous warbling.

She tore her gaze away, unsympathetic.

She had to get out. Get help.

With her bare feet, she kicked out the sagging, shattered pane of the rear window. It fell in on her, in one thick piece, but she shrugged it off and pushed her head through the opening, rejoicing in the cold, fresh air that hit her face.

With her hands bound, she squirmed out of the vehicle like a worm, rolled in a ditch that left her clothing sodden and cold. She staggered to her feet, struggling on the incline, her legs weak with the dizzying realization that she was still alive. *Alive!*

She struggled up out of the ditch onto an empty road, blinking as she took in the flat rural terrain. Withered cornstalks and copses of trees were all she could see in any direction. Surely a car would come along.

But all was quite, save for the pattering of snowflakes and the sounds of Ritter choking on his own blood.

She left the wreck, determined to intercept a house or dwelling of some kind, aware that her bare feet would soon be frostbitten. The snow was starting to accumulate. Her damp clothes were stiffening with frost.

If she could just find a phone to call for help. To let Joe and Lia know that she was all right. She focused on that warming thought to keep the numbing cold at bay.

When a humming sound carried over the unearthly quiet, Penny stopped and listened, her heart in her throat. *Help me, please!*

The running lights of an eighteen-wheeler emerged out of the vale of snow behind her. The truck was moving at a clip that made her heart accelerate. She stepped hastily off the road, unable to flag the driver down with her hands tied.

At the last second, the truck veered into the oncoming lane. He'd seen her.

With a shout for help, Penny watched it roar by. Her hopes plummeted toward despair, only to rise back up again when the brake lights flared. With a roar of deceleration and a hissing of hydraulic brakes, the truck slowed to a careful stop many yards down the road.

Penny started to run.

A bearded stranger leaped from the cab. Penny slowed, suddenly cautious.

'Ma'am?' he called. The concern in his voice was reassuring. 'Are you all right?'

'I need help!' she admitted, her voice cracking as the effect of the last twelve hours caught up with her.

His weather-beaten face was a picture of consternation as he bent down to peer at her. 'Good gravy,' he exclaimed in a thick local accent, 'you're the Price woman, ain't ya?'

'How did you know?'

'Saw it on the news; heard it on the radio. Whatcha doin' way out in here in Pungo?'

'Trying to get home,' she said, her eyes burning with tears.

'Well, I can sure help you with that.'

19

Joe was the first to step through the door of the Pungo County Sheriff's Office. In his eagerness to set eyes on Penny, he left Hannah and Rafe to catch the closing door.

He spied Penny the instant he stepped into the brick building, but the knot of fear cinching his stomach remained. She was huddled under a woolen blanket. Her hair was disheveled, one cheek swollen and bruised. She held a crushed paper cup in her hands. Her aqua-blue gaze tore into him as she glanced up.

'Joe!'

He reached her in less than a second, pulling her up and into his embrace.

She squirmed uncomfortably. 'I'm filthy; I smell bad,' she protested.

'No, you don't.' He craved her in his arms. But she kept him at arm's length.

'Where's Ophelia?' She peered past him to see Hannah and Valentino entering.

'Lia's still at the station,' Joe replied. 'We called her the minute we got news.'

'Penny!' Hannah hurried over. 'Boy, are we happy to see you,' she said, reaching out to

353

touch her. 'This is Special Agent Valentino, the heavy hitter from D.C.'

Valentino clicked his tongue in disagreement and murmured, 'My pleasure.'

'We're going to get you out of here,' Hannah said, casting a glance up and down the hallway. 'Let's go now.'

'They told me to stay here till the sheriff returned from the site of the accident,' Penny protested.

Joe wanted to hear more about her valiant escape. She'd managed a brief explanation in her phone call — a call that had made Joe dizzy with relief.

'Our people are already at the scene,' Hannah replied. 'Ritter's dead,' she added gently.

Penny's eyes glazed. 'I figured he would be,' she whispered.

She was so strong, so brave, that it was all Joe could do not to haul her into his embrace.

'So, let's go,' said Hannah. 'The sheriff of Pungo can wait for your statement.'

But then a deputy popped out of the nearest office. 'Just a minute, now. Who are you?' he demanded, swaggering up to them.

'Special Agent Lindstrom, FBI,' retorted Hannah, flashing her badge. 'We have jurisdiction on his case. The victim is coming with us. Take my card.' As she thrust it at the deputy, Valentino waved Joe and Penny through the exit.

Joe found himself back in the FBI official sedan, Penny tucked in beside him. As she released the edges of her blanket to buckle herself in, he noted the chafed skin on her wrists with a sense of shock.

What did he expect? She'd already told him that Ritter had been ordered to kill her. Tying her wrists was par for the course.

'She needs to go home and rest,' he gritted to the agents.

The dark eyes glancing into the rearview mirror were apologetic. 'Standard procedure requires that she be checked out by a physician. The faster we move on this, the better our chances of apprehending Ritter's boss.'

'He knows me,' Penny volunteered in a thin voice. 'That's why he wanted me dead. He considered me a liability.'

Hannah swiveled in the front seat. 'Do you want to talk to us now, hon? Or later, after a doctor sees you?'

'I don't need a doctor.'

'It's standard procedure, Penny. We need to process your clothes and check you for evidence.'

'I'll talk now,' Penny said, looking out the window.

Joe swallowed down his helplessness. He couldn't, wouldn't even think about what evidence Hannah believed the medical exam would yield.

'We'll need to record your statements,' Hannah added, producing a handheld recorder. She spoke into it first, naming the investigation and providing the date. She asked Penny to acknowledge that she was being recorded. Then the interview began. 'Can you tell us what happened as you left the hospital yesterday evening?'

As Penny recapped how she'd been chloroformed in the parking garage and had awakened, bound and blindfolded in a basement somewhere, Joe traced the scar that was throbbing and burning on his cheek. He willed his blood pressure to subside.

'Then I overheard Ritter talking to his boss,' Penny was saying. 'That's when I overheard his name. I swear I've heard it before, in a conversation.' She rubbed her forehead, closing her eyes in concentration. 'I just can't remember where.'

'Why do you think Ritter's boss knows who you are?' Hannah prompted.

'He sounded so distressed when Ritter told him my name. I could hear him on the other end. He told Ritter to get rid of me.'

Joe sucked in a breath at the stark remark.

'Did you recognize his voice?'

'No, not overhearing it like that.'

'What happened after that?'

'Ritter took my picture, as a memento. Then he left me for a while. Later, he dragged me out of the basement up to his car. He put me in the back seat and started driving.'

As she described her desperate bid for freedom, Joe had to open the window for fresh air. It was either that or throw up. At the same time, he couldn't be more impressed. There wasn't a woman in the world braver than Penny.

'What kind of profile do you have on this guy?' he demanded. It scared him to death knowing the ricin killer was still alive.

'We believe he's in the military,' said Hannah carefully.

'Penny sees guys in the military all day long,' Joe pointed out.

'We think he has a hang-up about friendly fire. He's taken it upon himself to avenge those he thinks are responsible for blue-on-blue engagement.'

'You mean those four officers,' said Joe.

'Yes,' said Hannah. 'They were all investigated for their part in friendly fire incidents and exonerated.'

Jesus, thought Joe. Everyone was up in arms about friendly fire these days. That didn't help to narrow down the list of suspects any. 'So, what now?' he demanded.

Valentino glanced into the rearview mirror again. 'We examine the evidence that Ritter left behind. Hopefully it'll lead us back to the ricin killer.'

Hopefully? Penny's safety was in jeopardy here. Joe wanted the ricin killer caught today. 'I want her protected, and Lia, too, twenty-four seven,' he demanded.

'Not a problem,' said Hannah, on a sympathetic note. 'I'll put in a request for U.S. Marshals, one for each of them.'

Placated, Joe glanced at Penny, hoping to see her relief, but she'd nodded off to sleep. He scooted closer, offering his shoulder as a pillow to lean on. The weight of her head was as much a comfort to him.

★   ★   ★

Joe drew down the blankets on his bed and realized that this was the first time Penny had elected to sleep in his bed, in his house.

Beyond the drawn blinds, the bright sky betrayed that it was just late afternoon, yet they were both exhausted from the events of the night before. 'Hop in,' he invited, fluffing the pillow as Felix took up residence at the foot of the bed.

With a murmur of thanks, Penny eased between the sheets wearing one of his T-shirts, long enough on her that it fell to her thighs. As she pulled the covers to her chin, Joe got in the other side, then wriggled to the middle to pull her close.

Her hands came up. 'I can't,' she whispered.

He released her, falling back against the pillows with deep concern. Penny had kept him at a distance since the incident. That and the mandatory examination by a doctor had left him fearing the worst. But he couldn't bring himself to ask. Even if she had been violated, it changed nothing for him. He only wanted to help her make the memories go away.

'It's not you, Joe,' Penny said, reading his thoughts as always. 'I'll be fine in a day or two. It's just . . . at the hospital they had to check me over, and — ' To his dismay, her voice began to quaver. 'He didn't rape me or anything like that,' she added.

'You don't have to say any more,' he begged, nonetheless aware of his relief. 'I just wanted to hold you until you realize you're safe and no one's ever going to hurt you again.'

'Oh, Joe.' She lifted a hand to stroke the line of his jaw. At the same time, her chin trembled, betraying troubled thoughts.

'What?' he asked turning sideways to see her better.

She shook her head, holding out on him.

'You know you can tell me anything, Pen,' he urged.

Tears seeped slowly from her eyes, each one leaving a gash in Joe's heart. *God*, he thought, *let me be able to handle this, whatever it is.*

'I was so afraid, Joe. All I knew was that he was going to kill me if I didn't do something. I didn't mean to stoop to his level; I just had to save myself.' A sob tore through her, and she turned her face into the pillow to hide it.

Joe's hands jerked her to him, nearly crushing her with the force of his embrace. 'Cry, damn it. Let it out, and then never think of it again. You did what you had to do, Penny. The accident killed him. Get that straight right now.'

'I know. I just feel so confused.'

He knew she was suffering the posttraumatic stress that followed terror, but still Penny's racking sobs made him feel so helpless. He'd never hurt so badly for another human being, would have given anything to strip her mind of those awful memories of her fight to survive.

To his relief, she accepted his comfort,

collapsing on and into him. He held her gently, murmuring reassurances until the storm of emotion passed.

He stroked her back, her hair, his touch comforting and platonic. At last, he felt her grow limp and slip into the sleep she needed to begin the healing process.

In the dim light, Joe studied Penny's pale, bruised face. How could he ever have considered her less than lovely? Her beauty came from within; it was timeless. It took his breath away.

He put his lips to her forehead, whispering the words that his heart felt so plainly. 'I love you, Penny. God *damn* it, I love you.'

She was sleeping. She couldn't even hear him, but it was better that way. Never once had Penny hinted at deeper emotions for him. Sure, she wanted a husband and a family of her own, but she'd never suggested that Joe might be part of that picture. He was just the hunk next door, a convenient screw, the man she'd taken as a lover to reawaken her sexuality.

And he'd fretted that he would end up breaking her heart! How ironic was it that he was the one with his heart in his throat, his chest swollen with feelings he'd never felt before?

With a despairing groan, Joe closed his

eyes. At least time was on his side. He had to convince Penny that he was worth keeping. By hook or by crook, he would prove that he was a worthy future investment, not just the playboy bachelor next door.

★ ★ ★

'We need to do this more often,' Penny exclaimed, sitting at the table by the restaurant window. Lia sat down across from her. Beyond the window, the Elizabeth River glinted under a gray sky. The moored boats clanged and rocked in their berths. Seagulls hunkered on the docks, looking miserable in the chilly weather. 'Do you always get an hour off for lunch?'

'As long as my story gets written,' said Ophelia, 'I can take all the time I want.' Wearing a sherbet-colored blazer and winter-white slacks, she looked the part of a professional journalist. 'What about you?' she asked. 'When are you going back to work?'

'On Monday,' Penny said, glancing at the menu.

Lia frowned across the table at her. 'Are you sure you're ready to go back?'

Penny glanced up, surprised to hear worry in her little sister's voice. 'Of course I'm ready,' she soothed. 'We can't live the rest of

362

our lives holed up out of fear. Besides, we have the Double D's watching us like hawks.' She nodded toward a table by the door where their personal shadows, Don Dawes and Gary Dirks, sat down to order their own lunch. Both were U.S. Marshals, assigned to them by the FBI — no more state police for them now that the FBI had a true case. 'How much safer can we be?'

'Yeah, but it bugs that hell out of me that the ricin killer hasn't been caught yet,' Lia grumbled. 'The bastard deserves to be strung up by his testicles.'

'Lia!' Penny laughed.

'Well, he does. And when he's caught, Hannah needs to give Joe a moment alone with him.'

'Hmmm,' said Penny, 'somehow I think he'd enjoy that.'

'Yeah, I've noticed you two are spending an awful lot of time together,' Lia fished.

'Do you want to split an appetizer?' Penny asked, steering the conversation to safer ground. Joe had been awfully attentive since the incident — so wonderful and smart and handy that it was scaring the daylights out of her. She found herself relying on him way too much for her happiness these days. She'd decided to take drastic measures to avoid the inevitable heartache.

'Go ahead,' taunted Lia, 'just ignore what you don't want to face. You always have. Let's try the stuffed crab shells.'

'Oh, that does sound good.'

'Anyway,' Lia added, drumming her fingers on the table, 'I have a surprise to show you.'

Penny glanced up from studying the entrées. 'What is it?' Coming from Lia, she knew it was going to be a doozy.

'Ahem,' said Lia, indicating her left hand, the one that was drumming the table.

There on her fourth finger glinted the loveliest little diamond that Penny'd ever seen. 'Oh, my God!' she cried out, grabbing her sister's hand and pulling it closer. 'It's in the shape of a heart! Oh, I love it! When did he propose?'

As Lia launched into a detailed account of an evening cruise on the *Norfolk Star*, Penny struggled to contain her envy. Never in her wildest dreams had she thought Lia would become engaged before her. *She* was the one who'd wanted marriage and a family. Wild, irrepressible Lia would surely take a while to settle down.

But seeing the joy that danced in Lia's eyes as she recounted how Vinny had gone down on his knees, right there in the crowded dining hall, where every passenger on board bore witness to his vulnerability, all trace of envy disappeared. This was what Penny had wanted for Lia for years: to be adored by the man she loved.

'Oh, honey,' she choked out, 'I'm so happy for you.'

They embraced over a carnation bouquet, then dabbed their tears with the cloth napkins as they sat back down.

'So, here's the deal,' said Lia, sending her an apologetic look. 'I won't be here for Thanksgiving.'

'Oh,' said Penny, feeling privately relieved.

'I'm going with Vinny to Philadelphia to meet his mother and sister.'

'Oh, boy.' Penny could tell she was daunted by the encounter to come.

'What if his mother hates me?' Lia cried. 'You know how mothers are with their sons.'

'Honey, you have nothing to worry about,' Penny comforted, even as she crossed her fingers in her lap. With Vinny barely out of his teens, his mother might be shocked and horrified to meet 'the older woman.'

'You think?' Lia asked. 'Vinny says she's really nice and that she'll love me the minute she sees me.'

'It might take her a little longer than that,' Penny cautioned practically.

Lia hadn't asked her what her own holiday was going to look like. She could hardly believe it herself, but if she didn't take a lengthy absence from Joe, she was going to buckle under her growing love for him, tell him how she felt, and send him running in the opposite direction.

No, the only option was to put distance between them, both physically and emotionally. If she came home to find another woman on his arm, so be it. She'd known what he was like when she agreed to an affair. Naiveté could be crippling. Penny had learned that lesson the hard way.

*   *   *

'Good morning, Admiral,' Penny called as she pushed open the door of the third examination room. Admiral Jacobs was here for his weekly therapy.

She found him seated on the examination table, his cane close at hand. 'Where have you been?' he demanded. His watery blue eyes impaled her, scrutinizing her in a way that struck her as odd.

'I took some personal leave time,' she explained. 'You shouldn't have canceled your last appointment just because I wasn't here. Commander Sparks is just as capable at keeping your knees from stiffening.'

'Nah,' the old man growled, waving away

the suggestion. 'She's too rough.'

'Well, I wish my contribution could be greater, sir, but I'm afraid I have some tough news for you. I've taken a detailed look at your statistics, and I'm going to have to recommend surgery at this point. We haven't made enough headway with manipulation techniques. You're going to need a double knee replacement.'

When her words got no visible reaction, Penny tried again. 'Do you understand what I'm saying, sir? You'll never walk normally again, climb stairs, tie your shoes, unless you have surgery.'

'Suit yourself,' he said, with a shrug and that same penetrating stare.

Puzzled by his reaction — after all, surgery at his age was a huge and unpleasant obstacle to face — Penny pulled a pen from her breast pocket and made a note for the surgeon. *Check patient's mental state.*

'I'm going to send Commander Huxley in to talk to today, rather than go into our usual routine,' she warned him.

The admiral kept quiet.

'You'll need to slip your slacks off,' Penny instructed, 'and put on a patient's gown.' She bent to fetch a gown from the drawer beside his feet.

As she placed it next to him, she saw him

reach into his pockets as if to empty them. She turned to make her way to the door when he lifted his cane, blocking her path. He startled her by leaping off the examination table, moving faster than she would have ever given him credit for.

'I hate to do this, Lieutenant,' he rasped, gripping her arm to keep her from stepping back. 'But I can't take unnecessary risks.'

Perplexed and thinking he'd lost his mind, Penny opened her mouth to soothe him. But then she saw what looked like the needle of a syringe flash in his left hand. Dear God! In the next instant, she felt the needle prick her skin.

'No!' she exclaimed, jerking her arm back, backing away from him. 'What are you doing?' she cried.

'Cleaning house,' he answered, chasing her. 'I had no idea you were Danny Price's daughter. Price is such a common name.'

Penny sought to hold him off, but he was amazingly strong and swift. To her horror, he seized her, whirled her around, and clapped a hand over her mouth, hauling her against his bigger frame. 'Now hold still,' he growled, 'or this will leave bruises.'

She twisted with all her might, managing to wrest free. 'Wait,' she gasped, backing away from him again, eyeing the door on the far side of the little room. 'Wait! I'm sorry about your son,' she stammered, as all the loose pieces fell into place. 'It's a travesty what happened to him, what happens to so many of our soldiers. But I had nothing to do with that, sir. You can't kill me. That would make you the guilty one. You're a patriot, sir, not a murderer.' She filled her lungs, preparing to scream for help.

'In times of war, my dear, even a patriot is forced to do the unthinkable.'

'But I'm not the enemy.' Strange, but her voice seemed to come from a great distance. A sudden ringing filled her head. The floor beneath her feet tilted, and she collapsed, falling across the therapy table. Oh, God. Whatever was in that syringe had gotten into her blood. She was going to die, after all!

★ ★ ★

Joe leaned an elbow on the clinic's counter and cast Petty Officer Davis his most winning smile. 'Good afternoon, PO3.'

She looked up, recognized him, and smiled back. 'Well, hello, sir. Do you have an appointment today?'

'No, but I was hoping you could work me in.' He needed just fifteen minutes of Penny's undivided attention. He had something important to ask her.

'Ah,' the aide winced, 'I don't know. The lieutenant's with Admiral Jacobs right now. That usually takes a while.'

An unpleasant feeling stitched through Joe. Ah, yes, the admiral who'd known so much about him. 'I'm sure she'd want to see me,' he cajoled, glancing into the offices behind the aide. 'Where's her U.S. Marshal?' he wanted to know.

'Oh, he went to get a soda from the snack machines,' said the aid.

'Really?' Joe's consternation mounted. 'I need to talk to Penny,' he said, with no leeway in his tone this time.

She eyed the schedule earnestly. 'Okay, sir. How about if I squeeze you in right after she's finished with the admiral?'

'Thank you.'

'Follow me on back, sir,' she invited, getting up to open the door.

Trailing Davis down the hall, Joe was aware of a rising sense of unease. He drew to a stop, ignoring Davis's inquiring glance, to query his nagging sixth sense. What was it about Penny being alone with the admiral that disturbed him so much? Was it just that the man had messed with Joe's mind, trying to convince him that someone was to blame for the failed mission? He'd seemed a little fanatical about it. Of course, he had lost a son to friendly fire, outside of Nasiriyah.

Friendly fire. The words exploded in Joe's head.

'What room is Penny in now?' he demanded of Davis.

'Sir, you can't — '

The clatter of a metal container had Joe pivoting toward a door on a different hall. Without pausing to knock, he depressed the latch and pushed his way inside. What he found scared the shit out of him. Penny lay on her stomach across the examination table, her grip slipping on the leather and the paper sheet. Admiral Jacobs hesitated in the act of rounding the table with a syringe in one hand. He swung his gaze between Penny and Joe as if deciding which of the two presented a greater threat.

'What did you do to her?' Joe demanded as Penny continued to slip. He rounded the table from the opposite side and hooked an arm around her waist, catching her before she hit her knees. The admiral lunged in the same instant, bringing the needle down on Joe's back, but it slipped on the canvas material of his jacket. With a hundred-and-eighty-degree turn, and Penny in one arm, Joe lifted a forearm to deflect another jab. The syringe flew out of the admiral's hand and struck the wall.

'Get help!' Joe shouted at Davis, who stood at the doorway, gaping. Davis took off. Penny lolled limply in Joe's one-armed embrace. The thought that she'd become the admiral's latest victim nearly paralyzed him.

But the admiral was going after the syringe, struggling to retrieve it from the floor.

'Leave it!' Joe commanded, torn between caring for Penny and going after the admiral. He satisfied himself by rushing the old man and shoving him off his feet. Jacobs collapsed on the floor, and Joe kicked the syringe out the door. He then lay Penny on her back across the table. 'Penny, sweetheart, talk to me!' he begged.

The admiral groaned, unable to rise again. Joe's heart stopped as he felt for a pulse and couldn't immediately find it — but then there it was, throbbing gently beneath his fingers. With a whimper of relief, he bent toward her face to see if she was breathing. The sweet exhalation of her breath on his chin reassured him enough that he reeled away. He lifted the admiral off the floor by fisting the collar of his shirt and looked him straight in the eye. 'She'd better not die, you sick son of a bitch! Is that ricin in the syringe?'

The old man set his jaw, refusing to answer. Joe shoved him into a chair. 'Don't move,' he warned, 'or you're dead.'

He was bending over Penny when three people rushed into the room: Penny's U.S. Marshal, Davis, and Doctor Huxley. The U.S. Marshal looked from Penny to the syringe he'd apparently picked up in the hall. 'There are still 4 cc's in it,' he said, reaching for a paper towel to wrap it in. 'Get a poison specialist in here, ASAP,' he said to Davis.

As the U.S. Marshal dealt with the admiral, slapping handcuffs on him and questioning him to no avail, Dr. Huxley turned to Penny. With his heart in his throat, Joe watched him check her vitals and try to revive her. To his knee-weakening relief, her lashes fluttered and her eyes slowly opened.

'Penny!' Joe cried, nudging the doctor aside. 'How do you feel?' No question, the blue of her eyes was the most beautiful color in the world.

'Okay,' she replied after several blinks. Lifting her head, she watched the U.S. Marshal grow disgusted with the admiral's refusal to talk. 'I guess I fainted,' she explained, sending Joe an apologetic smile. 'Sorry. It was such a shock.'

Joe's knees jittered. He felt in danger of fainting himself. To keep that from happening, he leaned heavily on the table and put his arms around the woman he loved.

Jesus, to think that she'd almost been wrested from him as second time!

★ ★ ★

An hour later later, Penny still lay stretched out on the therapy table. Joe was hovering. The room, which had buzzed with doctors, security personnel, and lab techs, was finally quiet. The U.S. Marshal had hauled Admiral Jacobs off to FBI Headquarters, where Hannah and Valentino would question him further. The poison specialist who'd drawn Penny's blood had stepped out to check the results of the tests being run.

'I'm going to be okay, Joe,' Penny insisted, wanting to chase that shadow of worry from his eyes.

'We'll know soon,' he agreed, rubbing her forearms briskly, as if to keep her blood flowing.

'I can't believe it was the admiral all along,' Penny marveled, shaking her head. 'I thought he was such a sweet man.'

'I'm sure he was,' Joe answered. 'War has a way of blurring the lines of right and wrong. He was a POW in 'Nam for years. Who's to say what kind of effect that had on him? And then to lose his son. In any event, it's over now.'

She let the finality of his statement sift through her, feeling, at last, a sense of closure. 'Thank God,' she whispered, reviewing what had happened. 'You saved my life,' she realized suddenly. 'If you hadn't rushed in here, he'd have injected me on his second try. Why were you even here?' she asked him.

'I just happened to drop by. I wanted to ask you something.'

Her heart performed a slow backflip. No, it couldn't be what she was thinking . . .

'You know how Thanksgiving is coming up soon?' he added, building the suspense.

It was hard to breathe . . . 'Yes.'

'Well, I went to buy tickets for a flight to Nevada and I thought, 'Maybe Penny wants to come with me.' '

His words further fanned her hopes. 'You want me to meet your parents?' she guessed.

'Well . . . yeah.' He turned faintly pink beneath his tan.

'Why?' she forced him to clarify.

'Well, 'cause . . . you're my best friend. I wanted to show you Red Rock Canyon, so you could see it in person. Besides, you've been through a lot this fall. You deserve a vacation.'

She wanted to ask, *Is that the only reason?* But it wasn't fair of her to put him on the spot. This was Joe, after all, a man who lived for life's thrills and challenges. She loved him for who he was, not what she wanted him to be.

'I'm afraid I can't,' she said, revealing her plans for the first time. 'I won't be here at Thanksgiving.'

'Where will you be?' He looked perplexed.

'Flying over the Atlantic Ocean. I'm going to take the place of medics on emergency medical flights,' she explained, watching his expression for any suggestion of heartbreak.

'Why?' he asked, merely looking bemused.

'So that medics with families can come home for the holidays,' she reasoned.

For a second, he did look bereft, but then the creases on his forehead disappeared. 'Okay,' he said slowly, processing her news. 'When will you be back?'

'The day after Christmas.'

His stoicism slipped a second time. 'You won't even be here for Christmas?' he asked incredulously.

'Most of the crews have families,' she pointed out, 'whom they haven't seen in months,' she added.

'What about Ophelia?'

'She'll be fine. She has Vinny now. And she's going to meet *his* family over Thanksgiving.'

Joe said nothing to that. Penny searched his

dark-green eyes for any clue as to what he was feeling. It would take the barest suggestion that he was looking for commitment, not just an adventure with her in the Nevada canyons, and she'd scrap all of her plans to be with him.

But he didn't go where her hopes wanted him to. With a forced smile, he bent his head and kissed her cheek. 'I should've guessed,' he said, sounding disappointed, not heartbroken. 'You always put other people before yourself. That's something I admire about you.'

As their gazes met, Penny's eyes stung with the abundance of love in her heart, love she dared not reveal lest he feel awful for not returning it.

He admires me, she thought, answering his smile with a pained smile of her own. If he felt more for her than admiration, this would have been the moment to tell her; after all, she could have died today.

'Good news,' came the voice of poison specialist, startling them both as he bustled into the room. 'Your blood looks absolutely normal, Lieutenant Price. You're in the clear.'

'Thank God,' declared Joe, stepping away to pump the doctor's hand. 'It's over, Pen,' he declared, turning back. 'Come on.' He reached for her to help her sit up. 'Let's go home and celebrate.'

Home? thought Penny with a pang. Home was a place you shared with your family, not your lover. And a family wasn't something Joe wanted to give her. Good thing she'd seen this impasse coming and taken desperate measures to avoid it.

20

On the eve of Thanksgiving, the Norfolk International Airport was a madhouse. 'I can't believe the Navy put me on a commercial flight,' Penny fretted, eyeing the departure monitor for cancellations and delays. 'Well, look at that. It's still on time,' she marveled.

'So is mine,' said Joe, studying the next screen over.

'I guess that makes us some of the lucky ones,' she quipped. They'd spent the last hour browsing the gift shops, listening to other passengers fret about their delayed flights. She'd secretly hoped that her own flight would be delayed, giving her more time with Joe, whose flight wasn't for another three hours. He'd been kind enough to come early just to see her off.

Now the reality of Penny's impending departure put a leaden feeling in her stomach. She wasn't ready for this.

'Well,' he said with reluctance, 'guess we'd better head to your gate.'

Ignoring the fact that she was traveling in uniform, Penny reached for his hand and clung to it. Why not? It was possibly the last time she might get to hold it again. She was headed into a war zone. Life didn't come with guarantees.

As they made their way through security and the swarm of human traffic, voices over the intercom announced departures and delays. Babies squalled. Frantic passengers argued with counter personnel.

The tension in the atmosphere seeped through Penny's thin skin, tying her stomach into knots. Strangely, though she was headed to D.C. and then to Iraq, it wasn't her physical well-being that concerned her. She could feel the pressure of her impending sorrow cracking through the veneer of her heart.

Yes, it was her idea to do this — to rescue herself from potential heartbreak. But with the moment upon her, she didn't want to go through with it.

Would she find him in the arms of another woman when she returned? The thought decimated her. How could he dote on her, make love to her, cherish her the way he had these past weeks if he didn't love her and her alone?

'See anywhere to sit?' he asked her as they slowed beside her gate.

'I don't want to sit down,' she confessed,

placing an arm across her midriff.

With a discerning gaze, Joe put their travel bags at his feet and pulled her against him, holding her firmly.

Tears sprang into Penny's eyes as she submitted to his comfort. There was nowhere in the world she'd rather be than here, with her head against Joe's chest, listening to the steady beat of his heart, breathing his clean male scent. It was everything she needed to be happy.

How frightening was that?

'God, I'm going to miss you, Pen,' he said gruffly, holding her even tighter. In the background came the first announcement for her departing flight.

He sounded so sincere. Plumbing the depths of his feelings for her, Penny gave a watery laugh. 'Yeah, sure. In five days you'll forget about me. I know you, Joe Montgomery.'

To her surprise, he nudged her chin up. She caught her breath at the frown on his face and the passion in his eyes. 'I don't think you do,' he quietly accused. ''Cause I only just figured that out myself.' To her astonishment, he jammed his fingers into her hair, loosening the bun at the back of her head, and kissed her hard.

Drowning in his fervent kiss, Penny could

scarcely think. On and on he kissed her, in complete disregard of the crowd lining up to board the plane.

What did he mean he'd just figured that out himself? What was he trying to tell her?

She savored his explosive kiss, absorbed it like a flower soaking up sunlight. Her world revolved around him. She would have let him kiss her forever, but at last, he sealed it sweetly and raised his head.

Several people applauded, but Penny was too stunned to care.

'Now go,' said Joe gruffly, his face flushed, his eyes smoldering. 'Go do good things for other people, Penelope Anne Price. But you'd better come home safe and sound to me. And that's an order,' he added.

Penny struggled to find her voice. Hope shot roots deep into her heart. 'Aye aye, sir,' she managed to choke.

Dazed, she accepted the carry-on luggage that he thrust into her hands. She stepped obediently into the quick-moving line, groping for her boarding pass and ID.

They maintained eye contact right up to when the attendant took her ticket. Joe lifted a hand in farewell, his bereft expression touching her heart.

'I love you, Joe!' she shouted out at the last minute. His eyes flared, and a stunned look overtook his sorrowful expression.

With a hot face and fearing the ramifications of her impulse, Penny turned and fled down the ramp.

If that didn't make Joe run, then maybe nothing would.

Oh, God, please let him be waiting when I get back.

★ ★ ★

As Vinny parallel parked before a line of clapboard row houses on the east side of Philadelphia, Lia wiped the sweat off her palms. She felt like she'd stepped onto an alien planet where the buildings were closer together and trash fluttered in an inhospitably cold wind. 'Which house is it?' she asked, suffering butterflies in her stomach.

'Right there.' He pointed to a butter-yellow home with flaking paint and a sagging front porch.

Lia swallowed hard. Would the fact that she and Vinny were from different worlds affect their future together?

He cut the engine and caught her look of uncertainty. 'I love you,' he said, leaning close to put his forehead against hers. 'Don't be nervous. I've told you a hundred times, they're gonna love you.'

383

'If you say so,' she said, blowing out a breath.

They'd barely stepped out of the car when the front door of his home flew open. A dark-haired girl rushed down the porch steps and, with a squeal of delight, threw herself into Vinny's arms. As he spun her around, Lia realized that the wild-haired creature was his fifteen-year-old sister, Isabella.

'Bella,' he said, putting her on her feet. 'I want you to meet someone. This is Lia.'

Cherry-brown eyes widened as they assessed her. 'Hi,' said Bella shyly. She was all knees and elbows, having yet to grow into her colt-ish body.

'Nice to meet you,' Lia murmured. *She hates me*, she thought. The front door opened again, and she braced herself for worse.

'Vincente!' cried the woman rushing toward them with her arms thrown open.

Buxom and brunette, with just a hint of silver in her hair, Vinny's mother engulfed him in a hug. She gave him a big kiss on both cheeks, then put him at arm's length. 'Vincente, *figlio mio*,' she crooned. 'Every time I see you, you grow more handsome.'

'Mama, please,' he said, shrugging out of her embrace. 'I want you to meet Lia.' He reached out to tug Lia closer. 'This is the woman I told you about. I asked her to marry me.'

Mother and daughter gaped. The city noises seemed to swell in proportion to their sudden silence. 'Dio mio,' his mother breathed, her gaze jumping to Lia's left hand. She looked horrified.

Vinny looped an arm over Lia's shoulders. Her mouth was dry; her heart galloped. Their love was doomed. But then —

'Welcome!' cried Vinny's mother. Clasping Lia's face, she planted kisses on both her cheeks. 'Vincente has told me so much about you,' she added. 'I should have guessed he would want to marry you.'

'Thank you,' Lia murmured, both stunned and disconcerted by the woman's sudden warmth. She looked at Vinny for an explanation.

'What'd I tell you?' he said with a shrug.

An hour later, Lia, Vinny, and Isabella sat around a tiny kitchen table, which Rosa, Vinny's mother, had covered with a lace tablecloth. Producing a bottle of wine and crystal goblets, she'd toasted their engagement, then threw herself into a frenzy of cooking.

'Amore!' she sighed, scraping diced cilantro into the bubbling spaghetti sauce. From time to time, she glanced at Lia and Vinny, who sat with their shoulders touching, and dabbed her eyes with the hem of her apron. Isabella, who had overcome her shyness, regaled them with news of her social life.

'Why are you friends with so many boys?' Vinny interrupted firmly. 'Boys are trouble. You stay away from them.'

Isabella rolled her eyes. 'I'm not a little girl anymore, Vinny,' she informed him.

'Yes, you are.' He leaned across the table to fix her with a stern look. 'As long as you're my sister, you're still a little girl.'

'*Basta*, Isabella,' Rosa called from the stove. 'Let Vinny's *fidanzata* talk. Do you work, *cara* Lia?' she inquired.

'I'm a reporter,' said Lia, 'for a television news station.'

'She's gonna be famous, Mama,' Vinny inserted. 'On her first story ever, she exposed the ricin killer. You know, the guy that poisoned four military officers, the ones involved in friendly-fire situations.'

'I read about that in the newspaper,' piped up Isabella.

'What're you doin' readin' newspapers?' Vinny scolded. 'You don't need to know what's going on out there.'

Isabella looked at Lia and sighed. 'How do you put up with him?' she asked.

'Your parents must be so proud of you,'

Rosa marveled at the same time.

Sorrow pricked Lia's heart, delaying her response.

'She doesn't have any parents, Mama,' Vinny said, in that gentle tone that made Lia want to crawl into his lap.

'What!' Rosa cried, dropping the ladle into the pot.

As Vinny explained that Lia's mother had abandoned them and her father had been murdered by the ricin killer's hit man, Rosa clucked her tongue and wrung her apron. Tears welled up in the woman's dark eyes, and Lia felt her own eyes sting.

'*Povera figlia!*' Rosa exclaimed, approaching Lia's chair to kiss her, yet again, on both cheeks. 'I will be your mama,' she declared.

'Boy, will she,' muttered Vinny under his breath.

Rosa wagged a finger at him. 'You hush,' she told him. 'Every girl who's getting married needs a mama. When is date of the wedding?' she asked.

Vinny and Ophelia just looked at each other. 'We haven't set a date yet,' Ophelia answered quickly.

'Her career's just getting off the ground,' Vinny explained. 'And I have to decide if I'm reenlisting or goin' to college.'

'I see,' said Rosa, looking disappointed. She

went back to stirring the sauce. 'In that case, Lia will have to share a room with Isabella tonight,' she said airily.

'Mama!' Vinny protested.

Lia hid a wry smile behind her glass of wine. Separate bedrooms or not, Vinny would find a way to be with her.

As the banter continued, a sense of well-being stole into Lia's heart. Strange, but in this unfamiliar environment, surrounded by people she hardly knew, she suddenly felt right at home.

★　★　★

Joe felt like Old Man Scrooge himself, climbing the steps to Gabe Renault's beach house. The sounds of merriment that drifted out of the lofty contemporary nearly had him turning around. But it was Christmas evening. As commander of the folks in there celebrating, he was obligated not only to attend the party, but to pretend he was enjoying himself.

His crisp knock was answered by Gabe and Helen Renault's daughter, a teenager with a ready smile and a grinning Labrador retriever. 'Good girl,' said Mallory to the dog, who sat obediently at the threshold. 'Hi,' she said to Joe, who'd gotten to know her several weeks ago when the Renaults had him over for dinner. 'They've been taking bets on whether or not you'd show up.'

'Oh, really.' He'd learned to expect just about anything out of Mallory. 'Guess I've been a real grump lately.'

'Oh, don't worry,' she said. 'You're not the only one.'

He had no time to ponder what that meant. Gabe Renault rounded the corner and said, 'Mallory, stop talking his ear off and show him in.'

'See what I mean?' said the teen, stepping back to let Joe in.

Gabe's wife, Helen, bustled over. 'We're so glad you could make it,' she said, accepting the bottle of sherry he gave her. 'Oh, this'll go great in the sangria I'm making.'

Joe couldn't believe the bulge on her slim, athletic frame. 'Wow, the baby's grown a lot in the last three weeks,' he commented.

'You know, I noticed that,' she retorted wryly, taking the sherry to the kitchen.

'I'll take your coat, sir,' said Gabe, who hung Joe's coat in the closet. 'I think you know almost everyone here,' he added, leading Joe into a great room with a soaring ceiling. The lit Christmas tree shed a cheery glow on many guests. Christmas music played softly in the background. 'On second thought, I don't think you've met our old master chief, Sebastian León. Sebastian, this is our new commander, Joe Montgomery.'

A lean, dark-complexioned gentleman leaped from an armchair to extend a hand. 'It's a pleasure, sir,' he said, his grip firm. 'I'm almost sorry I retired,' he said in lyrically accented English. 'From what I've heard, it would have been a pleasure to serve you.'

'I've heard good things about you,' Joe replied honestly. Sebastian León — the Sandman — was a legend in his own time.

'This is my wife, Leila,' Sebastian said, introducing the slim brunette on the couch, 'and my daughter Esme.' The baby was all cheeks and sparkling black eyes. 'Her twin brother, Kaspar, is with the senior chief.'

Joe spied Solomon McGuire sitting cross-legged on the floor, blowing raspberries on a squealing baby's belly. The vignette of Mako's gentle interaction with the baby overlaid all of Joe's assumptions about him, changing his opinion in an instant. Who would have guessed the man had a soft spot?

'And you met Chief McCaffrey last night,' Gabe added, still playing host.

Joe sent a nod at the sniper whom he'd released from the team just last night so that he could spend his last four months of his enlistment with the woman he loved. 'Sir,' said the ponytailed chief. He removed an arm from around his female companion and tugged her over to meet Joe. 'This is Sara,' he said, saying her name with reverence and a western drawl. 'She flew in with her son last night, makin' it the best damn night of my life, sir.'

A slim woman with blond hair and blue-gray eyes sent him a shy smile. 'Thank you so much,' she said, regarding him that same way Penny did — like she could see the real Joe. 'You've made Chase so happy — and me, too, of course,' she added, blushing.

From what Joe had heard of her history, the woman deserved to be happy. 'Don't thank me,' he said, feeling undeserving of her gratitude. 'Lieutenants Renault and Lindstrom were the ones pushing for his early release.'

'But you listened to them,' she insisted.

Her faith in him also made him think of Penny. God, he missed her!

The doorbell rang and the dog barked, and Gabe went to greet the newest arrivals. 'There you are. I was starting to give up on you,' Joe heard him say.

'It's my fault we're late,' sang out a familiar voice. A moment later, Hannah Lindstrom breezed into the great room in a dark red pantsuit that offset her flame-red hair.

'You didn't get a call from the office, did you?' Helen asked her as she carried in a tray of iced Christmas cookies.

'No, I had a bout of morning sickness,' Hannah announced, 'at eight o'clock at night!' she added with disgust.

'Hey,' Luther chided. 'You ruined my surprise. I was going to pass around my stocking present.' He handed Gabe an EPT stick.

'Damn, son,' Gabe exclaimed. 'I thought you two just started trying.'

Luther shrugged his massive shoulders. 'All I did was give it my best shot,' he said with a killer grin.

With an outraged gasp, Hannah punched him.

'Ow.'

'Stop taking all the credit. We're the ones who have to do all the work, right, Helen?' Hannah snatched a cookie off the tray that Helen passed under her nose.

'That's right,' Helen agreed. 'It all comes down to female fortitude. You guys are just in it for the ride,' she said, extending the tray to Sebastian and then to Solomon McGuire.

'What ride?' Gabe grumbled under his breath. 'I haven't had a ride in weeks.'

Ah, now Joe knew why his XO was grumpy. He felt a grin coming on.

'Just wait till those sleepless nights hit you,' Leila warned from the couch. 'Don't even try to be heroic, ladies. That four A.M. wake-up has 'Daddy' written all over it. Sebastian enjoyed it, didn't you dear?'

'I thought the twins would never sleep through the night,' the man replied without actually answering the question.

'Man, I can't wait,' said Luther, grabbing his wife. 'When are you going to look pregnant, huh?' he asked, rubbing her flat belly.

'It's not a genie bottle, honey,' she said, removing his hand. 'Oh, Helen, please don't tell me you made sangria and I can't drink it.'

'You're not the only one, sweetie,' Helen replied.

'Yeah, but you're almost out of the woods,' said Hannah, taking in Helen's girth. 'Good lord. When is this baby coming?'

'Yesterday. Can we not talk about the due date?'

'These cookies are fantastic,' said Hannah obligingly.

A thought harpooned Joe's consciousness: *Penny should be here.* An image of her, her belly round with child, flashed in his mind. And with heart-stopping certainty, he realized he wanted that, too, more than anything. He expected the thought to terrify him; instead, it thrilled him like no other rush he'd ever experienced.

'So, Joe, are you able to communicate with Penny?'

Startled to hear Penny's name on the heels of his epiphany, Joe met Hannah's inquiring gaze. 'We've sent a few e-mails back and forth,' he replied. And how many times had he wanted to write: *Did you say you loved me?* The terminal had been so noisy that day. What if he'd misheard her, hearing only what he'd wanted to hear? Her e-mails these last four weeks had been strictly factual, giving him no hope whatsoever that she harbored deep feelings for him.

'Well, next time you write, tell her that Admiral Jacobs pled guilty, so there's no need for her to stand witness at his trial.'

'Excellent,' said Joe. 'I know she wasn't looking forward to that. But I don't have to write her. She's coming back tomorrow,' he added. 'I'll tell her in person.'

Saying it out loud made his heart beat faster and his palms sweat. Having wrapped himself up in his work to forget how much he missed her, he hadn't grasped that their time apart was almost over.

What would it be like seeing her face-to-face after all these weeks? He sensed a monumental shift within himself — a reordering of priorities that was gaining momentum, approaching the most important moment of his life.

He couldn't believe it: at last, despite all odds, he'd found a love as pure and strong as his parents'. He didn't have to avoid their expectations any longer, seeking thrills and chills to take his mind off a lifetime of loneliness. No more running. Having Penny in his life was all he needed.

Solomon McGuire stood up off the floor. With the baby still clamped in one arm, he scooped a handful of nuts off the coffee table. 'Sir, do you have a sniper in mind to take Chief McCaffrey's position?' he asked Joe.

'Yes, I do,' Joe admitted. He'd given it some good hard thought. 'His name is Sean Harlan, goes by Harley. Best chief I've ever had the privilege of working with.'

'Harley,' piped up Chief McCaffrey. 'Yeah, I know 'im. Great guy. He really knows his shit — sorry,' he apologized to Sara, who elbowed him.

'He does,' Joe agreed. The question was would Harley ever want to work for him again? He'd sent him an unofficial inquiry and heard nothing back yet.

Solomon regarded Joe with his weird, unblinking eyes as he chomped on nuts. 'I know Harley,' he volunteered.

Something in the man's tone trapped the air in Joe's lungs. He and Solomon exchanged a long look, and Joe realized with a tingle of alarm that the senior chief knew that Joe was the survivor, that he'd taken Harley's place that awful, fateful night.

The man popped the rest of the nuts in his mouth and nodded as if to confirm Joe's guess. 'He'd be honored to work for you,' he added unexpectedly.

An invisible weight seemed to ease from Joe's chest, making it easier to breathe. 'You think?'

'A lot of commanders forget what it's like to be out in the field,' Solomon added. 'But you wouldn't forget that, would you, sir?'

'No,' Joe agreed, thickly. The senior chief's confidence summoned his gratitude. 'Thank you,' he added, wondering if the other guys knew, as well. Looking around, he found them all regarding him steadily. Not one of them seemed to judge Joe the way he'd judged himself.

Penny was right. He, more than most leaders, knew how much he asked of his men.

Thinking of Penny again flooded him with a feeling similar to that of jumping from a plane, only better. He was going to throw caution to the wind tomorrow and risk everything, most especially his heart.

Epilogue

Lugging her carry-on bag behind her, Penny followed the soldiers filing out of the C-141 Starlifter. Over the decrescendo of the jet's dying engines, she discerned the cheers of family and friends welcoming their servicemen and women to the Oceana Naval Air Station.

Penny's heart beat faster, but she was quick to squash the hope that Joe was among those waiting. She wasn't even supposed to be on this flight. At the last minute, she'd sought standby seating on the most direct flight home. As far as Joe was concerned, she was still arriving at Norfolk International this evening.

Stiff-limbed in the wake of a transatlantic flight, Penny was greeted by a sizable, cheering crowd withstanding a wintry morning as they waited for their loved ones to descend to the tarmac. About a hundred people stood behind the metal barricades, waving banners, screaming out names. With her heart in her throat, she watched as husbands rushed into the arms of their wives. Mothers wept. Young fathers snatched up their children and whirled them in the air.

At the back of the crowd, the words MARRY ME had been painted across a sheet that snapped in the breeze.

God in heaven, it was good to be home! Despite the bite of the winter air, the sky was impossibly blue, without a cloud in it. A fresh breeze, smelling of the ocean, buffeted Penny's uniform trench coat, but the sun felt warm on her shoulders.

As she wended through the crowd on her way to the terminal, the joyful reunions taking place around her brought tears to her eyes. She would need to call a taxi to get home.

A hand settled warmly on her arm. 'Can I help you with that bag, ma'am?'

'No thanks, I've got — ' Snatching her gaze upward, she was astonished to find Joe standing there, a crooked smile on his face. He wore civilian clothing — boots and a denim jacket that made him look so virile and handsome that her head spun.

'Joe,' she cried. 'What are you doing here?'

'Meeting someone,' he said, his green gaze cutting keenly into hers. 'Someone special.'

'Oh.' She checked the impulse to throw herself into his arms. Had he found another woman already?

'I meant you, Penny,' he added with

concern when she just stood there, stricken with doubt.

'Me?' The tarmac seemed to shift. 'But I wasn't supposed to be on this flight.'

He jammed his fingers into his pockets. 'You weren't trying to avoid me, were you?' he asked with an uncomfortable glance over her shoulder.

'No, of course not. How did you find me?' Shock gave way to the sensation that she was floating off the concrete.

'I woke up a lot of people last night,' he said, his smile reappearing.

'Really?' She looked down to see if her feet were still on the ground.

'You, uh, you didn't read my sign yet, did you?' he inquired.

'Sign?' The question had her turning to follow his gaze. There were dozens of signs, posters, and pictures bobbing in the hands of those gathered. She read the ones that she could see:

WELCOME HOME, HARRY!
DADDY IS MY HERO.
WE LOVE OUR E-3.

Behind them all was that enormous banner painted on the sheet. Looking closer, she saw that it was strung between two poles, held aloft by two very buff, stone-faced men with baseball caps pulled down over their eyes.

This time she read the sign in its entirety.

MARRY ME, PENNY?

The blood drained from Penny's face. Elation welled up in its stead, leaving her light-headed. 'Me?' She couldn't believe it.

'I don't know any other Penny,' said Joe, his smile growing forced, 'or even anyone like you,' he added. 'I think you said you loved me when you left?' he added self-consciously.

'Oh, Joe,' she breathed, putting her hands to her face. Out the corner of one eye, she realized some kid was taking her picture.

'You didn't need to leave to make me realize that I love you, Penny,' Joe added gruffly. 'I already knew that. What I didn't know was that I wanted you in my life, every day of my life, for the rest of my life — which is why I made the sign,' he explained, nodding toward the sheet. 'Plus, Gabe and Luther owed me a favor.'

To her amazement, he pulled a velvet-covered box from his jean jacket and sank down on one knee. In front of God and everyone, he grabbed her left hand.

Penny tottered. A hush stole over those bystanders close enough to take note of the proposal under way. The girl with the camera grinned as she held it to her eyes.

Joe opened the box and looked up at Penny. A cluster of diamonds glittered in the morning sun, but it was the love blazing in Joe's eyes that made Penny's heart stop.

'Copper Penny,' he said, in a voice thick with emotion, 'You'd make me the luckiest man alive, if you'd agree to marry me.'

'Aaww,' sighed several women in the crowd.

'Check out the sign he made,' pointed out a man.

'Come on, ma'am!' shouted a petty officer who'd sat beside her on the plane. 'You can't disappoint him now.'

'Forever?' Penny whispered.

'Forever,' Joe confirmed as the nearby camera continued to flash at a fast pace.

Penny's knees jittered. Tears flooded her eyes as she leaned forward to ask, 'Am I on *Candid Camera*?'

'What? No, that's Mallory, Gabe's kid. She insisted on coming along.'

'Oh, well, in that case,' Penny flashed Mallory a grin and then said to Joe, her voice wavering with emotion, 'You had me all along, Joe. I'd be honored to marry you.'

'What'd she say?' asked a bystander. 'Did you hear her?'

'I think she said yes.'

'Hell, she'd better say yes, or I'll take him home,' cackled an elderly woman.

With a click of her camera, Mallory caught on film the world's most perfect kiss.

Other titles published by
The House of Ulverscroft:

DRAGONSHEART

Jacqueline Webb

When Isabella Wyndham-Brown returns to London to celebrate her twenty-first birthday, she anticipates being able to direct her own life away from the restraints of her interfering relatives. But events conspire against her: she discovers that she cannot take control of her fortune until she is twenty-five, and then finds disturbing evidence that her father had a mistress . . . Nevertheless, there are compensations, including meeting her handsome French cousin, and being reunited with Peter Bennett, who saved her life in Egypt. However, when she discovers that her father may have found the lost family treasure, the Dragonsheart diamond, Bella's problems really begin . . .

STORMCROW CASTLE

Amanda Grange

On visiting Stormcrow Castle, Helena
Carlisle is disturbed to find that her aunt,
the housekeeper, has disappeared. Helena
takes on the role of the new housekeeper,
but it is not long before strange incidents
begin to unnerve her. The castle's owner,
Simon, Lord Torkrow, frequents the
graveyard at night; the portrait gallery
conceals a secret room; identities are
hidden at a masked ball; and the key to
the attic is missing. As the secrets unravel,
Helena finds herself drawn into a world
where nothing is as it seems, and she must
fight for her chance of love . . . and to
survive.